*W*hat do you think?" she asked him. She continued to look in the glass, watching the reflection of his image, pretending his presence did not affect her. She reached for the veil and fit it over her head, arranging the netting over her face. *So this is what it feels like to be a bride.*

Trevor, deliberate and unhurried, walked over to Julia's side. He gently took her right hand with his left and pulled her around to face him. Julia simply stared up into his eyes. Ever so slowly he traced a gentle course from her fingers to her wrists, along her elbows and shoulders. His actions sent shivers down her spine.

"What are you doing, Trevor?"

"What I should have done months ago," he said, his voice low and earnest. Julia did not breathe as he continued to draw his fingers along the graceful curve of her neck. Silently he pulled the delicate veil away from her face and settled it carefully over her head. Then he bent and met her lips with his own, kissing her first softly, then urgently, then softly again.

Torchlight

LISA TAWN BERGREN

Torchlight

WATERBROOK
PRESS

Ben

TORCHLIGHT
PUBLISHED BY WATERBROOK PRESS
2375 Telstar Drive, Suite 160
Colorado Springs, Colorado 80920
A division of Random House, Inc.

Scriptures taken from the *Holy Bible, New International Version*®. NIV®. Copyright © 1973, 1978, 1984 by International Bible Society. Used by permission of Zondervan Publishing House. All rights reserved.

The characters and events in this book are fictional, and any resemblance to actual persons or events is coincidental.

ISBN 1-57856-469-7 (formerly 0-88070-806-9)

Library of Congress Cataloging-in-Publication Data
Bergren, Lisa Tawn.
 Torchlight / Lisa Tawn Bergren.—1st WaterBrook ed.
  p. cm. — (The full circle series)
 ISBN 1-57856-469-7
  1. Inheritance and succession—Fiction. 2. Young women—Fiction. 3. Maine—Fiction.
4. Large type books. I: Title.

PS3552.E71938 T67 2001
813'.54—dc21

00-068627

Printed in the United States of America
2001—First WaterBrook Edition

10 9 8 7 6 5 4 3 2 1

To Jansey, for your steadfast friendship,
love, contagious laughter, courage,
and tenacity as you look for the Light.
I love you, my friend.

The sun will no more be your light by day,
nor will the brightness of the moon shine on you,
for the LORD will be your everlasting light,
and your God will be your glory.
ISAIAH 60:19

CHAPTER ONE

*J*ulia Rierdon traveled along what she assumed would be the equivalent of Vermont's Glory Road come fall. The verdant countryside flanking the narrow, winding road shouted spring. *Alive! Awake!* The sprouting leaves seemed to wave at her as she drove quickly by in her restored red convertible. This was what she had hoped for when she had left the crowded freeways of San Francisco headed for Maine. The power of this vista, the overwhelming sense of homecoming, was the magnet that had pulled her away from her career, her parents, her social circles, and, quite possibly, from her boyfriend.

Miles had been so angry when she left. Would he ever speak to her again? She hoped so. They had spent four years together; certainly their relationship could handle a little separation. But how long would they really be apart? For the hundredth time, Julia shoved the question from her mind. She had things to get straight, in her head, in her heart. And it was at Torchlight that she would be able to do so.

The air still held a hint of winter's edge, but the sun was out and, despite the chill, Julia could not resist pulling the car top down when she pulled to the side of the road to stretch. She grabbed a blue duffel coat from her bag and a matching beret, which she slipped over her head, leaving her long, golden hair hanging beneath its edges. Julia took a deep breath and reached toward the sky, then easily hopped over the car's door and turned the key in the ignition. The engine roared to life, and she blasted the heater so at least her feet would be warm. "Almost there," she announced to herself and pulled onto the highway once more.

An hour later Julia crested a hill at a place where the trees thinned, allowing her a spectacular view of the Atlantic. She cried out at the sight of the deep, blue waters she had gazed upon as a child from the windows of her family's Maine estate. Her memories of the mansion and lighthouse were dim. Both had stood vacant now for twenty years, in need of repair and someone with the passion—and finances—to take on the project. Now it was hers for the taking. She could not believe her good fortune.

Julia was so lost in her memories, she paid little heed to the motorcycle that had begun to tail her. She slowed as she passed through a quaint seaside fishing village, then sped up again upon reaching the north side of town. After four more miles, the motorcyclist casually crossed into the opposite lane, and Julia caught sight of him in her sideview mirror. He drew up alongside her car, keeping his eyes on Julia and not the road in front of him.

The man wore faded jeans and cowboy boots, and a weathered denim jacket covered his broad shoulders. Julia blushed at his obvious attention, although unable to see his face behind the dark shadows of his helmet. His lackadaisical attitude toward the risk of oncoming traffic made her anxious. *He's toying with me. Well, two can play this game.*

She lowered her sunglasses on her nose and stared back the next time he glanced at her. The man threw back his head, apparently laughing, when he could not stare her down.

Just then a logging truck rounded the corner, loaded high with thick, felled pine trees.

Her heart pounding, Julia stepped on her brakes, and the man easily slipped into her lane, in front of her. The trucker laid on his horn and shook a fist out the window as he thundered past.

The motorcyclist waved once to Julia, then opened the throttle.

He was out of sight within seconds.

It took several minutes for Julia's heart to return to a normal pace.

After passing three fishing villages and several roadside shacks labeled LOBSTER, Julia came to a peeling sign that announced her destination in OAK HARBOR, POPULATION 435. It was late afternoon, and bright spring sunlight still illuminated the valleys, inlets, and wide natural basin surrounding the town. The houses were made predominantly of white clapboard, with sunny porches and large yards that already showed signs of new spring flowers. A few brick buildings were interspersed among the homes, along with two picturesque churches, each with a bell tower and steeple. A covered bridge stood farther up the shoreline, crossing a harbor inlet.

Famished after her long drive, and stiff after several days of travel, Julia pulled up to a café that bore a sign that made her smile: TARA'S GOOD FOOD. As she entered, she realized there were no other customers—too late for lunch, too early for dinner. The café was partially decorated in the simplified Federal style made famous by the Shakers, although the rich wood of the bar made Julia surmise the building had once been a tavern.

Pine board walls had been laboriously painted matte terra cotta, giving the entire room a warm, reassuring feel. An elaborate, hand-stenciled frieze capped the walls above cream-colored molding. *Classy,* Julia thought. *Someone has some artistic talent.* She sat down on a tall cane stool and waited for someone to help her. From the kitchen came the sounds of someone humming and, apparently, chopping food.

When no one emerged after several minutes, Julia called out, "Hello?"

The chopping and humming stopped. An attractive young woman peeked out the window through which food was passed from the kitchen to the dining area. "My goodness," she said with a slight New England accent. "How long have you been sittin' there?"

"Not long. Sorry if I interrupted. Are you open now?"

"Always open when I'm here at work. What's the sense of havin' a restaurant if you close it?" The woman grinned and walked into the main restaurant area, wiping her hands on a bleached white dish-towel that was thrown over her shoulder.

"The name's Tara. Welcome to Oak Harbor."

"Thanks. It's wonderful to be here," Julia said with feeling.

Tara raised her eyebrows. "You sound like you really mean that."

"Oh, I do. I've been driving for days, and it's good to be home. I've come to renovate my family's estate—make it into an inn. I'm Julia Rierdon."

"Rierdon? Not a familiar name 'round these parts. Which estate might you be speaking of?"

"My great-great-grandfather was a shipbuilder named Shane Donnovan. He built the mansion beside the lighthouse on the point. The Torchlight estate."

Tara's eyes grew wide. "That's wonderful news! It's high time someone came and looked after the ol' girl. I love that mansion. I even climb the lighthouse steps from time to time to look out from up top." She blushed. "I guess I just confessed to breaking and entering…or at least entering. The lock was picked long before my time. Probably by some bored high-school kids. Sorry," she said hurriedly. "I guess I won't be trespassing anymore now that the owner's home."

Julia immediately felt a bond with the woman who loved the estate she had dreamed about for years. "You won't be trespassing anymore. You'll be my guest."

"Well, that's kind of you. Say, since you're new in town, why don't you come over to my house Saturday night for dinner? I'll invite some townsfolk over and introduce you around…make you feel right at home. But listen to me go on! You came here to eat. What can I get you?"

"What do you have?"

"I can fix up almost anything you please. Right now, I have a pot of clam chowder on the stove and sourdough bread in the oven. If you care to wait five more minutes and pass the time of day with me, you can have some fresh."

"Fabulous. Oh, and a cup of coffee would be great too."

The woman smiled warmly and moved down the counter to get Julia the coffee. Julia watched her as she poured the steaming liquid into a cup. Tara was shorter than Julia, with a more curvaceous figure, and she had rosy apple cheeks. Her short brown hair swung as she walked, and her eyes danced when she spoke. Julia looked forward to getting to know her better. *No wedding ring*, she thought. *Maybe we single gals can hang out together.*

"Here you be," Tara said as she served Julia minutes later. She poured herself some coffee and scooted up to sit on the counter behind her, to sit and face her guest. She watched her eat and looked amazed when Julia accepted a second bowl of chowder and blueberry pie afterward. "How do you keep that figure?" she asked pointedly.

Julia blushed. "Obviously, I eat like a pig. Lucky genes."

"I guess so," Tara said.

Julia smiled along with her. "Did you decorate this place? I love it."

"My great-great-grandparents were Shaker farmers. I think they'd be proud to see I turned the town pub into a sober café."

"Are there any Shaker colonies still around?"

"Very few. One up at Sabbathday Lake. Nothing like a penchant for celibate marriages to kill off a tradition." Tara smiled mischievously. "What about you? What made you decide to fix up Torchlight?"

"I've been on the fast track for a while—San Francisco CPA. I had a great office, top salary—but I was miserable. I'd always dreamed of coming here to restore Torchlight and opening an inn. When I hit thirty, I decided it was time. I came into some Donnovan family money on my birthday and thought the best place to spend it would be on the old estate."

"No one else wanted the estate?" Tara asked incredulously.

"My brother's pretty entrenched on a ranch in Montana—he loves it there—and my parents are wrapped up in their lives in San Francisco. I've always been the one who was interested in the old place, in Oak Harbor. We used to come up summers when I was a kid. When my grandparents died, we stopped visiting, and the place was closed up." She looked from the window to her hostess. "How about you? How long have you been a restaurateur?"

Tara scoffed at the lofty title. "I've spent my whole life here. A lot of my friends have left, looking for something bigger and better. But I can't imagine leaving. It'll be an adjustment for you, but I think you'll like it. The restaurant has been mine for, let's see, two, almost three years now."

Julia glanced outside then down at her watch, looking worried. "I've enjoyed my first meal in Oak Harbor, Tara. Thanks for your hospitality, but I'd better get going if I want to make it to the estate and get settled before dark."

"You can't sleep in there tonight! You'll freeze to death. Look, why don't you stay with me? We're practically neighbors, and you can head over to explore at first light tomorrow."

"Thanks, Tara, but nothing's going to stop me from getting home tonight. I'm so excited, I can hardly stand it."

Tara looked at her resignedly. "Well, if you can't get a fire goin', you just head on over to my house. I'm a mile south of you on the left side of the main road. I get home 'round ten, and the guest bed is always made up. Good luck… You have your work cut out for you."

"Thanks for the warning. " Julia smiled and walked toward the door.

Tara liked her new neighbor and hated to see her go. But the entrance of Benjamin DeBois and his son, Mike, quickly distracted Tara just as Julia was leaving. Ben met Tara's eyes, looking curious.

Mike beat him to the question. "Who's the babe?"

"The babe, as you so rudely put it"—Tara swatted him across the shoulder with her damp dishtowel—"is my new neighbor, Julia Rierdon."

"Julia who?"

"Rierdon. The heiress to Torchlight. She's come to rebuild the old lady and make her into an inn."

"Wow. A gorgeous babe and rich." The boy was the spitting image of his father—sun-burnished brown hair, wide, soulful blue eyes, and ruddy cheeks. They settled in at the counter, side by side, to chat with Tara, as was their habit three afternoons a week.

"Humph," Ben grumbled. "Just what we need. More rich folks coming in here and driving our property taxes up."

"Bad day, pumpkin?" Tara teased.

He allowed a smile. Tara believed she could kick his bad moods faster than any other person in the county could. "Sorry. Even with spring coming, the fishin's been lousy. If this keeps up, I'll never get Mike to college."

"Aw, who needs college?" the fifteen-year-old interjected.

"You do."

"You didn't need a college degree to fish," Mike argued.

"Son, we've been through this. The lobsters aren't gonna be around long enough for you to make a livin' off 'em. It's time you start facing reality." Ben's voice was low and firm.

"I don't care. I wanna be out there. If it's not fishin', I'll find some other way to be on the water."

Tara broke into the familiar conversation. "How 'bout some chowder?"

Both sun-bleached heads turned toward her.

"Sounds great, Tara," Ben said, smiling at her shyly.

CHAPTER TWO

*J*ulia followed Tara's directions but could have found the old place without them. The Donnovan estate, dubbed "Torchlight" by Julia's great-great-grandfather, was the largest structure in Oak Harbor. As the sun set in the west, the water to the east of the old house became a deep blue-gray. Waves crashed against the rocky ledges that protected the old lighthouse, which George Washington had commissioned in 1791. In the early days the beacons had been critical in guiding the numerous seafarers who navigated the dangerous reefs and shoals of Maine.

Beside the lighthouse was a small structure that had served as a home for those who manned the post. When Shane Donnovan had bought the property, he had allowed the lighthouse keeper to live on his land. According to the family's oral history, Shane had a deep love for lighthouses, no doubt because they routinely saved many of his vessels, while his wife, Anna, simply considered the entire pointed headland a romantic and wonderful place for a home.

Home. As Julia stood before the iron gates that guarded the entrance, she agreed with Anna. Torchlight was as wild and wonderful as she remembered. From the looks of the rambling mansion that had fallen into disrepair, it would take a lot of elbow grease to tame it. She paused to roll up her sleeves; she was bound and determined that Torchlight be restored to its original grandeur.

Giving up on the rusted-shut wrought-iron gates, Julia threw a duffel bag over the old stone wall and carefully climbed up and over, the way she had as a child. She landed hard. *I'm not as limber as I used to be.*

She pushed aside overgrown branches that blocked the front walk and moved toward the old house's steps. Along the way she paused to take in peeling white paint, shutters hanging from loosened hardware, and easily visible holes in the roof above the porch. *I've got my work cut out for me, all right.* Rotting boards and rusted nails, long unaccustomed to human company, groaned their disapproval at the visitor's approach.

The screen door came off its hinges as Julia pulled. Laughing, she set it to one side, then turned the oversize key in the lock. The huge oak door opened inward, surprisingly without a squeak. She resisted the urge to call out, "Hello? Anybody in there?" and shook off the chill that ran down her spine. Spooky. *Maybe I should've taken Tara up on her offer.*

Smells of dust and mold invaded her nostrils, and she unzipped her bag to search for a flashlight. The shadows were deep, and in the fading daylight the covered furniture made her think of oddly shaped ghosts. Julia was relieved when her fingers closed around the flashlight and the bulb illuminated her way. She stood in the grand entry and gazed up at a dramatic staircase that rose straight up and then divided at the landing into a Y, each arm leading to a separate wing of the house. The rust-colored carpets were dingy and faded, and the solid oak banisters needed refinishing. But it was clear that, with a little repair, the entry would be grand indeed.

Julia moved to her left, stepping into the kitchen and a puddle of water. She moaned at the damage that had been done to the wood floors and shuddered at the thought of what she might find upstairs.

Her flashlight's beam reflected off blue-and-white tiles that decorated the large old kitchen's counters and backsplashes. Copper kettles still hung from their rack, as if someone had left the house just the day before.

Most of the mansion's contents had been abandoned, unwanted, when Julia's grandfather, James, died at the age of ninety-eight. His descendants were making their own way in the world—mostly on the West Coast—and doing well at it. They had their own kettles. The family had maintained the house for ten years after his death, thinking they'd get a chance to visit it more often, but eventually closed it up for good.

Julia was delighted with all that remained. She idly opened a cupboard drawer, marveling at the craftsmanship that allowed it to roll so easily, even after so many years. The drawer lay empty. *But*, thought Julia, *so many drawers to explore!* She moved on, entering the dining room through the swinging wooden door. The dining table was huge, built to seat as many as eighteen. Julia pulled off the dusty sheets that covered the ancient cherry masterpiece and moved to expose each of the chairs that surrounded it. *Unbelievable. How could the old place have escaped burglary through all these years?*

The china cabinet was a spectacular matching cherry piece, with a large center door of convex glass and oval glass shelves where heirloom china and crystal had once been displayed and would soon be again. Julia's aunt, Linda, had promised to send down to her at once the pieces that remained. "They belong in the old house," she had said, accepting no argument from her niece.

"Well, I have no one to invite for dinner, but I sure could put on a show." Julia moved into the hall as the house grew darker. The next door led into the room that had been her favorite as a child: the library. The odors of mold and dust and leather permeated the air. Huge, leather wing chairs sat in idle pairs here and there in the giant room; wooden tables of various sizes stood beside them. But it was the books, the hundreds upon hundreds of leather-bound volumes, that intrigued Julia.

She flashed her beam left and right, hoping that the books, which she considered to be the real treasures of the house, still remained. The library was vast, as Anna had been a devoted reader and self-taught scholar. Julia looked forward to spending countless hours in the room. She walked to the window and peered through leaded-glass windows to the dim form of the lighthouse against the dark sea. The shadows were deepening further, and Julia wanted to see the upstairs before night completely descended. She headed through a unique arched doorway that led back into the living room, then walked upstairs and turned left where the stairs divided.

As she reached the top stair, the house groaned, sending another shiver down her neck. *Come on, Julia, be brave.* She quickly circled the hallway that bordered the staircase, taking stock of the rooms as they lay: the tiny room her great-grandmother had called a water closet, several guest bedrooms, a master bedroom with its own water closet, three more bedrooms.

Two bathrooms for all these people. It's grounds for murder. Julia returned to the master bedroom. Spying the wood stove, she thought about lighting a fire but decided instead that climbing into bed early would be easier. She rubbed her arms, chilled even under the wool sweater and duffel coat she wore.

Julia unzipped her duffel bag again and brought out a fresh set of sheets. She uncovered her great-great-grandparents' huge four-poster bed and quickly pulled the clean linen over the mattress. She would need her sleeping bag; the only blankets that were left in the house were eaten half away by moths. *Tomorrow,* Julia decided, *I'll find some quality blankets in town to replace them.*

She drank from her small bottle of water and climbed into bed before eight. She was asleep by eight-thirty. Even the loud groans of the house, spurred on by gusting northern winds, were unable to interrupt her dreams of descending the grand staircase, wearing a beautiful ball gown, to a party held in her honor.

Julia awoke to find herself folded in the center of the old bed, which sagged badly in the middle. She giggled at her plight as she struggled to rise. *I'm in a big feather taco. I guess I'll need a new mattress.* Her mind was filled with a thousand things she needed in order to get started. It was so cold in the house that her nose—the only part of her body that peeked out of her Arctic-ready sleeping bag—felt numb. Taking a deep breath, she unzipped her polyester cocoon and ran across the room to her duffel bag. She lifted one foot and then the other, attempting to keep them off the freezing floor as she dressed.

No water for a shower. No electricity for the old refrigerator in the kitchen. *First things first,* she resolved, considering her rumbling stomach. She would find the water main and then head to town for breakfast and her first load of supplies.

Julia spent a larger part of the morning at Tara's restaurant than she intended to, caught up in easy conversation and laughter.

"Enough, Tara, I can't eat another bite! And I have a ton of things to do! But let's talk again tomorrow, okay?"

"Okay."

"Why don't you come out to the house and see her before I get the work started? I'll show you what I've got planned."

"I'd love to. I'll even bring my camera and take 'before' shots."

"Great idea. Say around ten?"

"Perfect. Breakfast crowd's gone by then, and I have an hour break before I have to get back for lunch."

"Good! I want someone to share this with me. Say, where do I go for supplies? I'll need all the basics—mattresses, blankets, towels."

"Hit the old woolen mill on the north side of town. They have wonderful things, and the best deals on linens and bedding. You'll have to go to Portland for a mattress."

Julia first stopped at the hardware and grocery stores, businesses so tiny they would have been considered small markets in San Francisco. Each store clerk met her at the counter and gazed in wonder at the amount she purchased. "Sure, we'll send a boy with your delivery," they agreed, delighted with the newcomer who was such a good customer.

Before she headed over to the woolen mill, Julia stopped again at Tara's to use the restaurant phone. From there, she arranged for her own phone line to be connected and the electricity to be turned on. She discovered that one of the luxuries of living in a small town was fast service; what would have taken days in the city was accomplished in twenty-four hours in Oak Harbor.

Tara was singing old hymns in the kitchen, and Julia listened with pleasure to the woman's beautiful mezzo-soprano voice. She hated to break in, but she needed to get back to Torchlight. "Tara?"

The singing stopped, and her new friend peeked through the kitchen window. "Are you off again?"

"Yep. I've gotta get going if I want to bring some order to the house. Which reminds me: I need to hire some help. Do you know of any reliable men in town? Most important, I need a general handyman who can work for a good solid year."

"None of the locals comes to mind. Most are fishin' this time of year. There is one new guy who's been around 'bout a week, lookin' for work. I'll put the word out. We'll find you somebody."

"Thanks, Tara. See ya."

"Hey, wait! Don't forget dinner at my house tomorrow! Six o'clock sharp."

"I wouldn't miss it. Thanks for inviting me."

"You're welcome. And pay no mind if some of the people are a little distant at first. It takes awhile to get to know folks 'round here. They're soft as marshmallow once you get past the crusty exterior. Most of them are harmless."

Julia grinned at Tara. "I'll remember."

She hurried back toward home, anxious to return during the full light of day. On her way, Julia stopped at the old woolen mill Tara had recommended. She had found stack after stack of plastic-wrapped, locally woven blankets and linens inside the cold warehouse. A small wood stove kept the clerks and customers warm, and Julia stood close to it as she gazed about in wonder. "This is incredible," she said to one motherly looking saleswoman.

"Best blankets Down East," she said proudly.

With the clerk's help, Julia purchased four thick blankets, two sets of sheets, two huge bath towels, and a handmade cream-colored comforter for the bed. *I'll come back when it's time to decorate the other bedrooms,* she thought happily, dreaming of the different color combinations she would create.

Around three o'clock Julia laid a fire in the living room fireplace to test it out. When the paper burst into flames and the kindling crackled, she smiled in satisfaction and began to drag several carpets out to the porch where she could clean them in the fresh spring air. She had just begun to pound the rugs with an old carpet beater she'd discovered in a closet when she heard a motorcycle approach the main gates. Moments later a man pulled up outside the wrought-iron fence and shut off the engine. Casually, he stood and carefully parked the vehicle. As he walked up to the gate, he took off his helmet and peered through at her.

It was the man from the highway.

Julia's heart pounded.

The guy looked back at the red convertible parked beside his motorcycle, then grinned at her. "So we meet again," he said, his voice low and self-assured.

Julia slapped her hands against her jeans to remove the dust from them and descended the porch stairs, acting sure of herself. She stopped ten feet from the gate. "If you call a near-suicide attempt a 'meeting.' Can I do something for you?"

Trevor stared at her. She was gorgeous. More beautiful than he had been able to see from the road. Without her sunglasses and hat, and out from behind the wheel, he could take in her almost perfect figure, smooth golden mane, and violet eyes. Not to mention those lips…

Julia repeated her question, looking a bit uneasy under his scrutiny. "I said, 'Can I help you?'"

Her question shook him out of his reverie. "I hope so. Trevor Kenbridge. I'm a newcomer to Oak Harbor too. And, lucky for you,

I happen to be an excellent carpenter, plumber, and general handyman."

She stared at him blankly.

"Tara sent me. Tara, from the restaurant? She said you needed some help in fixing up the old place." He glanced beyond her. "It's a beauty. I've found myself dreaming of lighthouses a lot lately, not to mention a certain gorgeous driver I met on the road. Feels like I've been led here."

She appeared disturbed by his directness. Or was it his flirting? "I don't need any help," she said, her tone guarded.

"So why'd you tell Tara—"

"Look, I need someone reliable, trustworthy. And I can handle things myself until the right person comes along."

Trevor nodded. "So you parked outside because you wanted to?"

"Well…the gate's rusted shut," she admitted.

Trevor went to his motorcycle and dug through to the bottom of a bag attached at the rear. He came back to the gate holding a crowbar and grinned at Julia, who looked at him in surprise. "Always carry one with me, and a hammer, too. You'd be amazed how often they come in handy." Lodging the tool between the gate and latch, he pulled quickly and forcefully, and the two pieces separated. Creaking and groaning, the gate soon opened so that nothing stood between Trevor and Julia.

Julia's heart pounded. He was *so* handsome. He moved as if he owned the world and could put anything right. As he smiled and approached, she felt guilty, thinking for the first time of Miles and how she shouldn't be admiring this stranger so openly.

Resolving to be strong, she stared up into his deep brown eyes.

"I think I'm looking for someone else. I need someone stable, not a person with a wish to resemble road kill."

"Perhaps I'm more trustworthy and reliable than our first meeting has led you to believe. I'm really good at spotting trouble and finding solutions. Let's just say I was distracted on the highway. I think I'm your man."

Julia shielded her eyes and looked to the ocean, then back to him. "I don't think we're a good match. Flirting on the highway is not an auspicious beginning for a business relationship. I have a boyfriend in San—"

"Ma'am," he interrupted, ducking his head with a smile. "I need a job. Not a girlfriend."

"I…I think it's best if you go."

"Hmm. Before I put out the fire?"

"Fire?"

"The one in your house."

Julia turned around and gasped as a plume of dark smoke escaped the open living room window. She left at a dead run and disappeared into the house.

Following close behind, Trevor quickly located a kettle in the kitchen, filled it with water, and rushed into the parlor behind Julia. The fire was small and still contained to the fireplace, but Julia was struggling with the flue. Calmly Trevor bent over and doused the flames.

Smiling, he wiped a large smudge of soot from Julia's cheek. She backed away.

"Thank you. You've been a help. But, like I said, I think I'm looking for someone else."

"I think you're wrong. This is a small town full of fishermen and mill workers. While I, on the other hand, have a variety of skills that perfectly suit me to this job."

"Boy, you sure don't have a confidence problem."

"No. I don't think you do either. Which is why I'm confused. Why would a confident, smart woman not hire the right man for the job?" He moved several inches closer, but Julia held her ground, resolutely staring back into his eyes.

Flustered at his audacity, she lowered her gaze and pointed to the door. "Go."

He shrugged and followed her direction. At the door, he paused. "The fireplaces are probably clogged with soot or birds' nests. I've done some chimney sweeping and repair. You can't use them until they're thoroughly inspected."

"Out."

"It was nice to meet you. If you come to your senses, I'll be 'round for a while yet."

CHAPTER THREE

The following night, after a hard day's work, Julia bathed in preparation for dinner at Tara's. Tired of her hair, she pulled it back into a French braid and dressed quickly. She picked out a black wool turtleneck sweater, which she tucked into slim jeans, then put on a thick black belt and boots to match and, finally, silver earrings. After a quick check in the mirror, she took a deep breath and went to meet her new neighbors.

Warm light poured out of Tara's windows, welcoming people as they drove up. She had invited more than twenty people and was serving hors d'oeuvres and setting up the buffet when Julia knocked.

"Come in! Make yourself at home. You'll have to introduce yourself, or better yet, come with me and I'll give you a tray to pass 'round—it will give you an excuse to approach these Down Easters."

Julia followed Tara into the kitchen, smiling shyly at many of the guests. Tara's house was of the classic New England style—lots of windows, clean lines, whitewashed wood, and airy rooms with high ceilings. "It was built just a few years after Torchlight," Tara said, seeing Julia look around.

"It's very homey."

"Just the way I like it. Here. Pass these around and say hello to everyone."

Julia picked up the tray of fruit, cheese, and crackers and did as she was told. She began in the living room where she spotted a familiar looking man and boy. They were obviously father and son; they each had a head full of bleached-by-the-sun blond hair and sparkling blue eyes. It was clear that the boy would soon share his father's broad, lean frame as well.

"Julia Rierdon," the man said easily with a smile. "We've heard all about you. I'm Ben DeBois, and this is my son, Mike."

Mike turned as he heard his name and flushed at the sight of Julia. She did not understand his embarrassment but smiled kindly and chose to ignore it. "It's nice to meet you both. Guess in a town this small it doesn't take long for word of a newcomer to get around."

"You're right. You and Kenbridge over there have been the only interesting things to hit Oak Harbor this year."

She froze at his name. She turned, slowly, casually, and glanced to the other side of the room. Trevor raised his glass to her and mischievously smiled. She turned away without acknowledging him.

"So, Ben, what do you do here?"

"I'm a fisherman." He had such a warm, easy way about him that Julia instantly felt relaxed.

"Ah. I'd like to hear more about that sometime. I'm looking for a handyman out at Torchlight. Do you happen to know anyone?"

"Just Kenbridge. Seems like just the man. Has he been out to see you?"

"Yes. But I think I'm looking for someone…different."

He nodded, but his face belied his confusion. Again, Julia wondered why she was so cowed by the tall stranger in the corner. Tara and Ben had thought he would be perfect for the job. What was it about him that made her uneasy, wary?

Julia changed the subject. "So, how do you know Tara?"

"Been friends since we were little. She was my wife's best friend."

"And yours now," Mike piped in.

"Nah. You're my best," Ben said, nudging him on the shoulder.

"*Dad,*" Mike squirmed under his father's arm. "I think I'll go talk to Jessica." He left without waiting for permission.

"Adolescence," Ben said with another easy smile, shrugging off Mike's action. "He still misses his mom."

"Oh. Are you divorced?" she asked carefully.

"No. Sharon died in a boating accident ten years ago. I sure could use her help in dealing with a teenager."

"I bet. They can be a handful."

"Here. Let me introduce you to some of your new neighbors."

Across the room, Trevor's eyes never left Julia. She held herself in an elegant manner and moved easily through the crowd of strangers, introducing herself and talking intermittently with Ben. Trevor fought off a feeling of competition. Ben was just being kind. Trevor had already picked up that the man had a thing for Tara.

The distance allowed him to watch Julia without interruption until an old man next to him broke into his concentration.

"A beauty, eh?"

Trevor followed his cataract-glazed eyes. "Yes. She is."

"Still. Not from these parts, so she can't be much. Her people built Torchlight, but they haven't been 'round in years. We can't have people just up and comin' to the Harbor and making their way in."

"Why not?"

"Well, son, I like it just the way it is. Someone should blow up the bridge down there in Kitteredge to keep the tourists from poisoning these parts—present company excluded, of course."

"Of course," Trevor said with a smile.

Another elderly man nearby roused at the idea of blowing the bridge at Kitteredge. "Keep out the summer complaints, I say." Then he settled back into the couch, having spoken his mind.

Trevor enjoyed the way New Englanders didn't pull any punches. He liked their droll manner of speaking and their one-liners. When conversation turned to themselves, they became more withdrawn.

"You retired?" he tried, hoping to draw out his companion.

"Yep."

"How do you spend your days?"

"Work some on my son's boat."

"How big is she?"

"Forty-footer."

"Where is she moored?"

"The bottom. Winter storm."

Trevor laughed under his breath. "Are you gonna get her running again?"

"Not where she is."

"Are you going to raise her?"

"Yep."

Tired of the game, Trevor turned his eyes once more to Julia.

"Spittin' image of Anna," the old man said.

"Anna?"

"Anna Donnovan, her great-great-grandma. There's a portrait of her up in the library."

"Oh? I'll have to see that."

"She is much more interestin' in real life."

"That she is."

A week later the only people who had shown up looking for work were the town drunk and a swarthy man Julia instantly distrusted. As she scrubbed the wooden floors to see what kind of shape they were in, her thoughts turned once again to Trevor Kenbridge.

As much as he aggravated her, she had to admit that he might be the best man—perhaps the *only* man suitable—for the job. She had thought of him often in the last week. Julia sat back on her heels and wiped her brow. She needed Trevor, and he might be leaving soon. What was to keep him here? He needed work, and as it stood, there weren't enough fish to go around. Even with the inheritance, she had to get the inn up and running soon, to start bringing in some income. There would be a ton of money going out in the next nine months.

Coming to a decision, she bathed quickly in the ancient, deep, freestanding tub, grimacing as the faucet spewed half-dirty water from the rusted old pipes, and dressed in jeans and a purple turtleneck, before heading into town. She spotted Trevor's motorcycle in front of Tara's restaurant and pulled in beside it.

Trevor allowed his eyes to rest upon her for a moment, then deliberately turned back to his late-morning breakfast. She sat a ways down the counter from him and greeted Tara enthusiastically.

"Hi there, Julia," Tara said, pouring her a cup of coffee. Then, louder, she asked, "Have you found that handyman yet?"

Julia pointedly stared at Tara.

"Uh, I think I better get workin' on dinner. Expectin' quite a crowd tonight." Tara bustled out of the front room and back into the kitchen, humming loudly.

"I think you get more gorgeous every time I see you," Trevor said, looking calmly down the counter over his mug of coffee.

"I think you speak out of turn. I think you should remember I have a boyfriend. And I think you know I still need some help at Torchlight, thanks to Tara." Julia spoke loudly so Tara could hear her in the kitchen. The humming stopped. "Mr. Kenbridge, I'm in a bind. My better judgment tells me not to hire you, but I need help and I need it right away. The whole house will need to be rewired and new plumbing put in. I plan on basically gutting her and starting over. I want to make Torchlight into The Torchlight Inn. And I want her up and running in less than a year, this fall, if possible. Overwhelmed yet?"

"No."

"Do you do electrical work?"

"Yes."

"You said you're an adept plumber."

"Yes."

"Carpentry?"

"Yes."

"Do you mind some grunt work as well as the big jobs?"

"No."

"References?"

"Uh, yes. Most are out of the country."

She paused. "Out of the country?"

"Yes. My last three jobs were in Afghanistan, Greenland, and Zaire."

Julia frowned. Just as she had thought. A vagabond. "How long in each place?"

"Three, sometimes four, months."

"And is that how long you plan to stay here?"

"Want me to stay longer?"

"Mr. Kenbridge, I need someone trustworthy. No more games. No more flirting. I need to be able to count on the man I hire. To know he'll be here until at least the major jobs on Torchlight are complete. I don't want to start with you and have to hire another to take your place. If we work together, find some good people for each project, we could be done in four or five months, and you'd be free to go."

He stared into her eyes for an inordinate amount of time. She refused to look away.

"You can count on me, Julia. No games. We'll get the old mansion into tiptop shape."

She sighed, still studying him. Why did this feel like a mistake? *Stop me, Lord, if this is wrong,* she prayed silently. Hearing no response from her Maker, she said grudgingly, "You can bring your stuff and stay in the lighthouse cottage."

The next Saturday night, Tara again invited Julia over for dinner.

The two ate at her kitchen table and gabbed about Trevor and Ben and life in Oak Harbor. Julia gushed over the food.

"I'm serious, Tara. You should write a cookbook. You could even call it *Tara's Good Food.* It's quaint! And the recipes…people all across America would kill for your baked beans."

Tara waved her off. "Please. I can't write an entire cookbook."

"You run a restaurant! Of course you can. Don't tell me you don't have enough recipes."

"Oh, I have enough." She paused and fiddled with her napkin. "I have thought of it once or twice—"

"Then it's settled! My dad has some friends in publishing in New York. A few phone calls, and I can get you a chance to pitch your ideas. Send 'em a vat of beans, and you'd win 'em over in seconds flat."

"Seconds flat, eh?"

"Seconds flat."

"Well, maybe," Tara said shyly, still toying with the idea. Apparently, for a woman born and raised in tiny Oak Harbor, the idea of reaching out to the world seemed daunting.

"Do this for me: Pull together your top hundred recipes." Julia looked around Tara's kitchen, which was artfully painted and stenciled, and remembered the restaurant's exquisite decor. "Did you do all this?"

"Yes."

"I've got a great idea! You obviously have an artistic bent. Along with the recipes, include some sketches and homey notes. Publishers love a gimmick."

"That might be fun. I'll think about it."

"Just remember who to dedicate it to when it's published and you're rich and famous."

Tara paused a moment and then shook her head. "Imagine that! Beans making me rich and famous!"

The two laughed together like old friends.

Trevor and Julia's first days together at the mansion seemed to revolve around one trial after another, but it felt good to Julia to have someone else in on the planning. Alone it was overwhelming. But Trevor's take-charge attitude, while vaguely disturbing and stimulating to Julia, also relieved her burden. He was careful and polite from the start, arrived on time, and often worked late. And it had been Trevor who decided they needed an architect to help them plan the additional bathrooms, as well as to confirm their plans to take out a couple of walls and move another to expand the kitchen.

"I found the guy," he announced on the third morning as she sat sipping some coffee.

"What guy?"

"The architect. I called my cousin Bryn in Boston, and she knew just the right one. Just out of school, hungry, but smart, and he has a penchant for old houses. Shouldn't cost you much, but he'll know what we need to know."

"Wonderful!" She rose. She could at least be polite. "Would you care for a cup of coffee?"

"Please. Black."

She walked to the coffee maker and poured him a cup. As she handed it to him, she asked casually, "Do you have much family here?"

"Bryn is my cousin, doing her medical residency in Boston. She's one of the few left. But she's part of why I wanted to come to the coast. Went for a visit, then started searching the tiny towns along the Eastern seaboard, looking for the next right place for me. And work," he added with a smile.

"What about your parents?"

"Died. When I was little. Bryn's parents, who separated when I was in high school, raised me. I took off after graduation to travel a bit. Returned for college."

"You have a degree?"

"Five credits short of the degree. Got most of my knowledge on the job."

"In Afghanistan, Zaire?"

"Yes. And elsewhere." He looked at her curiously. "You don't think much of my traveling, do you?"

"No, not at all. I think it's just…interesting. I've done a little traveling but have spent most of my time making a life, friends. Hasn't your…*moving about* kept you from some of the good things in life?"

He took a long sip. "Like what? I have friends in virtually every country of the world. I've experienced more than most will ever think of doing." Trevor set down his cup to gesticulate left and right. "This is a huge, wonderful world, Julia. God has done amazing things, everywhere I go. Isn't that why you are here? To explore what he has for you to see next?"

"Maybe." What was it about his explanation that left her disgruntled, confused? "But mostly, I'm thinking I need a sense of place, a sense of me." She clammed up, well aware that she was sharing too much, letting things get too personal.

But he didn't let her off the hook. "Let me guess. Society girl, right? Debutante? The right schools, the right clothes, the right car. College in four years, maybe grad school. Right job, right condo, right church. Even the right boyfriend—how long have you been dating?"

"Four years," she said, wondering how to extricate herself from the conversation. His presumption irritated her, regardless of how close he was.

His chin rose in surprise. "Four years. But you left and went to the opposite coast. Is he moving out here?"

"I don't know. Listen—"

"Ah. I've met a lot of people like you on the road, in the middle of the Sinai, in Rio. You're wondering if it's right at all, if you're meant to be somewhere else, doing something else. You're wondering if you were ever home at all. That's why you're here at Torchlight, far from Frisco and family and boyfriend. To discover the truth of it."

"And what about you, Trevor?" she asked, conscious that her voice was barely more than a whisper. "Have you discovered the truth?"

He studied her for a long moment. "I've discovered the pertinent truths; now all I need is a home. And as I've told you, I've been dreaming of lighthouses lately."

She coughed and turned away, intentionally breaking up their intimate moment. She didn't need this now, a man who thought he knew her, who invaded her privacy and urged her thinking toward darker unknowns. The places she longed to go but didn't dare. It simply wasn't wise. She'd ventured far enough, coming here.

"I was thinking that we could start in the master bedroom today," she said, her voice strong and clear. "I'll need help clearing it of furniture before we begin ripping up plumbing."

She waited for him to answer, busying herself with buttering a cold piece of toast.

"I'll be waiting," he said, setting down his cup. He left the kitchen.

She knew he wasn't speaking only of the plumbing project.

Julia was poring over the ancient blueprints of the house when he came into the dining room to ask a question about some work he intended to do in the cottage. The sight of her brought him up short.

She was so intent she did not hear him enter. Her hair fell over one shoulder, and she brushed stray strands from her eyes as she continued to study the original plans for the house. In the soft afternoon light, she looked like an angel to him—so quiet, so serene.

Dear God, he prayed silently. *Give me the strength to control myself around this woman. Help me to wait on your timing.*

"How long have you been standing there?" She stood with her hands on her hips, angry to find him spying on her.

"I…I'm sorry. I was just—"

"I don't need to be looking over my shoulder all the time, Mr. Kenbridge."

"You can call me Trevor," he quipped, hoping to elicit a laugh. What was wrong with her? Ever since yesterday, in the kitchen, she had her walls back up… He had apparently edged too close, pushed too far.

"Did you need something?"

He scowled at the hard edge to her tone. "Look, I just came to ask you about the cottage. I think it would be a much nicer place if I took out the small wall between the two rooms. I'll ask Bryn's friend about it when he comes tomorrow—"

"Fine. Do what you want with the cottage. But be ready to begin on the main house soon. Anything in the cottage will have to come last, or on your own time." She was staring back at the blueprints, obviously pretending to have him already out of her mind.

"Anything you want, *Ms.* Rierdon." He turned and walked out, letting the front door close loudly behind him.

CHAPTER FOUR

dozen roses arrived every three days for Julia, a gift from Miles. "So you don't forget me," the card would read, or, "Thinking of you every day." It was thoughtful of him, and the roses made Julia miss him a bit. Maybe this separation would be good for them, help them to determine if they wanted to finally make more of their relationship in marriage, or call it off. As constant companions they had been on the fence for years and had become fairly comfortable with how things stood.

And so it was that when the car pulled into the drive Julia half expected the florist. She looked out the leaded window from her bedroom, where she was stripping wallpaper, and wiped her sweating brow. Trevor appeared below, walking quickly toward the Toyota and opening the passenger-side door. His grin was wide, and when an attractive brunette emerged, he gave her a long, brotherly hug. Who was it? A man appeared from the driver-side door, and Julia roused herself from the window to hurry downstairs.

"Julia?" Trevor yelled, opening the front door with a half knock. "Julia?"

"I'm right here," she said, moving down the staircase as she had been taught to move in ball gowns as a teen. Even in jeans and a T-shirt, she could still be a lady.

The woman on Trevor's arm looked up to grin at her. She was lovely—olive-skinned with long, dark hair, as if she had Native

American blood. They'd be a beautiful couple, but her demeanor was more sisterly than that of a woman with romantic intentions.

"Julia, I want you to meet my cousin, Bryn Bailey. This is her friend, Dan Lindgren, the architect." *Oh, that explains it,* she thought.

"Oh! Welcome." She reached out to shake the woman's hand, and then the architect's. "Please, come into the dining room. I've got some coffee on—"

"Water would be great," Bryn said. "May I help you?"

"No, no. I can handle water."

"I'll take coffee," Dan said gratefully.

"I'll be right in. You can spread your things out on the table," Julia said, gesturing toward Dan's case. Dan and Bryn turned to admire the front foyer and staircase, then moved toward the dining room, while Trevor followed her into the kitchen.

"I'll grab the coffee," he offered.

"Okay. I'll get your cousin's water." She paused as she poured from a filtered jug—the house's water was not yet suitable for drinking. "I didn't know she was going to come up today."

"Neither did I. I hope it's okay. She said something about wanting to see the old place; I've talked so much about it."

"It's fine, fine."

"Well, good." He gestured toward the dining room. "I'll be in there. Coming?"

"Yes. I'll just grab a plate of cookies and be right in." The door swung shut behind him, and Julia stared after him. *I've talked so much about it,* he'd said. And he and his cousin were apparently as close as she and her brother, Jake, were. She mused over her own smile. Maybe Trevor Kenbridge was more stable and at home here than she had given him credit for.

The next few days went smoothly enough. Hours were eaten up by the demanding tasks of inspection: foundation, electric system, plumbing, timber framing. The list went on and on, and their to-do list expanded accordingly.

The following day, a week after Trevor's arrival, Julia left with Dan Lindgren to file renovation plans at the county courthouse in Portland, two hours away. Unlike the bureaucracy of the big cities on the West Coast, approval could come within days. Still, the lines and the forms and the interviews took all afternoon.

When Julia drove back into Torchlight, she smiled at the wreckage, imagining how it would look within the year. The vision invigorated her. She wondered what Trevor had accomplished in her absence, and her heart sped up strangely as she imagined him coming out the door to greet her.

Catching sight of the convertible as it came through the gates, Trevor paused at the kitchen window and watched Julia park and jump out of the car. His heart seemed to stop, then beat again more quickly. *What is it about her?* It irritated him that a woman could so captivate him. *I'm a freewheeler, so why do I feel like my feet won't move?*

Realizing he would be seen in the window if he didn't change positions, Trevor forced himself to go back to tearing out the electric stove and wiring, in preparation for a new gas range. *You always want the unavailable ones,* Bryn had teased him. She had recognized his attraction for his new boss from the start. They had traveled together, spent hours on the phone together; she knew him like a brother. And she was right. He always set his sights on the unattainable… It made him angry at himself. He gave the wiring a fierce yank, and instead of trailing out, it ripped through the wallboard. *"Oh!"* he growled in frustration, clamping his mouth shut lest swearwords emerge.

The door slammed shut, and Julia came into the kitchen to drop off the few groceries she had picked up. "Hi," she said.

"Hello," he responded, not looking up at her.

"How's it going?"

"Fine."

"I thought you'd be done with this by now."

He stood up and wiped off his forehead. "Yeah, well, I thought I'd take the afternoon off while the boss was away. I just sat outside in the hammock and dozed."

"No need to get sarcastic, *Mr.* Kenbridge."

"No need to check up on me, *Ms.* Rierdon."

She put away her groceries silently, her tense shoulders telling him of her anger at his impudence.

As she turned to leave, he caught her at the door. "Look, Julia, I had to move the rest of the stuff out of the basement so the guys could work on the pipes tomorrow. It took all morning and part of the afternoon. All the stuff is in the shed—you need to go through it and decide whether you want to save or toss it."

She looked down at her feet and then at him. "I'm sorry. I was checking up."

"I'm a trustworthy man. Give me some room. I've told you; you won't be sorry."

She paused a moment, then: "What'd you find in the basement?"

"It looks like mostly junk to me. But go on down and check out the wine cellar. I unearthed it behind two old couches."

"A wine cellar? I don't remember that."

"Maybe your great-grandparents were teetotalers who buried it before you were born."

Julia moved over to the basement door and opened it. It smelled musty, dank. She yanked a chain attached to a bare light bulb, and the old cement stairs were immediately illuminated. Fighting off her childish fear of dark basements, she walked down. The basement was an empty warren of makeshift, half-walled rooms. *It must've taken Trevor forever to empty it.* And she had jumped all over him...

"Boo!"

Julia jumped. Realizing it was just Trevor behind her, she turned around and slugged him on the arm as hard as she could.

"Ow! What'd you do that for?"

"You creep!"

"I was just playing around. Lighten up."

"I thought you had something to do."

"I wanted to show you some things." He rubbed his arm and frowned at her. "Come on."

She followed him to the left, noting the rough-hewn beams and posts that made up the timber framing of the first floor. Here and there stood walls of shelves, full of empty canning jars, paint, brushes, and various tools. To the right of the wine cellar was a huge assortment of wine jugs and soda bottles, all full of a clear liquid.

"What do you think those have in them?"

Trevor smiled. "I thought you'd want to see that. I was thinkin' that Gramps had gotten into the moonshine business, but it didn't make sense with the little that I know about their lifestyle. Anyway, Ernie, one of the plumbers, told me to open one and check it out."

"What was it?"

"Water. He said that back in the forties they had a severe drought. Apparently your relatives were stocking up for another sunny day."

Although she was still upset with him for spooking her, Julia had to smile. "And the way basements go, they never returned to empty or clean 'em out."

"Nope. This way, ma'am." Twelve more feet to their left was the wine cellar, festooned with a huge hand-carved timber depicting luxurious grape leaves and their bounty. "Check it out; natural refrigeration at its best." He opened the door and Julia peeked inside.

"It's really cold in here!" The small room had ten steps that descended another seven feet below ground. The walls were hewn granite. "It must hold more than two hundred bottles, when it's full."

He jumped the last three steps and landed beside her. "Probably's been empty since Prohibition."

"Probably. But I bet it was full when Shane Donnovan was man of the house. Grandmother said he loved to have either a quiet evening with his family or a big party. Anything in between left him restless."

"Sounds like a man I would've enjoyed knowing," Trevor said, as they climbed back up into the basement again.

He closed the wine cellar door behind him. "There is something else you should see. Over here." He pointed into the corner of one section of timber framing, shining his flashlight carefully.

Julia crowded in to see, with Trevor close behind her. "What?" His proximity and her own reaction to it irritated her. She felt herself flush from head to toe.

"No termite damage."

"No termite damage?"

"None whatsoever." He calmly remained poised behind Julia, clearly enjoying her proximity.

She turned to get out of the corner. When Trevor didn't move, she pushed him backward. "You couldn't just tell me that?"

He shrugged innocently. "I thought you'd be happy with the news."

"I am. But...oh, forget it." She shook a finger in his face. "Boundaries. Remember our boundaries. No flirting. I'm your boss. You're my employee. *That's it.*"

"Right. Boundaries," he said mischievously. "You have a boyfriend. And the flowers. I've seen the flowers. From him, right?" Was he taunting her, testing her?

She kept her stern look and nodded once, staring him down. "Yes. They're from Miles." But as she climbed to the main floor and he silently followed behind, Julia couldn't keep a tiny grin from escaping.

The old house reverberated with a loud groaning and squeaking noise.

"What is *that?*" Tara asked.

Julia and her new friend sat at Torchlight's kitchen table, drinking tea from delicate china cups. "Creepy, huh? It's the heating lines. Cast iron. They *have* to go. Unfortunately, it's very ugly, dirty, heavy work. The men get rid of the lines in chunks, using a pipe wrench, a hammer, a chisel—whatever works. You should see their hands. I don't know if they'll ever get them clean."

"How is Trevor working out?"

"I have to admit, he's a godsend. My life would have been miserable without someone like him on board." She wrinkled up her face. "But I have this weird thing going on with him. It's like we're at each other's throats all the time. I say one thing, he says another. I do one thing, he does another. We're constantly at odds."

"Could it be that he's so spectacularly handsome that he makes you edgy?"

Julia looked up at Tara in surprise. "What are you talking about? I already have one man in my life, and that's quite enough, thank you very much."

"Just a suggestion. Tell me about your man," she invited.

"Miles. He's an attorney in San Francisco. Handsome, talented, stable, reliable."

"And generous," Tara said, fingering the petals of giant red roses.

"Yes."

"How long have you been dating?"

"Four years."

"Wow. That's a long time. What's the deal? Are you in love? Almost married?"

"Not exactly." Julia frowned slightly. "I guess we've been heading toward marriage all along, but there's something that niggles at me, something missing. I guess I thought coming out here, gaining some distance, would help us figure it out. Our relationship is solid, comfortable. Maybe too comfortable. I think I just need a break to see it more clearly. For him, too."

"I see. Kinda like if he moves out here, or you can't stand to be without him, you'll finally know?"

"Kind of," Julia agreed.

"I know what that's like. Ben and I have been buddies so long, I don't think he can see me in any other light. But I'm tired of the way things stand. It's time for a change."

"Maybe we can form a support group," Julia quipped.

"Yeah." Tara turned back to the roses. "How handsome *is* Miles?"

"Oh, attractive. Tall, blond. Sophisticated. More basketball player than football."

"More handsome than your hired man?" she egged her on.

At exactly that moment, Trevor emerged through the basement door, carrying a huge chunk of cast-iron tubing; his arm and chest muscles bulged from the effort. Sweat ran down his face, and his T-shirt was soaked. Yet he passed them with a bright smile that crinkled up his eyes warmly in the corners. The three plumbers passed by as well, carrying their own smaller segments.

"Just a question," Tara said lightly. "Tell me more about yourself."

"Well, obviously I was born into a family with great taste in property, and I was blessed with that trust fund that turned over when I hit the big 3-0. My grandmother didn't want anyone marrying me for my money, you see, before I was old enough to spot 'em for myself... Not that there's ever been any danger." She paused to look around her. "All my life I've dreamed of coming back here. Somehow it feels more like home than the house I grew up in.

"I tried to please my parents and go the professional route; I did all right as a CPA. But it just wasn't me. It was like God was calling me home." She grinned. "I mean to Torchlight, not to heaven. And he wouldn't let me rest until I listened."

"So you're a believer."

"As of a year ago."

"I see. What happened? If you don't mind my asking..."

"Not at all! My brother, Jake, works as a foreman at a ranch in Montana. After he got married, I stayed with Dirk and Rachel Tanner, the owners of the ranch, for two weeks. They had an incredible impact on me, and I realized how hollow my faith was. They helped me discover what it means to me, personally.

"That's another reason why I had to come here. I needed some time to myself...to grow. It feels good to be on my own. Away from my family and my boyfriend—at least for a while—and my old life. I'm thirty years old! It's high time I figured out what I believe...and live it. I've got a long way to go."

Tara reached across the table and squeezed her hand. "Me, too. I hope we can be there for each other. Would you want to go to church with me sometime? I think you'd enjoy getting to know our pastor and the congregation. It'd be a great way to meet some of your neighbors."

"I'd love it. I've been so busy since I got here, I haven't had time to stop and think about it."

"Well then, I'll just badger you until you actually come." Tara stretched and looked at her watch. "I'd better head back to the restaurant. But consider this: It might please God to see you cut Trevor a little more slack. The man's a believer too."

The news so surprised Julia she didn't know what to say.

"Don't look so shocked!" Tara looked at her strangely. "Why are you so suspicious of Trevor?" she whispered.

"I don't know," Julia admitted. "There's just something vaguely...dangerous about the man."

Tara frowned with concern. "Dangerous, physically dangerous?"

"No. No. I feel perfectly safe with him that way. It's more...I don't know."

"No?"

Julia squirmed under her gaze as Trevor came through the door again and disappeared into the basement.

"Are you sure you don't know what bothers you about him?" Tara asked leadingly, narrowing her eyes. "Or do you know exactly what throws you off center?"

"Isn't it time for you to leave?" Julia asked her saucily, tossing a napkin across the table.

"Oh no," Tara said. "We're just getting started, my friend."

"Well, you may be," Julia said, rising. "But I've got work to do. Can I pour you a cup of coffee as I go?"

"No. I get the hint. I'm goin', I'm goin'. But we will talk more about this someday, Julia."

"Maybe. Have a good day, Tara." She grinned. "Thanks for stopping by."

"My pleasure." She leaned forward. "Now don't work that poor man into a lather. You decide if you're interested or if you're not. Don't mess with his heart."

"Good-bye, Tara."

"Bye," she said, obviously aware that she had stepped on Julia's toes and caring not a whit.

The workers wrapped up the removal of the old boiler and cast-iron heating lines within three days and moved on to the plumbing and wiring. One night late Julia found Trevor still in the kitchen working on leveling and supporting the sagging ceiling.

"Isn't it time to call it quits?"

Trevor looked down at her from his ladder, frowning and rolling his neck to ease the tension. "Yeah, maybe now that you mention it..."

"You know I never intended for you to kill yourself on the job."

"I want to get the kitchen, master bedroom, and main systems on line quickly. Then I'll ease up. I like to get the grunt work over fast and take my time with the finish work."

"Painting, wallpapering, and all?"

"Yes."

"Closet artist?"

"Maybe." He climbed down from his ladder and held out his hands. "Still black. I'm hoping one day to get back to my natural color."

She smiled. "Have you had dinner?"

"Hadn't thought of it until you came in."

"How 'bout some leftover tomato basil soup?"

"That'd be great."

Trevor made a valiant attempt to wash his hands as Julia heated the soup and toasted some bread. They sat down at the table, each trying not to feel awkward. It was the first time they had intentionally sat down alone together. Fortunately, both were famished, and the food afforded a welcome distraction.

"This tastes great," Trevor said.

"Thanks. Got the recipe from Tara."

"Figures. That woman can cook better than anyone I know."

Julia fought off a ridiculous feeling of jealousy. She stood. "I'd better turn in. When we get the kitchen in shape, I'll make you my famous fried chicken, regardless of what it does to our arteries." Julia's forward manner surprised even herself.

He rose with her. "Or you can come over to my place and I'll cook you dinner."

"I don't think so. I feel more comfortable here, in the big house."

He brushed by her lightly as he exited the breakfast nook. "Of course."

Something in his manner disturbed her. "Look, maybe this wasn't such a great idea—"

"Not a good idea? No, I think that if you really listen closely, maybe you'll hear that you're attracted to the man you hired."

She frowned in consternation. "Of all the arrogant... Have you talked to Tara?"

"No. Why, do I need to talk to Tara? Does she know something?"

"Not at all!"

"Good night, Julia." He ducked out of the kitchen, walked quickly to the front door, and opened it.

"I have something else to say to you—"

"I think we both had better turn in now. We have a long day tomorrow." He shut the door before Julia could respond, leaving her utterly frustrated.

The phone rang, as it almost always did about this time of night. *Probably Miles.*

Julia sat down and let the phone ring until it ceased.

CHAPTER FIVE

*H*i, Sally," Ben said to the new waitress as he sat down at the counter in the restaurant. The slim blonde automatically poured him coffee. "Tara in?"

"She took the day off. She's workin' on her cookbook. I'll be fillin' in on Thursdays for the next couple of months so she can spend her time on that."

Ben nodded and lifted his coffee cup to his lips, pretending to be unmoved by the news. Tara was always here, always ready to cheer him up, make him smile. It disgruntled him that she would leave the restaurant to pursue her lofty dreams of a cookbook. What a waste of time, of money! She should stay where she was meant to be, which was here, at her restaurant, ready to pour him a cup of coffee and talk over the latest about Mike, or…

He frowned at his own explanation. He was miffed because Tara wasn't here, waiting on him like she always had. What right had he to be so presumptuous? To assume she'd stick around just to see him? They were just friends! He chatted with some locals sitting down the counter from him, then left a dollar under the saucer. Pausing outside, he debated between going home and going to see Tara.

He decided to head home. *No sense giving her the wrong idea.* It was only a short walk to the docks. Directly before him stood a large group of cottages that faced the sea. This was where he had been raised. After Sharon had died, he had given up the house on the hill and settled Mike back in the little cottage of his youth. It wasn't much, but it had given him a sense of security that nothing else could.

Mike was outside, sitting with the old-timers on boxes at the dock and working with Henry Abrahms, nailing oak laths and frames into lobster pots. The boy loved to listen to the old-timers talk fishing, and he spent hours with them, building pots or painting buoys the DeBois colors of red, gold, and purple. Each fishing boat had its own distinctly colored buoys, which were attached to the traps on the ocean floor, making it easy to decipher whose pots were whose.

"Ben," Henry nodded in greeting.

"Hi, Dad."

"Hi, Mike. Done your homework?"

"Not yet."

"Better get to it."

"Dad…"

"Better get to it."

Mike stomped off. Unfazed, the old-timers just kept on with their talk about the weather.

"Least it wasn't so bad as las' winter," Henry said.

"Yep. That was a lousy trap-bustin' winter. Practically had to start from scratch with new pots. Even had the missus working on 'em with me."

"With these prices, a body can't afford to be short one pot."

"With these prices, I can't afford to eat lobster. I'll have to eat steak."

"Prices don't matter much when you catch half what we used to," Ben broke in.

"The bottom is crawlin' with snappers," Henry said. "It'll be better this season."

"Don't think so," Ben said. "We take too many because we all have families to feed. But a lot of them are first generation. We're going out farther and taking more. How long can it keep up?"

"The snappers will always be there," Fred Nearing said gruffly.

"Fred, you told me yourself that you remember gathering the lobsters *on shore* at low tide. When's the last time you saw that? When's the last time you caught anything less than a thousand feet down?"

Ben looked around at the group of honest, straightforward men who had spent a lifetime doing difficult, backbreaking work. The men were silent. They had braved heavy seas and gale-force winds and spent their lives in pursuit of the great clawed vermilion, *Homarus americanus.*

I've spent half my life doing the same. And for what?

Feeling defeated, he followed Mike into the house.

The old-timers resumed their conversation, picking up with the raising of Danny's boat that had sunk in the severe sou'easter of last season.

Tara watched the sea become an inky gray, scalloped with whitecaps from the spring breeze as the sun faded from the sky. From her kitchen window, she could nearly see the fishing village in which the DeBoises now lived, and she wondered again if Ben had come into the restaurant looking for her.

She turned back to her easel, willing herself to focus. *Humph. Would serve him right not to find me exactly where he always thinks I'll be.* She debated calling Sally to check but decided against it. *No use anyone thinkin' I'm unduly interested.*

Sharon had been a fine woman, a dear friend. But this thing that had developed over the last few years between the deceased woman's husband and Tara had come to a head. Like Julia said she was trying to do with Miles, Tara had to do the same with Ben. *Fish or cut bait, Benjamin DeBois,* she thought angrily. If not for her, for Mike! The boy needed a mother and clearly adored Tara. Was Benjamin a blind idiot? Or just a stubborn nor'easterner, set in his ways and unwilling to change?

If he continued on, refusing to acknowledge what had happened between them—love, was it?—then, well, Tara would just move on. She would. And this project was her first step away from him, out into the world on her own. Maybe she'd meet a handsome bookstore owner, or a chef who had his own show and invited her on as a guest host…

Cherries jubilee. This border will be fun to paint. She dipped her brush into a bright red wash and set bristle to paper to create a design far merrier than she felt inside.

"Julia!" Miles's voice greeted her across the crackling telephone line. Just another thing that needed work, Julia ruefully mused. "I was worried when I couldn't reach you last night."

"Oh yes, I'm fine," she said, not feeling like explaining herself. "Thanks for the roses, Miles," she added, hoping to change the subject. Wearily, she sat down in an old padded chair. "You really don't have to send them every three days. It's too generous."

"Nonsense. If you were here, I'd be taking you to dinner every night. It's the least I can do to help you remember what you've left behind."

"Believe me, sweetheart, I remember. It's not easy being away, doing this alone."

"Maybe you won't be alone for long."

"What do you mean?"

"I'm checking into some career opportunities in Boston."

"You are?" She leaned forward, then frowned. "You said you hated the East Coast."

"Let's just say that it got a lot more attractive when you moved there. And since your heart is set on staying there awhile, I thought I could at least see what might be available for me. It's obviously what you want, and I want whatever will make you happy."

She paused over his words. *This is new.* "Any leads?"

"A few. I'll keep you posted. In the meantime, may I come and visit?"

"Yes! I'd love that, Miles. Come and see Torchlight."

"And you."

She paused a beat. "Of course. Yes. I think it would be good."

"Consider it done, darling. You can show me your little project, and I can take you out for a well-deserved dinner or two."

"Oh. Yes, okay."

"Julia? Are you all right?"

"Fine, fine. Why wouldn't I be?"

"There's just something odd in your tone of voice. Would you rather…prefer I not come?"

"No, no! Miles, please come," she encouraged him. But as they said their good-nights and she hung up the phone, she heard only his words—*your little project*—and Julia was overwhelmed with a sense of foreboding. Did he think her coming to Torchlight was merely a temporary distraction, a hobby to keep her busy for a few months?

Because the longer she remained here, the clearer it was: She was home. And what she needed was a man who could call it home too.

⌐⌐⌐

Two weeks later Miles Beckley arrived. And Trevor immediately disliked him.

The feeling was mutual.

Trevor was on a ladder tacking the shutters back into place when a white sports car screeched through the front gates. Placing his hammer in his tool belt, he watched as a tanned, healthy-looking man jumped out of the car and swung Julia into his arms. Trevor fought off a pang of jealousy.

"Trevor? Trevor!" Julia looked up at him, her eyes alight, her hand in Miles's. "Come down and meet my boyfriend."

"On my way!" He forced a note of cheerfulness into his tone and pushed aside his feelings of competition. *This is the guy Julia chose. There must be more to him than meets the eye.*

Miles watched as the man descended, his own smile fading as he realized that the contractor Julia was so relieved to have found was not a doddering old genius, but a man young enough to be trouble. *I don't like this.* Was he the reason that he couldn't reach her on the phone every night?

Trevor smiled and raised his hand to meet Miles's. Julia introduced them, and Miles shook the handyman's hand, checking out the competition with steel-gray eyes. *Commoner. Out for something other than work. Julia's money? Julia herself? I've seen his kind before.*

Trevor made his own assumptions. *Schmoozer. Out for himself, not Julia. She works well into his plans and looks good on his arm. What a leech.*

They chatted idly, then quickly parted ways.

Miles wasted no time in talking with Julia about him over dinner. They sat at one end of the huge dining room table, lit only by the candelabra, eating off century-old Wedgwood china that had just arrived from Aunt Linda.

"I'm so happy things are going well, darling," he purred. "Life in New England, despite being so far from me, seems to be agreeing with you. You're more beautiful than ever."

"Thank you, Miles."

"Have I lost you? Will you be here forever? Or will you get your little inn up and running and then come home to me?"

"You never seemed to be overly concerned with having me around when I lived in San Francisco. You're gone half the month on business. We agreed on this, Miles. I need my own life."

"An entire continent away?"

"I love this old place. I'm going to make it my home. And you could follow those leads to Boston, if you want to be closer to me."

"I just may do that."

His second affirmation astounded her. A part of her had assumed he had only been testing her, that he wasn't really serious about moving. In the four years they had been dating, he had never made her his priority. They both assumed they'd marry eventually, after Miles pushed his law practice to the top. Their families came from the same circles of San Francisco society, and as everyone said, they seemed made for each other. They laughed at the same jokes, liked the same authors. Both enjoyed theatre and dining out.

The problem was that when she turned thirty, Julia was not at all sure that those commonalties were enough. She wasn't sure "everyone" was correct.

Julia looked over at Miles, smiling at her in the candlelight. He was handsome and a successful lawyer. Her mother, Eleanor, was crazy about him, and Jacob, her father, got along with him. But there no longer seemed to be the zing she thought should be there; had it ever been there? That pause in her heartbeat, the electric bolt she sensed every time Trevor came around? She dismissed the thoughts even as they passed through her mind. *Miles would always be here for me—he's even willing to move for me! He's the right one. Trevor will be here a few months, then leave.* She smiled back at Miles.

"Look, darling, I know I've only been here for several hours and have just met the man, but what do you know about this Kenbridge? I don't like it that a man we barely know is living in the cottage right next door to you."

Julia took a bite to cover her feelings of guilt and any risk of a telling glance.

"What if he's some mass murderer or something?" Miles went on. "Have you checked him out?"

She stifled a laugh at his intimation. "I've called four references. He comes highly recommended. And I'm sure our local sheriff is on top of any wanted posters coming through the fax machine; there's not a whole lot of crime here to distract him."

"There's just something about Kenbridge I don't like."

"Maybe you're jealous," she teased.

"Do I have cause to be?"

Julia covered his hand and gazed up into his eyes, willing her soul into the words. "Of course not."

Miles stayed for the weekend, then left to meet a potential law firm associate in Boston. Before he departed, he sought out Trevor and found him in the kitchen taking apart the pipes to install a disposal.

"Kenbridge?"

Trevor ducked out from under the sink and looked up at Miles, dressed elegantly in an expensive olive-green suit, perfectly contrasting tie, and a camel's-hair overcoat. Trevor stood, wiped his wet, grimy hands on his jeans, and met the other man's eyes.

"Look," Miles said shortly. "I'll make my point so I can get out of here and back to civilization."

Trevor watched him calmly, not saying a word.

"I don't want you anywhere near Julia. You are her hired man and nothing else. You touch her and you'll pay."

"Worried?" Trevor baited him.

"Not at all," Miles lied. "Just a warning in case you ever think of making a move. I plan on Julia being my wife someday. I know it's hard on a man like you to be near such an attractive woman. But don't touch. She belongs to me."

"Julia doesn't strike me as a woman who likes to be owned."

Miles moved within an inch of Trevor's face, but Trevor did not budge. "Don't mess with me, Kenbridge," he warned.

"Something tells me that I'd take distinct pleasure in 'messing with you.' We've just met, but I know you. I know your kind. And from what I've seen of Julia, you're not the man she needs."

"Miles?" Julia called from the entryway. "Miles, you'd better get going if you want to make your train."

He turned on his heel and stalked to the kitchen doorway, then faced Trevor once more. "You don't know anything. Cause any trouble between us, and I'll personally boot you out of here."

Trevor could hear Miles speaking with Julia in low, earnest tones as they stood in the entry, and he could not resist peeking around the corner to look at them. Miles bent his head to kiss her good-bye, and Julia quickly gave him a perfunctory peck on the cheek, not the passionate, warm kiss Trevor assumed would be natural between a couple in love.

He went back to his work, whistling a bright little tune he had heard Tara humming the day before.

"Julia!" Trevor called from the southwest corner bedroom. "Julia!"

She hurried up the stairs, wondering what had happened now. After patching the roof temporarily, Trevor had moved on to the task of expanding the two existing water closets into full bathrooms and adding a third.

She walked through the doorway and almost into Trevor, who was on his way out to get her. "There you are!" he said. "Check it out…"

He walked to the corner of the room and paused beside a wall panel that had not yet been removed. Reaching behind an exposed wall stud, he pulled a wire, and a hidden door popped open.

Julia gasped. "A hidden doorway! Where does it go?"

"I don't know," Trevor said with a mischievous twinkle in his eye. "Let's explore."

"I'll go grab my flashlight!"

"Grab mine, too, while you're at it. It's downstairs by the kitchen sink."

Julia returned within a minute, slightly out of breath after running up the stairs. She smiled at Trevor. "Let's go."

Trevor nodded excitedly. "Ladies first."

Acknowledging his dare, she passed him smugly, accepting the challenge. The passageway was tiny, dusty, and full of ancient cobwebs. Scrunching up her face, she plunged forward with Trevor close on her heels.

"What do you think old Grandfather Donnovan wanted with a hidden passageway?" Trevor asked.

"Who knows? I don't think he was into anything illegal. Weren't hidden rooms the thing when this old house was raised? Maybe he just liked having secrets." The passageway turned sharply and plunged down a cramped, steep stairway. "Going down," she warned.

At the bottom, they turned to the right and then right again. Straight ahead, the upper half of the passageway was blocked, forcing them to duck as they crawled through the narrow opening. "I think this space must be one of the dining room windows," Trevor said. "I thought they were unusually deep."

"I bet you're right! Here's the other one!" Julia ducked, crawled through, and moved on. She was so excited she didn't wait for Trevor. Julia reached the end of the passageway and scanned a series of shelves that held volumes of leather-bound books and sheaves of paper. Several were too high for her to reach. "Trevor, could you reach those?"

There was no answer.

"Trevor?" Julia turned and flashed her light back down the passageway. It was empty. *He's trying to scare me.* She ignored Trevor's silence and looked back at the shelves, grabbing the nearest book.

She blew the dust from its spine and coughed at the resulting cloud. "Whew!" Julia opened the pages.

Anna Serine Donnovan, 1839

"Oh! Trevor! Come quick! I know you're there! Look what I've found."

He crawled through the last window frame space and stood behind her, holding the flashlight beneath his chin to light up his face eerily. "I'm coming," he said in a monotone. Getting only a distracted giggle from Julia, he gave up his game, and his voice returned to normal. "You won't believe what I found."

"Look what *I've* found! My great-great-grandmother's diaries. Think of the family history stored in these. And look! She wrote a ton of them! This was Anna's passageway, not Shane's."

"And if this works like the dining room passageway…," Trevor began, searching the walls. He found an exposed wire and pulled, and an entire bookcase swung outward into the library, letting in the afternoon light.

Julia's jaw dropped. "How in the world…"

"The dining room china cabinet moves the same way."

"You're kidding. None of the china was hurt moving it, was it?"

"No. Whoever designed these was ingenious. Check out the tiny lips that hold the books in place. It's the same in the china cabinet. And the way these swing—so level and so smooth—nothing budges, even with the weight and momentum of the pieces."

"That's amazing. I would think that the settling of the house over the last hundred years would have thrown them off-center or something. Here, help me take some of these diaries into the library."

Julia grabbed two more volumes from the shelves and walked

through the huge secret doorway into the room. She placed the books on a table near the window, which faced the lighthouse and sea, then turned to take five more volumes from Trevor's hands. "Is this all of them?"

"That's it."

"What about that tin box up high? Could you grab it for me?"

"Can do."

Trevor emerged from the passageway a moment later, then carefully shut the bookcase behind him. Setting down the tin, he went to work looking for the secret latch that opened the case from inside the room, while Julia began reading.

Finding the first of the volumes by date, she opened the first page and began reading Anna's elaborate, flowing script.

25 December 1839

My Shane has convinced me at last. Perhaps it's the cheery and hopeful mood that surrounds the celebration of our Lord's birth that made me susceptible at last to his dreams and aspirations. Having made captain the same day as making me his fiancée seems to have sent him floating on air. I find it most difficult to even speak with him of the details, but I must say it is enjoyable to see him in such high spirits. He says it's as if the world's at his feet, now that I have agreed to become one with him on 18 January 1840, despite my parents' concerns over his dangerous seafaring occupation, and his desire to emigrate to America. It will be quite a trip, indeed.

"Julia?" Trevor stared at her. She was so absorbed in Anna's journals that she didn't hear his voice. Her distraction afforded him the chance to watch her intently, observing how her hair shone in the soft light of the lamp beside her, and how her violet eyes eagerly took in the words upon the pages before her.

"You are beautiful," he said simply. But she did not hear him even then. "You are quite possibly the most beautiful woman I've ever encountered," he said, more bold.

This, she heard.

She raised her head slightly and looked up at him. Her eyes threatened to melt his heart. Never had he encountered a woman like her. After only four weeks, he knew he was in trouble. "I've only seen eyes like yours in the Middle East. There are people there who have eyes the color of teal or the impossible violet of your own. Yours are amazing. I could sit and stare into them for hours."

"Trevor…"

"I know, I know," he raised his hands in immediate surrender. "You're practically engaged to our friend Miles, and I'm the hired man. Still, you should know that I'm intrigued, Ms. Rierdon, and it takes a lot for me to be intrigued. You can take it or leave it. I just have to be honest. I agreed to no games when you hired me. I'm not flirting. I'm…declaring."

She was apparently at a loss for words. "Thank you," she said lamely.

He smiled at her. "You're welcome."

Chapter Six

*B*en finished his blueberry pie as Tara served another customer and then returned to him to continue chatting. "And anyway, she said she'd put me in touch with some big New York publishers. Maybe it could really happen!"

"Well, don't count your chickens before they hatch."

"Oh, Ben, dream a little with me! Think of it. I could finish this cookbook, maybe another. Maybe I could even do a local cable cooking show in Portland."

"Aren't you getting ahead of yourself?"

"Why are you being so negative?" It made her cross that he was bringing her down from her high mood.

"I just don't want to see you disappointed."

"Well, *you're* disappointing me. I thought you'd be happy for me."

"Happy that you might up and leave to be a big-city author? Happy that you might start your own cable show in Portland? I like things the way they are."

"And how are things, Ben?" she asked, crossing her arms in front of her.

"Well, you know." He squirmed in his chair.

"No. I don't."

"I can't talk to you when you're like this." He got up and laid a five-dollar bill on the counter.

"When I'm like what?" She raised her voice. The other customers in the tiny restaurant were watching them. "When I finally push you to tell me how you feel?"

"Good night, Tara."

She turned away from him. Their relationship had reached a stalemate. She would *not* be the first to confess. It had to be his move.

Tara put her hands on the back countertop, not turning to face him. "Good night, Ben."

All eyes followed Ben as he put on his hat and walked out the door.

"I know something that will make you happy as a cow in a field of clover," Trevor announced as he arrived in the living room, where Julia was moving furniture. He wiped his greasy hands on a shop towel, and grinned from ear to ear.

"Don't know if I like the comparison to a sister of the bovine species, but I'll bite. What?"

"Come with me."

Obediently she followed behind as he led her to the kitchen. He nodded at the sink. "Try 'er out."

"No! The water? It's done?"

"Give her a whirl," he said, like a daddy playing as Santa.

"Oh, Trevor! If I have clear water, I *will* be pleased as a cow in a field of clover." Tentatively, she reached out and twisted the knobs. The faucet sputtered and spit and then ran quickly with the first clear, clean water she'd seen since arrival. "Oh, Trevor!" she repeated. Without thinking, she turned and gave him a quick hug. She was in his arms before she realized that it was rather unorthodox behavior for a boss and her employee. She pushed away and focused on the running water. "Thank you, thank you," she said lightly. "I'm ever so grateful."

"How 'bout I make you dinner to celebrate?" Trevor asked.

Julia had been working with him and the men all week, ripping out the walls in preparation for the new plumbing and bathrooms while the guys did the primary work in the basement. She and Trevor had at last reached the master bedroom and were almost done with the ripping work. She glanced at him as he yanked at a piece of kitchen wallboard covered with layers of wallpaper, but she was careful not to look too long. He hadn't made another move toward her since his declaration of admiration in the library a week before. She had pretended his offer was a casual one of friendship and camaraderie, and yet she had carefully placed Miles out of her mind.

"Sounds great," she said, after an awkward moment of silence. "What are you going to make me?"

"I'll surprise you. My place or yours?"

"Mine," she said. Trevor had managed to fix up the lighthouse cottage in the month since he arrived, in addition to the work he had accomplished on the main house. The cottage was quaint and very livable, and Trevor enjoyed its easy access to the lighthouse. But, as she had made clear earlier, she felt surer of herself in her own living space.

"Okay," he agreed. "Seven o'clock?"

"Great." Then she said deliberately, "This is just dinner between colleagues, right?"

"It's anything you want it to be."

"It's a platonic dinner. Let's keep the lines clear."

At five minutes to seven, Julia looked at herself in the mirror one more time. After taking a long, luxurious bath in the blessed clear, and hot, water, and redressing, she was at last ready for dinner. She chided herself for being nervous and thought of Miles, due to arrive again later that week. "Why am I more excited about dinner tonight than my upcoming weekend with Miles?" she asked her image in the mirror.

The thought of Trevor downstairs cooking dinner distracted her. What an amazing man. He had traveled the world. He was good with a hammer and in the kitchen. He could make rusty water clean. And he was obviously infatuated with her. "In-fat-u-at-ed," she enunciated at her image, just in case she was thinking it was anything more. Then she turned and walked downstairs.

Obviously not wanting to put Julia off, Trevor had set a table in the brightly lit kitchen rather than in the darker and more intimate dining room. When she entered, he glanced at her briefly, then looked again as if to make sure what he had seen was true. "You... you're stunning."

"Thanks. Thought I'd dress for dinner."

Julia wore a lavender silk blouse, which brought out the color of her eyes, tucked into a slim black denim skirt that tapered to her lower calf. Her hair was pulled up in a graceful chignon.

Trevor looked down at himself. He wore jeans and a white Henley, with a handwoven vest. "Sorry I couldn't dress up more. My luggage should be arriving any day." He had been living out of his duffel bag for an entire month, but it hadn't mattered to Julia. To her, his easy ways and simple, if slightly foreign, clothing were reassuring.

Trevor turned back to his work at the sink. "That Miles is a very lucky man. Glad you're with me tonight and not him."

Me too, she reluctantly admitted to herself. *I'm just not in the mood to see Miles.* "So what's for dinner?"

"A bit of Thailand. Curried chicken and all the fixin's."

"Hmm. Been to Thailand, too, eh?"

"Ten years ago. Fascinating country, fascinating people."

"You've wandered far and wide."

"I've done my share."

"Why? I mean, I like traveling just as much as the next person does, but Europe and a couple of other trips have pretty much sated that desire. What drove you to see so much?"

"I wanted to see it all. I really started after college and didn't stop for twelve years. Here we are in this huge, wonderful, diverse planet—I wanted to see it. I wanted to know other cultures, other people, learn other views. It was a passion. I worked my way through four continents and forty-two countries."

"Forty-two?" She reached for some cheese to put on her cracker.

"Forty-two." He opened the fridge and pulled out a salad.

"So what happened? Did you see all you needed to?"

"I just reached a point where I felt like I'd gotten a solid overview of the rest of the world. I wanted to come home. I'll always want to travel, but that won't be my entire focus anymore. I told you I'd been dreaming about lighthouses. And Bryn was in Maryland, so I went there and started driving north. Which led me to Torchlight." She felt as if he wanted to add "and you," but his lips had quit moving.

"Is that how you've always done it? Just found your way, followed your nose, until someplace tickled your fancy?"

"Pretty much. I'd run into someone friendly or interesting or find a place so gorgeous I knew I had to stay and see it through at least one seasonal change. I've seen some amazing places, met some fantastic people."

"I bet." She chewed another bite of cracker and cheese, thinking back on her postcollege trip. "I saw Europe, briefly. Twelve countries in a month."

Trevor smiled knowingly. "Dead guys' grave sites, big buildings?"

"Yes," she said, aware of what was coming.

"You missed the people, the texture. Are they all jumbled together in your memory, hard to decipher, one from the other?"

"Somewhat. Language changes help."

"Uh-huh. I decided right away that it took at least three weeks in a country to get a real sense of it." He turned to stir a pot, and Julia studied him. He was so worldly, so earthy, so sensual…so different from Miles, who considered himself worldly-wise.

Trevor handed her a tiny clay cup with hot green tea and raised his arm to toast. "To Torchlight."

"To Torchlight," she echoed.

After dinner they sat in the living room and settled into two chairs drawn close to the fire. Trevor had had the fireplace fixed right away so Julia could get heat from the wood-burning fireplaces and not just from the more expensive electric floorboard heaters. Heatilators were installed in each fireplace, making efficient use of the fire. Still, Julia and Trevor both pulled blankets over themselves.

"So where's Grandmother Anna today?" Trevor asked with true interest. Julia had been reading Anna's diaries nightly, and each day she was keeping him abreast of the news.

"Oh, Trevor! She was a wonderful writer. They're still in the middle of the Atlantic, and she describes everything so well that it's like I'm traveling with her."

"Would you read me some? I'd like to hear what you're so charged about."

Julia's smile was warm. "I'd love to."

As she went to retrieve the diary from the library, she felt his gaze rest upon her. When she came back into the firelight, she paused to turn on the lamp beside her chair. "Sorry," she apologized as the white light intruded upon their cozy atmosphere.

"The better to see you with," he quipped.

She ignored him and began to read.

> 10 June 1840
>
> I watch Shane in command, and my heart swells with pride. He is a good, fair captain, and the men respond to him with genuine appreciation. Despite the pain and problems of such a long voyage, the ship is still a happy one. I continue to spend most of my days here in the captain's cabin, reading or working at my cross-stitch. If we ever reach this land called America, I shall kneel upon it and kiss the ground. I do not understand a sailor's calling to live upon the waves.

Julia paused and looked up at Trevor. He smiled at her.

"Are you listening?"

"Of course! It's wonderful."

Julia continued reading.

> My love deepens for Shane, quite possibly because I no longer have the distractions of family or society about me. We are as Adam and Eve in the Garden, ready to

make this world our own. Explorers. Conquerors. Partners. With him I have found the best companion I could have and a lover, too. What a blessing that God saw fit to match us!

20 June 1840

The voyage continues, and I grow increasingly anxious to reach land. My stomach sails with the waves, even at this late date in the voyage, although by now my seasickness should have ceased. I cannot keep even hardtack down. I am growing weaker, and I can see the concern in my Shane's eyes. He mumbles words such as "The sea is no place for a woman" and scans the horizon for a hint of land. He curses the slow pace of the ship and yells at his man above decks to "look harder."

28 June 1840

Land ho! America has been sighted, and not a moment too soon. I find myself too weak to even rise from my bed and have discovered the reason. I carry Shane's child. I am exhausted, but the thought fills me with joy.

10 July 1840

Shane has found a tiny apartment for us here in this bustling city called "New York." It looks little like the York of England and has many more people than our village at home. Shane says we will not be here more

than a few months. He is off on a voyage again. He will
travel around South America to a place called
"Kalifornia," earning money to buy us a home. America is
more expensive than we were ever told.

Julia continued to read, completely absorbed in her ancestors' world. After an hour, she glanced up at Trevor, who looked back at her sleepily.

"I love your time warp, but I have to admit I'm getting tired," he said. "I think I'll go finish the dishes and then turn in. The plumbers are coming early in the morning." Sitting there watching her read was like pure torture. *Look, but don't touch,* Miles had warned. And all he wanted to do was touch her, caress her cheek, kiss those lips…

"I'll finish the dishes. It's the least I can do—you cooked me such a marvelous meal. And fixed the water!"

"With some help from the guys." He stood. "Okay. I'll be a poor host and let you at the dishes."

"It will give me another chance to gawk at the water," she said with a smile. "It's amazing how you appreciate something like running water when you've been living with ol' rusty for a while."

"There're a lot of things you notice you miss when you have to go without it."

They walked together to the door. Julia shivered slightly at the cool night air upon her neck.

Trevor noticed her tremble and fought the urge to take her in his arms. What was it that drew him? She was beautiful, to be sure, but he had met hundreds of attractive women in his travels. *Why this one, Father?* His anguish consumed him; Julia's heart clearly belonged to another. She was his boss, nothing more. He closed his eyes and imagined Julia embracing him, returning his eager kisses…

"Trevor?" Julia questioned, noticing his closed eyes.

He started and blinked. Swallowing hard, he said with a melancholy tone, "Good night, Julia."

"Good night."

He paused with his hand on the door handle. "Julia?"

"Yes?"

"Do you think we could do this again? I enjoyed the company and sharing the Donnovans' story, but I don't want to cross any lines. I want you to be comfortable too."

"Thank you. I think…I think we could."

Trevor smiled as he walked out the door and headed for the cottage. But as he walked, he couldn't help but wonder if he should keep on walking. Because back there, at the house, was surely trouble.

Tara turned off the lights and locked the door to the restaurant. Now that it was spring again, she could walk home in the evenings. She enjoyed the cool night air after a long shift in the humid kitchen.

Ben emerged from the shadows and began to follow her, undetected. It was his habit to see that Tara got home safely. But for some reason he could never tell her or escort her openly. *It's easier and safer this way,* he told himself. *We're just friends.* It had really gotten complicated last summer. Their friendship had deepened over the past year as Ben had shared with Tara his struggles over raising a teenager alone. Mike and Tara were crazy about each other. She was a logical and attractive choice for the widower.

But whenever Ben saw her laugh, his mind spun crazily back to times he had watched her laugh with Sharon in the kitchen of his own home. Sharon. He wondered if the ache in his heart would ever end. *Oh, Sharon, I miss you.*

He justified his reasons for following Tara home, for eating at her restaurant three times a week, and for often visiting her at the house on Saturdays with Mike. *It's for Mike. The boy needs a mother figure around.* But Ben had to admit, he enjoyed Tara's company too. The thought of her moving away threw him for a loop. He stared at her diminutive figure, bundled in a fisherman's coat, and concentrated on quietly keeping pace with her. He wouldn't confuse the issue by outwardly escorting her home.

During his second weekend in Maine, Miles slept at a tiny inn, refusing to stay at Torchlight, which was again without any running water while the crew worked on the upstairs plumbing. He tried to talk Julia into staying with him, but she refused, ignoring his obvious insinuation.

"Come on, Julia, we're practically engaged."

"But we're not really engaged, are we, Miles? And even if we were, I still wouldn't sleep with you."

"Hmm. Can I help it if I find you incredibly attractive? But play by the rules; I respect that. In any case, it's not sanitary to live in a place without water. Come into some semblance of civilization. Stay with me. I'll sleep on the couch."

"No, thank you. We'll have water back in a few days, and in the meantime, I've made do with a shower at Tara's every couple of days. I reserved some water for sponge baths before they shut off the main. Really, Miles, where's your sense of adventure?"

He looked at her askance. "I could ask the same question, but I'll ignore that comment because I don't want to ruin our weekend together. We have some wonderful plans."

"We do?"

"Well, don't look so surprised. Your old Miles has a trick or two up his sleeve."

She smiled at the glint in his eye. "Such as...?"

"I'm going to show you the town."

"Miles! I'd love that. I haven't had much of a chance to see anything, with all the work to be done here at Torchlight."

"Good. Then it's a date."

He was moving to kiss her when Trevor walked in the front door. Miles scowled at him as he and Julia parted. "Don't you knock?"

"Good to see you, too, Beckley. Guess you didn't realize, this house is my work zone. Julia stays in her room if she wants privacy." He looked at his boss for the first time. Trevor clearly understood he had broken up a romantic moment and was doing his best to stifle a smile. "That's still the arrangement, right?"

Julia shifted, obviously uncomfortable with the way Trevor was drawing her to his side of the sparring. "That's true—"

"There you have it. Straight from the boss's mouth."

He brushed by as Miles bristled. "Isn't it a bit late for work?"

"I get paid for overtime." Trevor's eyes twinkled with mischief. He headed toward the kitchen to meet the plumbers in the basement, but paused in the doorway. "Oh, and Miles, too bad you haven't been around more. There have been all sorts of interesting developments lately."

Miles glared back at him.

"Would you two knock it off?" Julia asked, looking from her agitated boyfriend to her general contractor.

Miles's face was an angry red, and the veins on his temple bulged. He looked at Julia accusingly as Trevor disappeared. "What's been going on around here? Has he made a move on you?"

"No. Of course not." She shifted uncomfortably. "We're just friends. We've shared a few evenings of reading and such, but that's it."

"Are you sure?"

"Miles!"

"I'm sorry, but something about that man drives me crazy. I think he's after you, Julia."

She looked toward the door and back to Miles. "Even if he were, I wouldn't return his feelings. The man is a wanderer." She embraced the man she had known for over a decade, dated for the last four years. "I prefer to know that the man I'm interested in will be around, not to wonder when I wake up if he's off to some new territory."

Miles studied her in his arms, wondering if she was trying to convince herself just as much as she was trying to convince him.

"I'm not surprised you two don't get along; you're so different. But I would have thought the two of you would be mature enough to get along. For my sake at least."

Miles softened, inhaling deeply. "I'll try. I've certainly dealt with his type before." He paused in the entry.

Julia changed the subject. "You could put on your jeans and help us out here tomorrow morning. There's plenty to do."

Miles smiled down at her. "There's a part of me that wants to do just that. But I have business calls to make, letters to fax. Meet you back here at five?"

Julia's disappointment was evident. "Miles, are you ever going to help me?"

He took her chin in his hand and raised her face gently to meet his. "This is your dream. Chase it if you must. But do not expect me to. I have my own dreams. Isn't it enough that I visit, take part in the dream a little? Better than not at all, right?"

She sighed. "Five will be fine."

CHAPTER SEVEN

*T*hat afternoon Julia was working upstairs, removing molding to be refinished, when she heard a large freight truck pull up front. *What on earth is being delivered now?* She walked downstairs and opened the front door.

Trevor was already outside, talking to the driver and his assistant. He looked up and grinned at Julia.

"My luggage!" he explained excitedly. "Bring it around the side," he directed the driver and followed them toward the cottage.

Julia watched as the truck, loaded with several large trunks, three sizable wooden crates, and two suitcases, pulled forward.

"Where'd it come from?" she called to Trevor's back.

"Nepal," was all he threw back over his shoulder.

Miles arrived promptly at five, showing up at her door with a glamorous bouquet of spring flowers—purple irises, barely open, bright yellow daffodils, tulips of violet, soft pink, and pale yellow, and fragrant stock of several shades.

"Why, Miles, I've never known you to give me anything other than red roses."

"I thought it was time for a change," he said with a wink. "Spring flowers, symbolic of a new era for us." He leaned close and gave her a deep, searching kiss. Julia settled into his arms, longing to feel intimate with him, but the kiss did little for her heart. She gave him a tentative smile. *It's as if I'm giving him a smiley sticker for effort,* she chided herself. She turned and set the flowers in a glass of water, deciding to arrange them in a vase when they returned. Resolutely she took his proffered hand and stepped out of the house.

As Miles and Julia walked out onto the porch toward the Lincoln town car he had rented, Trevor drove past them on his motorcycle with a wave.

Julia stopped and watched him go.

"Julia?" Miles questioned, closely watching her.

"Trevor didn't say he was going anywhere."

"Does he tell you everything?" Miles asked.

"Not everything. But my goodness, Miles, we're working close together. We talk."

"Is that all you do?"

She turned to confront him. "Are we going out for our date, or are you going to grill me about Trevor?"

Miles looked from Julia to Trevor's departing figure, then opened the car door. "Shall we?"

Julia got in without a word. Why was she concerned about where Trevor was going? It was certainly none of her business. What was her business was Miles. Her dear, sweet Miles. The man with whom she had won sailboat races and danced until dawn at countless parties. He was the man she needed. Stable, strong. Hadn't he been with her for four years? If that didn't prove his devotion, she didn't know what would.

Mike, watching Julia and Miles pass through town, entered the restaurant with a puzzled look on his face. The speed was only twenty miles per hour down Main Street, making every passerby gawking material. "Why does Julia hang out with that dweeb?" he asked Tara, nodding his head toward the door.

"Dweeb?"

"The rich guy who cruises through town in those fancy rented cars."

"She thinks he's the one for her."

"Why? I mean, I like Jessica, but if she acted as hoity-toity as Julia's boyfriend does, I wouldn't spend time with her."

Tara dished up a bowl of chowder for the always-hungry boy. "Sometimes adult relationships can get complicated."

"Like you and my dad?"

Tara wondered if she looked as stunned as she felt. "What do you mean?"

"Come on, Tara. You know. I'm not blind."

"Obviously. Have you asked your father this question?"

"Yeah. He gets around it every time."

"He's pretty good at that."

Mike spooned chowder into his mouth as fast as he could, then smiled at Tara across the counter. He was the only one in the restaurant, as usual for this time of day. In the last two weeks, he had shown up for a bowl of soup after school almost every day and had then returned several evenings with his dad for dinner.

"You'd be a great mom, Tara," Mike said.

"Thanks, Mike. Maybe with some practice I could be even better."

"You can practice on me anytime."

That evening Miles took Julia all the way to Portland—nearly two hours distant—to show her "the town."

"I thought you were going to take me out in Oak Harbor. Can't you even try to understand my new home? To see the good in my life here?" Julia was hungry and becoming more irritable by the moment.

"Listen, Julia. I just wanted a quiet, romantic dinner with you. I wanted to do something special, not take you to Tara's. Was I wrong?"

Julia sighed. "No. I just wish you'd try."

"If I wasn't trying, I wouldn't be here at all. Let me get used to all this in my own time."

Julia looked at him sadly. She had the sinking feeling he would never "get used to all this." But she had to admit, the restaurant—a restored captain's home that overlooked the water—was wonderful. They dined on pot roast, potatoes, cabbage, and carrots.

"Takes you back to Anna and Shane's era, doesn't it?" Miles asked, pausing over his last bite to grin at her. "Come on. Admit it. You like this more than you thought you would."

"I admit it. I wasn't eager to leave Oak Harbor, but now that I'm here, it feels good. I haven't explored much of Maine yet. And Portland isn't really that far."

"Let's explore some of it together, darling. Come. I'll pay the bill, and we can take a walk down by the harbor, stare up at the old clippers. I'm told they have them all lit up. You can dream of Shane Donnovan and tell me what's transpired in Anna's journals."

"Not a whole lot," Julia said, wiping her mouth with the cloth napkin. "She's still awaiting his return from California, which she spelled with a *K*."

Miles smiled. *He really is handsome when he smiles,* she thought, staring across their intimate table for two. *And he is trying…*

"Let's go for that walk," she said, smiling shyly. Maybe they'd kiss again, and she'd remember a little of that spark she once had felt for him.

Trevor's motorcycle was not in its usual place when they returned.

"Do you think he's okay?" Julia asked Miles. She'd never known Trevor to be out so late. It was almost midnight.

"He probably had a date. Can I come in for a nightcap?"

Feeling oddly cross at Trevor's disappearance and not wanting to be alone, Julia welcomed the idea. "I have only coffee. Maybe I could brew some and read to you from Anna's journals."

They went in the house, and Julia went to make some coffee. Her drip machine had died that morning, and so she boiled water on the stove. After setting up a filter and measuring out the black, fragrant grounds, she retrieved the latest journal from the library. *How fun to share this with Miles, too.* She had explained to him a little over dinner how much the journals meant to her.

By the time she returned to the kitchen, the teapot was whistling, and she poured the steaming water through the filter. After fixing Miles's coffee carefully, with just the right amount of cream, she entered the living room with their cups on a tray.

Miles waited for her on the overstuffed couch, newly recovered in a rich tapestry fabric. He sat, relaxed yet regal.

"You look like you belong in this room," she said with admiration in her voice.

"Thank you. It feels good to be here with you, Julia."

Julia carefully laid the tray down on the coffee table in front of them and sat beside Miles. She handed Miles his coffee and, after sipping from her own cup, opened the journal to where she and Trevor had last left Anna.

"Anna is pregnant," Julia informed Miles. "She's waiting for Shane to return from his voyage to California."

30 July 1840

The heat is unbearable. Never have I endured such a sweltering summer as this New York seems to brew. Now four months along, my back aches, and I fear the way I perspire will dehydrate me and harm our child. Oh, how I long for Shane to return! It should be soon, but I am not patient. The thought of his touch makes me tremble. I want to dine with him, sleep with him, live with him, even in this, our meager little apartment. The only thing that matters is that we are together.

Julia blushed at this very personal journal entry, but Miles wasn't looking at her. He stared at the paintings that adorned the walls.

"Are you listening?"

"Of course. She certainly is passionate, isn't she? Is one of these pictures of Anna?"

"Above the fireplace," she directed, pleased that he was at least interested in part of the history of Torchlight.

"Why, you look just like her! Look at her lips. And her eyes. They're just your color. It's uncanny."

"I must admit, it feels a bit odd to look at that portrait. Apparently there's another in the town library, which she founded. People remark about the resemblance all the time. It's rather unnerving."

Julia resumed her reading and became so engrossed in her great-great-grandmother's prose that she failed to notice Miles walking up behind her. All at once he was kissing her neck.

"Miles…" She gently pushed him away with a grin. Now *there* was a spark.

He came around the couch to sit beside Julia, took her in his arms, and kissed her. His embrace felt warm, comfortable. After several moments, he drew back, his eyes taking in every inch of her. Holding her hands in his, he said, "I want to make our own history in this house. Together, in Shane and Anna's bedroom. I want to hold you where they held one another." His face was earnest.

Julia looked away, frowning slightly. "Miles…we've been through this before."

"And don't you think we've waited long enough, Julia? It's been four years. We can wait until we marry. Or we can consummate our love now. Come upstairs. I love you. Let me show you."

She looked into his hopeful, smoldering eyes. "Look, Miles. You're a handsome, desirable man. But I decided long ago that I would make love only to the man whom I would know for the rest of my life as my *husband*. I thought you agreed. It's the way God meant for it to be."

He leaned toward her, kissing her soundly, than nuzzled her neck, moving toward her clavicle and sending delicious shivers down her spine. "God created us as two people with desires," he muttered, still kissing, "a man and woman who want to be with one another."

"And who can have each other, body and soul, once they're married." She gently pushed him away.

He stood, his face red. "You know I'm only waiting to ask you to marry me because I want to make a decent life for you."

"I don't want to push you into it, Miles. Why do our arguments always have to revolve around you? This isn't only about you. It's about my dreams, and your dreams, and how they meld together. I haven't decided that you should be the man I marry. If you ever should decide I should be your wife, and you actually ask me rather than assume it will happen one day, I hope I know how to answer. But in the meantime, I wish we could just enjoy each other's company. Are we so accustomed to the action of the big city that we can't relate to each other without it?"

Miles ran a hand through his hair and looked up at the high ceiling. "Look, I'm sorry. You're right. We've waited this long… I want to marry you, Julia. You're the one I love. I knew you wanted to wait, so I didn't push. But with you all the way out here, in Maine, so far away… I just want us to be close, Julia."

"I want that too, Miles."

He sighed. "Look, we're tired. Let's talk about this tomorrow after we both get a good night's sleep."

Julia walked to the door and opened it for him. "No," she said slowly. "I think I came to Torchlight for a break, Miles. I need some time. Some time to figure out what I want. I long to be close to you, but I'm no longer sure that marriage is what will bring me that. I need to think! I need to think. Please, go. Go home. I'll call."

"What are you talking about? Just like that you're ready to end a four-year relationship?"

"I'm not ending it, Miles. I just want a break."

"We both know where separation leads, Julia. Maybe we should see a counselor, find someone to hear us both out." He reached for her, but she pulled away.

"Please. Miles. Please, just go. I'll call. I promise."

"Julia, when I say my vows to you, it will be forever. Let me love you. I'm sorry for pushing." His humble tone began to cool her anger.

"It's not the pushing, Miles. I...I need time to sort things out. In my heart, in my head."

"Julia—" He reached for her, but she held up her hand.

"Good night, Miles." And with that, she shut the door in his face.

She leaned into it from the other side, trembling, until she heard the engine purr to a start and the gravel slide as he left Torchlight.

Then she wept.

Chapter Eight

The following morning Ben surprised Tara as she was taking fresh muffins from the oven. "Good morning!"

His deep voice so startled her she almost dropped the pan. "Ben! You're not going out today?"

"Nah. Fishin's been lousy the last week, and I thought I could use a break. I had this idea…"

"Well, what is it?" Tara busied herself with removing the muffins from the tins.

"I was thinkin'…we could try it and see what you think…and you could say no—"

"What, Ben?" Tara turned to face him.

He squeezed his crumpled hat, unconsciously wadding it up into a tight ball. "You and I have been working hard since we were just kids. We've never taken more than one day off a week in our lives, and I was thinking I'm missin' out on a lot because of that.

"Talkin' to Trevor last night, and hearing about how he's seen the world, makes me want to get out there too. And then I thought, I haven't even seen much of my own home state. I've been to Acadia, and I've been hunting down west, but there's a lot I haven't seen. I don't want Mike growin' up the same way. And I was thinkin' you might consider doin' this with us."

"What?" Tara repeated gently.

"Well, after church Sunday, maybe you could get Sally to fill in—since it's a slower day than usual—and maybe we three could go explore."

"Ben DeBois, I can't believe you're saying this. Are you asking me out on a date?"

He studied her, long and hard. "A date?"

"A date," Tara said, lowering her gaze.

"Does it have to be?"

"Why, yes, Ben. I think it does."

"Call it what you will. I want you to come with us. It's important to me."

Tara smiled mischievously. "I'd love to go. Where should we start?"

"Let's sail to Egg Island next week on your boat. Mine's still in dry dock."

"Sailing! That means it's truly closing in on summer. Now sit down, and I'll pour you some coffee, and you can share one of these cranberry muffins with me."

The departing sound of Trevor's motorcycle woke Julia. In the early hours that Sunday morning, when Trevor had returned home from his night's activities, his bike's single beam had cast a shadow-and-light show on her bedroom ceiling. Now, he was apparently leaving again.

By the time she raced downstairs to ask where he was headed, Trevor was already roaring down the road. She stood in the grand entry, panting after her hurried descent and looking out the window to the open gates. She sat down on the bottom stair and sighed.

Why am I holding out? Why don't I just give in to Miles if he is truly the man I mean to spend the rest of my life with? Is it really so impor-

tant to God, or is it just old-fashioned idealism? And why am I racing after Trevor like some sick schoolgirl?

She placed her head in her hands and moaned loudly.

After showering and making herself some breakfast and coffee, Julia decided to go to the lighthouse. She had been to the top only a few times since her arrival, and she was eager to see the estate's namesake again. For once she was free from renovation questions, and she didn't need to entertain Miles. *I've earned a day off,* she assured herself.

She walked into the foggy morning, thinking that it looked the way she felt. It was during mornings and nights exactly like these that ships had depended upon the coastal lighthouses to guide their way. A huge foghorn stood atop the cottage. Lighthouse keepers had used it to warn ships away by sound, when the sailors could not see the beacon.

Where's my lighthouse? Where is my foghorn? Lord, I need some serious direction.

Julia entered the musty, dark, conical building. After pausing to let her eyes adjust, she moved toward the stairs, which were dimly lit by a shaft of light coming from the windows high above. She climbed the hundred and eighty steps that circled steeply around the edge of the building until she reached the top. "Whew! Better than a StairMaster," she said.

Julia looked through the windows to the waves crashing on the rocks beneath her, then looked out to the sea beyond. It was as soupy as London's fog, and Julia wondered how ships had ever made their way without benefit of radio and sonar. It seemed a miracle that any ships had been spared in these waters.

She shivered in the cold and wondered again where Trevor had gone. He had Sundays off, but he rarely left Torchlight, preferring to stay in his cottage and read, or look over magazines and books with Julia in preparation for the projects ahead. It was May, and they had completed the plumbing; next they had to replace the walls of the new bathrooms and find appropriate furnishings.

Julia fought the feeling of abandonment and thought again of Miles as she searched the dense clouds before her. As if on cue, Miles pulled through the front gates and parked in front of the house. She watched as he went inside, but did not go after him. The sight of him still made her angry.

After several minutes, Miles stormed out of the house, calling her name. He rounded the corner, and Julia watched him stride angrily toward the cottage. She felt like a voyeur. Did he assume she'd turn to Trevor's arms after denying him?

Is he right? When I couldn't sleep last night, would I have gone to see Trevor if he had been home? Not that she would have slept with him either—there was just something about Trevor that warmed her from the inside. Something that was tangibly absent inside when he left Torchlight. What would it be like when he moved on?

Her thoughts were interrupted by Miles's exasperated call. "Julia? Julia? Are you up there?"

"I'm here," she said softly, not truly caring whether he heard or not.

"Julia? Was that you? Are you okay? I'm coming up."

Julia turned back to the ocean, bracing herself for Miles's arrival.

He emerged from the stairwell, panting hard. "There you are! I was worried about you. Didn't you see me drive up?"

She didn't answer, didn't even look at him. He stood behind her and took her in his arms. "Quite a view from here, huh? If it wasn't so foggy, we could probably see for miles."

"That's the point of lighthouses," Julia said.

"Look, Julia, I'm sorry for last night. I had no right to push you as hard as I did. Can I help it if you drive me wild?"

He turned her around to face him. "Please, don't send me away, Julia, please. Please forgive me. For whatever I've done. Or for whatever I haven't done. I was a fool for waiting. I had this idea that I would buy you a house, surprise you with a ring, as well as the keys. I wanted to provide for you, let you know that you would be safe by my side, cared for."

"I don't know, Miles." She met his earnest, pleading eyes. *This is the man I've wanted for four years. I do love him. I do.*

"Maybe this will help." He bent down on one knee in front of her. "Julia Rierdon, will you marry me?"

Julia's eyes grew wide in shock. How long had she waited for this moment? But the questions that had taken root in her heart the night before wouldn't let go. She shook her head as if she could shake them out and into the sea.

He pulled a ring box from his jacket pocket and opened it to reveal a huge diamond surrounded by twenty smaller stones. "I've carried this around with me for a year now. I've been a fool to wait so long. You are the most intelligent, beautiful, fabulous woman I've ever met. I want you at my side forever."

She stood absolutely still, blinking.

"I'm thinking that an August wedding would be lovely. Here...San Francisco...anywhere you like."

Still, she did not speak.

"Julia?" He shifted uncomfortably in his kneeling position.

Julia looked from the ring to his face and back again. "I can't."

"Can't…what?" He looked concerned.

"I can't answer you now."

Miles sighed in relief. "Of course. How much time do you need?"

"I don't know. I need to be alone. Away from you."

A furrow appeared on his brow. "I don't like the idea of leaving you…alone." He paused. "What do you want, darling? A few days?"

"No. Longer. I don't know. A month maybe? Just leave me alone awhile, please. We've waited four years. Let's not jump into this."

Miles got up and brushed the dust off his trousers. He stood before her and smiled down into her eyes, encouraging her trust.

"Wear the ring, Julia," he said as he picked up her hand and placed it on her finger. It was stunning, the ring of girlhood dreams. The ring of a queen. "I'll be back soon for your answer."

He kissed her on the forehead, then walked to the lighthouse stairs, where he paused. "I trust you'll make the right decision, darling." With that, Miles smiled at her and then left without another word.

After descending the lighthouse stairs, Julia opened the door and stepped outside. Trevor was still gone. The cottage seemed to call to her. She glanced around, then walked up the steps. Julia knew it was wrong, but the urge was irresistible. She turned the knob. Unlocked.

Inside, the room was filled with souvenirs from Trevor's travels. Trevor had unpacked his many trunks and the few pieces of furniture that had arrived. She walked from table to shelf, looking at his things, wanting to know more about her mysterious employee. There was a hand-carved bowie knife, a brightly colored knit cap from South America…even a white cotton work shirt from Ecuador that reminded her of something Shane Donnovan might have worn. By the pedestal sink she saw an old-fashioned shaving brush and cream with a lid inscribed: Taylor of Bond Street, London, England. Several elegant oriental carpets lay beneath her feet.

Beside the door stood cross-country skis, a diver's mask and snorkel, and what looked to be handworked snowshoes. Beneath the window an antique globe sat atop its own wooden stand. Trevor's bed was an elegant Empire sleigh style with a rich, handrubbed patina. On top lay a soft cashmere afghan, thrown casually over the bedding yet appearing as if it had been artfully placed. She sat down on the bed and picked it up, musing over it and the other rich furnishings. He had taste, artistic taste. Taste for the fine things. She was somewhat surprised… He had always seemed more denim than cashmere to her, more pine than mahogany.

Handcrafted rods hung over the three wide windows, and from them, heavy canvas curtains gently cascaded to the wooden floor, billowing up at the bottom in generous rolls. A coffee table and a comfortable-looking overstuffed chair were beside the windows. She examined the book he was reading. *A History of Lighthouses.*

On the walls hung pictures of Trevor and friends from around the world: in the desert, in a jungle, on top of sky-high mountains; in Asia, Europe, Central America.

She squinted at each picture carefully.

"Never figured you were a snooper."

She whirled. "I…I…"

"I parked in front of the house. Thought I'd ask you out for lunch. Were you looking for me? Or did you just want to peek around?"

Julia found her voice. "I'm sorry. I have no excuse." She looked up at the devastatingly handsome man in front of her, waiting for him to throw her out. Her heart pounded.

Trevor draped his leather coat on a peg by the door. "It's okay, Julia. Glad to know you're interested. Thought you were too wrapped up in Miles to give me a second glance. I would've invited you in eventually. In fact, I think I did. But you declined."

Trevor paused and looked at Julia closely. She knew her face must be pale, her eyes wide. "Julia, are you feeling okay? You're as white as a ghost."

She sat down on the edge of his bed. "I'm feeling a bit confused. Where were you?"

"Church. It's time I got back in the habit now that I'm settled here in Oak Harbor."

"When did you become a Christian?"

"I've studied a lot of religions in the past years. Found the one true faith about ten years ago now."

Julia listened to the easy cadence of his voice and thought of the relaxed state in which he seemed to move and live. She saw that he carried a well-worn Bible in his hand. *Has he found his peace in the Scriptures?* Julia felt anything but peaceful at that moment. "I need to start going back to church again too. With all that's been going on here, I haven't focused on finding a church home. Tara called me to join her this week, but with Miles here—" She changed the subject abruptly as she fought off her sense of uneasiness. "Your place looks wonderful. Are you Indiana Jones in disguise?"

Trevor laughed. "No. Just a careful collector. I have an eye for great things. Which is why I suppose I'm attracted to you."

"Yeah, well, I'm not a collector's item at some Far East boutique."

"No. You're not. But you're worth more than anything in this house. A person can't own another human being, but he can value her for who she is."

Julia turned away. "Have a hot date last night?"

"You could say that."

"When have you had time to meet women?"

"When Tara found out you were wrapped up with Beckley, she went to work fixing me up with every single woman in Oak Harbor—of which there are about three near my age. I went to dinner at her house last night, to eat with her and Ben, and, you guessed it, one of the eligible bachelorettes was there. Tara said to say hello. I think she's disappointed that you two haven't had more time together."

"Are you sure Tara's not interested in you? Maybe she's just using me to get to you." Julia's voice sounded weary, without its usual teasing lilt. Trevor looked at her curiously. "Nah. I think she's got a thing for Ben DeBois. Great guy."

Julia stood and looked out his window while Trevor watched, wondering how to reach out to her. *Why is she here?*

Her hands rested on the freshly painted window sill. Trevor's gaze moved from her feet up to her fingertips. There he spied the ring. His heart stopped, and it took him a full minute to speak. "So, he finally popped the question." He forced light into his voice when he could not find it in his heart.

"Yes."

"Did you set a date?"

"I didn't answer him."

Trevor felt his heart pumping again. "When is he expecting an answer?"

"When I figure out what to say."

"When is he coming back?"

"I don't know. I wanted some time. A month. Maybe longer."

"How could a man who just proposed leave you for that long?"

"He has business." Julia continued to stare out at the sea.

Trevor walked over to Julia, started to reach out and pull her into his arms, but let his hands drop. Regret seized him. Why hadn't he met Julia sooner? Why hadn't God led them to Torchlight before things had progressed so far with Miles? And why was she considering a proposal from such a man?

He moved to her side and followed her gaze. "Do you want to marry him?" He forced his tone to be nonjudgmental.

"I don't know." She looked up at him. Although they stood a foot apart, she felt feverish at his nearness. "I have four weeks to figure it out." Why couldn't she feel this way about Miles? *We used to be this close...this magnetic. Didn't we?* Their passion seemed tame now in comparison to what she felt toward Trevor. But Miles...Miles would always be there for her.

"How come you never married?" she asked.

"Didn't want to be tied down," Trevor hedged. *Never met the right woman.*

"I thought so. Just one of those noncommittal types?"

"Maybe." She was wearing another man's ring. How could he expose his heart?

"What are your plans, Trevor? Are you moving on after you finish at Torchlight?"

"Most likely. What else would I do in this town? I've done my share of fishing in Alaska. Didn't care for it. And, well, there's nothing more to keep me here. Right, Julia?"

She glanced at him and then rushed toward the door, as if near tears.

He met her there, shutting the door as soon as she opened it a few inches. *"Right,* Julia?"

She paused a long moment, still staring at the door, then whispered, "Right."

Only then did he let her flee the cottage.

CHAPTER NINE

The weekend's developments left Trevor and Julia both feeling as if they were in a stupor. After three days, Trevor could no longer stand their silence. As they pored over catalogs, he deadpanned supposed interest in bright pink sinks and a tub in the shape of a lion's head.

"What? You're telling me you don't care for my taste?"

"Well, I guess not—at least not when it comes to my bathroom fixtures."

"Then I suppose you won't like this—"

"No, leopard skin toilet-seat covers are definitely out. Maybe if they went better with the house..."

"There you go! Think of it. We could redecorate Torchlight to be a safari getaway—it'd be the perfect tourist draw."

"Yes, and oh so classy." She looked up at him, and they both burst into hysterical laughter.

Wiping the tears from her face, Julia smiled at Trevor. "I guess I've needed a break from my heavy thoughts lately. Thanks."

"No problem." He stood up. "Look, we have to begin on the electric wiring of this old house tomorrow. I'm going to have a good week of long workdays in front of me. What do you say to getting out of here for the evening? Let's go get dinner. My treat."

"Your treat? Sounds like an offer I can't refuse. I'm paying you a fortune, after all."

"Yeah, right. Just bundle up. It could be cold where we're going."

"Hmm. Sounds like a mystery dinner."

Trevor only lifted his eyebrows mischievously and then walked out the door.

Two hours later he rumbled up in front of the mansion on his bike. Julia peeked out. "Don't you want to take the car?"

"Come on, worrywart. I'll be responsible."

"I've seen you ride, remember?"

Trevor stared her down with a simple smile as Julia climbed on behind him.

"Ever been on a motorcycle?"

"No. Never wanted to risk death on the road."

"Lean with me. Let me take the lead, and follow it smoothly. Don't try to counterbalance when we tilt on a turn. Just trust me."

"Uh-huh. Where's my helmet?"

Trevor handed it over his shoulder. He placed a hand on her thigh casually and lifted it so that she could see where to place her feet. "You can hold on to me or the bar behind you." His touch left her feeling warm, as if he had left a handprint on her leg. How long had it been since Miles's touch had made her feel that way?

Trevor pulled out. They cruised down the highway along the ocean, slowly, easily, as if they had all the time in the world. Julia felt precarious, holding on to only the small bar behind her; awkwardly, she wrapped her arms around Trevor.

Deep spring. Almost summer. Julia could feel the barely percep-tible change in the evening air. "I'm thinking an August wedding…" Barely three months away. She forced the thought out of her mind.

She wanted to ask Trevor where he was taking her but, with the interference of the helmets and engine noise, could not. They rode past Oak Harbor's tiny post office, the general store, TARA'S GOOD FOOD, and then were on the south side of town, driving down a picturesque stretch of highway that bordered the ocean.

"Did you see that?"

"What?" Tara looked up from table five to where Ben sat by the window, eating an early supper with Mike.

"Julia's finally with a decent guy," Mike said.

"Who's that?"

"Trevor Kenbridge," Ben said with a grin.

"Do you think—"

"Maybe she's beginning to see something good right in front of her face," Mike said, looking straight into his father's eyes.

"Maybe we shouldn't come to any conclusions," Ben said, returning his son's solid look.

Tara came over with the water pitcher, and Mike shoved his last bite of sandwich into his mouth. "Gotta go," he mumbled.

"Mike…," Ben said with consternation. Tara saw that the kid was making way for her and sat down across from Ben. "Maybe it's time we come to some conclusions of our own, Ben. When are you going to let me in? Why can't we be…together?"

Ben glanced out the window and then fiddled with his french fries. "I just don't know if I'm ready."

"Sharon's been gone a long time, Ben. She loved you. She loved me. I can't help but think that she'd enjoy the fact that we found each other."

Ben grimaced and fished a wallet out of his jeans pocket and threw a bill on the table. "Can we talk about this later? I'm just not ready. Maybe this weekend, when we go to Egg Island?"

"Fine, Ben. This weekend." She watched as he rose, leaned over to give her a quick kiss on the cheek, and then hurriedly departed. *What will it take to move that man off the fence?*

It seemed like decades since she'd had any time away from responsibilities and decisions. But here, no one expected anything of her. Julia swayed with the rolling turns, feeling free and at peace for the first time in days. The man in front of her was an enjoyable and scintillating companion. The evening was glorious. Again, Julia forced Miles from her mind, determined just to enjoy herself tonight.

After five more miles, Trevor pulled alongside one of the many roadside lobster shacks. He greeted the cook, Walt, and introduced him to Julia as a friend of Ben DeBois. The man had the ruddy, rough-hewn complexion and personality of a traditional fisherman and spoke with a Down-Easter's accent as thick as the fog rolling in. Julia instantly liked him.

They sat down at a weathered picnic table, and Walt brought out a red-and-white-checkered paper tablecloth, plastic bibs, a pair of stainless-steel shell crackers, and two tiny forks, which he set down in front of Julia and Trevor. "Preparation for battle," he explained. Then he returned from the old shack with a candlelit hurricane lamp. "Ambiance," he said.

Julia was delighted. She had not eaten at one of these old road-side shacks since she was a girl, and she had many wonderful memories of her entire family gathering around for a traditional lobster feed. Her grandparents had delighted in the paradox of "picnicking" on lobster. After they died, Julia's parents had let the tradition fade away, but Julia still found comfort in the sights and smells of lobster shacks. Trevor could not have chosen a better setting.

Walt opened a gigantic pot to stir the contents, filling the air with the aroma of steaming lobster. "You're my first customers this season," he told Julia. "Your man there talked me into a private dinner for two. Won't get a steady stream of tourists for another week or two, when the summer people start to come."

Julia blushed at Walt's implication about her relationship with Trevor but brushed the notion and her embarrassment off quickly. "Do you fish all day and then cook all evening?"

"Aye. Good way to make an extra buck or two, I've found. Especially since the lobster seem more and more reluctant to make their way into my traps. Not as good a livin' as it was twenty years ago."

"You must be exhausted when you get home."

"Nah. I start at three in the mornin', get in 'bout three in the afternoon. Close shop 'bout nine and get ta bed 'round ten. Not bad. Keeps me on the sea and out from under the ol' woman's foot." He laughed at his own private joke, a trait that seemed prevalent among New Englanders.

"Many of the locals depend on these little shacks to make it each year." Trevor was genuinely concerned for the welfare of the solid folk who piloted these waters for a living. His empathy warmed Julia's heart. Maybe she could bring Miles when he visited again. He'd get a sense of the place, begin to see what she had envisioned when she thought he was going "to show her the town." This, this was New England at its finest.

Julia closed her eyes and listened to Trevor talking with Walt and to the waves crashing on the rocky shore twenty feet ahead of them. She listened to the gulls venturing north and the occasional car passing on the highway. A romantic interlude. *Romantic.* Julia dismissed the thought as soon as it entered her mind.

She opened her eyes and smiled at Trevor, sitting beside the open fire over where Walt stirred their boiling dinner. In the fading light, the shadows caught the cleft in Trevor's chin and the deep dimples of his cheeks, highlighting his rugged good looks.

His eyes shone as they met hers and held her gaze, but Julia turned away, unable to listen to what his eyes were saying.

Trevor came to sit beside her, looking seaward with her at the view. Moments later Walt presented them with two earthenware plates, each piled high with potatoes, corn, and a whole lobster apiece, with a garnish of seaweed. "It's beautiful!" Julia said. "You're an amazing chef, Walt. I never could boil anything right."

"Well now," he said shyly, "you haven't tried anything yet. It does look purty, though, don't it? Always did like the solid red of a done lobster beside a good yellow cob of corn and dark green seaweed— that's my own idea. Come back this summer, and the corn will be American. Lot better than that foreign corn the missus buys this time of year."

"It's all wonderful," she assured him.

"Well, I'll leave you two. Just yell if you need anything. I'll be catching the baseball game inside the shack."

"Thanks, Walt," Trevor said. He looked at Julia and gently took her hand. Julia's heart skipped a beat at his touch. "Will you say grace with me?"

She found her voice. "Sure," she said lightly.

"Father, thank you for this gorgeous place, for people like Walt, and for this food. Thank you for allowing us to live here. We are blessed, and we acknowledge these gifts we've been given as coming from your hand. Amen."

Julia opened her eyes to the heaping plate in front of her. Her hand still tingled from his touch, and she tried to ignore the feeling. "How am I going to eat all this?"

"I bet Walt will give you a doggy bag if you can't manage it." Trevor lifted a huge claw and cracked it with one of the steel utensils Walt had laid out for them. Handpicked by Walt from his afternoon catch, the lobsters were bigger than any Julia had seen in San Francisco.

The two talked and ate and talked some more until the sun faded from the sky. Julia barely noticed that time was passing. Walt came out of the shack at nine-thirty.

"Well, folks, you're welcome to stay as long as you'd like, but I better head home." He threw a bucket of water on the embers beneath the huge cast-iron pot, sending a plume of steam into the night air. Trevor stood, reached into his pocket, and handed a wad of cash to Walt without counting it. Julia noticed that Walt did not count it either.

"Thank you, friend," their host said. "Come again this summer when it's warmer and the corn is better."

"You can count on it, Walt. It was a great meal."

"Glad you liked it." He cleared the table as Julia stood, moaning over her full stomach. "'Night. Nice meetin' you, Julia. Tara had nothing but good things to say 'bout you."

"Good meetin' you, too, Walt. Thanks again for a fabulous meal."

"'T'weren't nothin'."

As Trevor turned the key and revved the engine, Julia noticed how cold the evening was. She did not hesitate to put her arms securely around him for the ride home.

When they arrived, Trevor paused to let Julia off in front of the house. His body tingled with the desire to stand, pull her to him, and kiss her as she'd never been kissed before. He swallowed hard. She was still wearing Beckley's ring.

"Thanks for a great evening, Trevor."

"Thank you."

"Good night."

He nodded, unable to speak, and drove off to the lighthouse cottage.

Please, God, give me patience if what I feel is right. And if it's not, please make it clear to me very soon.

Dressed against the elements, Ben, Tara, and Mike entered the boathouse and approached the twenty-two-foot sailboat that was Tara's passion in life second to the restaurant. Even with the unseasonably warm spring weather, it was early for sailing. But the trio was dressed warmly for their excursion. They had even attended the early service at church in order to leave most of their day free.

The *Sea Maiden* had been dry-docked all winter, and Tara smiled at seeing her again. Tara loved few things more than the wind in her face, the sun on her back, and the spray of the ocean. She felt it was the perfect counterpart to cooking. Tara watched as Ben lowered the boat, allowing it to drop into the water.

"Come aboard, matey." Ben stepped in and raised a hand to Tara.

"Watch how you address the captain," she warned.

"Aye, aye. Forgot it's not my ship."

"Just don't let it happen again." The two shared a smile as they put their things away and began to get the boat ready.

"Why do we have to go on the island?" Mike complained. "Why don't we just sail? We have great wind today—we'd be flyin'."

"I've fished for thirty years 'round these islands. I figure it's time we see what's on top."

"Yeah, Mike," Tara added. "Imagine we're the first settlers who came here. Let's think of ourselves as explorers."

"Oh brother."

"Hoist the sail, or I'll make you walk the plank," Tara threatened.

Mike did as he was told, resigned that he was outvoted.

"Don't feel too bad, Mike. Another summer of lessons and I'll let you take her out on your own. The girls will all be after you for a ride."

"I like that idea. Especially with Jessica."

"Maybe I'll come along to chaperon," Ben teased.

"Dad…"

"Okay, boys, let's go!" Together, Ben and Mike pushed the *Sea Maiden* out of the dock and unfurled the mainsail, while Tara remained at the helm. Then they moved to the jib.

As soon as they cleared the dock, the wind filled the broad lengths of canvas, and they were off. The day was glorious. The smell of salt filled their nostrils as they turned their faces to the sun, which was doing its best to cut through the cool spring air.

After half an hour, as the mainland eased into the distance, Tara called to Mike and, pointing in the direction they needed to head, set him to work at the helm. Then she carefully made her way up to the bow, holding on to the guard cable to keep her balance in the small swells that pitched them upward and then fell away.

She sat down by Ben, enjoying the opportunity to close her eyes and feel the motion of the boat. Ben stared at her, observing her dainty nose, apple cheeks, and dimples, and the way her shiny brown hair blew wildly in the wind. Slowly he put an arm around her—not exactly holding her—just testing out the feel of it. He found he was holding his breath though, and when no pain but only pleasure greeted him, he sighed in relief and relaxed. He smiled at her and she shyly grinned back, then closed her eyes, obviously feeling the rhythm of the boat like a sensuous dance.

She was dressed in jeans and a thick, rust-colored fisherman's sweater. Over them, she wore waterproof pants and a jacket to ward off the cold sea spray. Absently she pulled her hood up to cover her head and retied the chin strings that kept falling undone. Ben enjoyed seeing her so utterly relaxed.

Suddenly she opened her eyes. Catching him still staring, she smiled impishly, then closed her eyes again, grinning from ear to ear.

Ben blushed a deep red and looked back to see if Mike had been watching.

He had.

"What are you lookin' at?" Ben called back.

"Well, what do you expect?" said the boy, smiling. "You're sittin' right in front of me."

Confronted with blunt logic, Ben looked away, careful not to let his eyes rest on the captain again for too long. "Tara, I noticed your CB is out again."

"Again? Man, I just had that fixed."

"I want you to promise me you'll get it fixed when we get back. It's dangerous. I don't like the idea of you out on the water with no way to radio home."

"Why, Ben, are you saying you care for me?"

"Well, of course I care about you!" He scowled and rose. "You'll get it fixed then?"

Tara grinned at him. "Yes, Ben. I'll get it fixed."

"Land ho!" Tara cried an hour later, sighting Egg Island among several other land masses. Beside Maine's shoreline were hundreds of islands, ranging from outcroppings that succumbed to each storm's waves to high lands covered with thick forests. Egg Island was one of the larger islands, roughly three miles around.

"There's a natural harbor on the southwest side," Tara called to Mike over the wind.

He nodded, acknowledging her directions. Within ten minutes, they had entered the quieter waters of the small bay. Ben waited until the last possible minute to weigh anchor, carefully watching the seabed rising beneath them. When it began to rise quickly, he released the weight as Tara pulled down the sail to slow their progress. After thirty feet of line uncoiled and submerged behind them, the anchor pulled the *Sea Maiden* firmly to a stop.

"Ben, could you set out the dinghy?"

"Sure."

"Mike, grab the backpacks."

"Aye, aye."

Together Mike and Tara climbed into the small rowboat while Ben set the oars into the sockets. They were only a hundred feet from shore, and Ben's strong arms brought them there quickly. Mike climbed out and pulled them up onto the pebbly beach.

"Where to?" Tara asked.

Ben took a field guide from his waterproof jacket. "Says here if we walk fifty feet north, we'll hit a trail."

Mike was off. "Sure enough!" he called. "It's kinda hidden—like a secret path!" He parted the thick, blossoming branches of two young maples and disappeared, with his father and Tara following closely behind.

They climbed silently for fifteen minutes, keeping their eyes on the steep trail that rose sharply from the beach below. When they reached the crest of one particularly steep hill, they paused to catch their breath. Mike's young lungs recovered faster than Ben's and Tara's, and he was off again quickly.

"Over here!" he called.

Tara rolled her eyes. "Let's make him carry *all* the backpacks next time to even the race."

"Sounds good."

Tara reached Mike first and gasped at what she saw when she emerged into the clearing. It had been years since she had been to the top of the island, and she had forgotten how gorgeous the view was. The sea spread out before them, and dark reefs spotted the sea. The sky was a brilliant blue, and fluffy white clouds blew over them, caught in the spring winds. The mainland appeared as a shadow on the horizon, seven miles distant.

"Cool, huh?" Mike said.

"Very cool," Tara said. "Well done, God!"

"Looks like a good place for lunch," Ben said.

Mike's stomach rumbled as if in response, and he grinned.

The threesome ate heartily, enjoying the picture-perfect picnic Tara had packed—fried soft-shell crabs Ben had gathered the day before, fresh apples, and pine-nut salad. They feasted heartily, carefully saving room for the grand finale, Mike's favorite: Indian pudding.

They talked about how everything must have looked to the first settlers and to the Indians before them.

"Why'd they name it Egg Island, Dad?"

"Well, for years, mainlanders came collecting eggs from the migrating seabirds. It wasn't too long before the seabird population severely dropped because of the heavy egging. People even hunted the birds for their feathers."

"Doesn't look too bad now," Mike said, watching a gull sail out from the cliff beside them and hover over the *Sea Maiden* far below.

"That's because they finally put a stop to the egging," Ben said.

As Tara opened the dessert's container, smells of cornmeal, molasses, ginger, and cinnamon wafted into the cool air.

"Indian pudding! Tara, you're the greatest."

"Well, I figured it was a special occasion and all—you know."

"If only we had ice cream," Mike said, licking his lips.

"Voilà!" Tara said with a smile as she dipped into the third back-pack for a thermos container.

"No wonder it took all three to pack a lunch," Ben said. "I'm not complaining, mind you."

"You better not, Dad. This is the best meal I've eaten in weeks!"

"Hey! You've been eating three times a week at my place," Tara said.

"No offense, Tara. This is way cooler than any restaurant."

"True," she agreed, looking to the view before them and feeling happy to be alive.

While their food settled, Tara and Mike listened as Ben read about the island's history. Then the three set out on a walk around the perimeter. Because the Nature Conservancy had preserved the island for day visitors only, buildings were not allowed. The island had been left as a natural northeastern Eden, with sights around every bend.

Mike led the way along the damp, narrow trail. Several times, Tara and Ben reached out to steady each other when the terrain became particularly rough. Along the beach at the northwestern tip of the island, they came to Crab Cove, a small inlet that bustled with migrating seabirds who came to feast on the delicacies they found there.

"Look!" Mike shouted.

Ben and Tara saw what he had spotted immediately. Among the sandpipers, plovers, oystercatchers, and gulls were several pairs of puffins. Years earlier, ornithologists had conscientiously reestablished the rare birds on the island. Since the animals had a tendency to breed on the islands on which they were born, the puffin population on Egg Island had grown exponentially.

Among the rough outcroppings of granite, Ben paused at a rock cairn that marked the trail. He smiled at Tara, his eyes crinkling in genuine pleasure. "I haven't seen Mike this happy in years."

"It feels good to me, too. Thanks for inviting me to come along."

"I wouldn't have it any other way."

Ben moved off again before she could press him on his comment. The trail climbed as they passed Crab Cove, then entered the

Cathedral Woods at the northeastern tip of the island. A thick stand of hundred-year-old red spruce shot upward above the damp, mossy forest floor. Their sturdy trunks cut the ocean wind to a gentle breeze. The result was a scene of such serenity that they agreed it felt like a cathedral.

"I almost feel like getting down on my knees," Ben's voice was barely more than a whisper.

"I know what you mean," Tara responded.

Mike led the way south on the trail, less appreciative of the trees than were his companions. Eventually the forest opened up into a beautiful, verdant meadow. Mike's sudden appearance surprised three white-tailed deer. They raised their graceful heads and froze, ears taut, as they scanned the meadow for sounds and movement.

"How'd they get here?" Mike asked in a hushed voice.

"Probably swam or were brought here by settlers," his father whispered.

"What's up?" Tara asked as she emerged from the forest. The deer caught sight of them and bounded off to safety.

"Oops. Guess I blew it, huh?"

Mike rolled his eyes and moved off again while Ben simply smiled.

On the southeast end of the island, they found the broken remains of a lighthouse that had been battered to bits by the surf long ago. "Probably warned off Boston whalers coming this way," Ben theorized.

"I'm glad Torchlight's lamp fared better," Tara said. The thought of it took her mind to Julia and Trevor. Would Julia ever see Trevor the way Tara longed for Ben to see her? They belonged together—

Julia and Trevor, just as she and Ben belonged together. But she was wearing Miles's ring. Would she really go through with it? *I suppose she just might,* Tara mused, *just like Ben may never make more of a move than this.* She sighed. *There's always friendship.* But the thought of it left her disgruntled and irritable. She wanted love. She wanted a family, a husband, a baby of her own. "Come on," she suddenly said to the men. "Let's go home."

They looked at her in surprise, but she ignored them. If Ben wasn't going to do more than put an arm around her, if he couldn't say *I love you,* then she'd just have to take drastic measures.

Chapter Ten

The following week Ben, Mike, and Tara invited Julia and Trevor to go kayaking after the early church service. Julia agreed, shaking off the awkward feeling of going with Trevor, as if they were a couple. They met up with the others at Tara's restaurant. It was a bright, sunny day, much like the weekend before, but even warmer. Summer was coming fast.

The men piled into one car, the women into another, and they headed south to the docks where the *Sea Maiden* was moored. They stopped in front of a sea kayak rental shop with a sign that read ATLANTIS and scrambled out of their vehicles.

Inside, they looked at the pictures, brochures, and sea-kayaking paraphernalia that filled the walls. "I've never been in one of these before," Julia said. "Do I need a lesson or something?"

"Nah," the clerk said. His young face was tanned already by his afternoons on the water, under the late spring sun. "I'll explain when we get out there. Just follow your instincts. There's nothing like it."

"I'm game."

They finished the paperwork and followed the young man out to Atlantis's dock behind the shop. There, twenty kayaks in varying colors were tied in individual slips.

"Now these aren't the kind of kayaks that tip over easily," their young instructor began.

"That's a relief," Tara piped up.

He continued. "Still, take the spray skirt, wrap it around your torso like this"—he demonstrated—"then hop in and attach it to the lip of the kayak's cockpit. There's a pull cord here for emergencies," he said, lifting his up for them to see. "You'll stay lots warmer that way."

They chose their boats and, after stowing their lunches inside and climbing in without incident, were off. Mike whooped with glee as he whipped his double-paddle through the water and gathered speed. His companions were not far behind. They left the shallow bay and headed south to Acadia National Park. The day was hot and windless, unusual for spring.

As Julia cut through the ocean swells, she thought about that morning's church service. The sanctuary was a quaint, refurbished building that had originally been erected in the early 1800s. It was the quintessential Northeast church: white clapboard, with the original bell still in the steeple, calling townsfolk to the services. The pulpit had been built to resemble a ship's prow—which had been common in the nineteenth and early twentieth centuries among the seafaring communities. Julia remembered attending with her grandparents as a small girl, holding her grandmother's hand and listening to her grandfather belt out hymns.

"Penny for your thoughts." Trevor's resonant voice caught her unaware. She had been paddling silently, alone.

"Actually, I was just thinking about church."

"What'd you think?" He slowed his stroke to match Julia's pace.

"It was great. That story of the prodigal son always gets me, but today...today I could almost see God with his arms reaching out for me. I've been caught up in my own things—moving, working on Torchlight. I forget too easily that my priority should be my faith."

Trevor nodded. "Sometimes I feel like I'm the constant prodigal—always coming home to the fatted calf, and then going to spend my inheritance again. It's a good thing our God is a God of grace."

Julia nodded. "It feels good to come home again. It's where I want to stay." She smiled at the man who by example had helped remind her of her priorities again. If he hadn't gone to church the week before, it would have been months before she had been moved to attend. Even with Tara urging her to do so.

The kayaks slid through the water with little effort. Trevor held his head high and leaned forward. *He is so at ease with himself, he commands respect from everyone with whom he comes into contact. He has a quiet dignity, a constant, strong presence. My friends like him, the men at the house respect him, and...*

He began to stroke faster, and Julia broke her thoughts to keep pace with him. Trevor grinned at her as each paddle dug to the port side, then starboard; port, starboard. The rhythm lulled her into a more relaxed state of mind. "This was just what I needed," she said to Trevor as they slowed their pace again.

"Me, too. Feels great, huh?"

"Wonderful."

He enjoyed seeing her out, away from Torchlight. Her blond hair flew as she stroked forward, and her face was a healthy pink from the spring sun and exercise. Her movements were graceful, and Trevor wondered how she would dance. *Confident, free, and easy,* he guessed.

They darted alongside Schoodic Point where broad, storm-washed ledges reflected the late morning sun. After pausing for a break and a snack, they set off across the water to Mount Desert Island, the heart of the park.

Tourists were few and far between, and it seemed as if the five friends had commandeered the park as their own private paradise. They lunched in the saltwater fjord of Frenchman Sound, riding the gentle swells that ventured inward from the sea. On either side, granite cliffs tinged with pink climbed dramatically upward. In some places the rocks had been worn smooth. Other areas were rough and foreboding. Stands of birch, beech, oak, and maple broke up the dark, dense spruce and fir that lined the shore.

They spent the remainder of the day exploring the myriad inlets and coves, chasms and large bays that made up Acadia. Julia was resting and rubbing her aching shoulders, wondering how she'd make it back to the kayak shop, when she heard a splash and felt cold salt water wash over her.

Trevor was off and paddling. "Time to go home, I'd say." He dug deep into the water as Julia's shout of disbelief cut the air.

Julia was determined not to let him get away with it. She met each of his strokes with her own, not gaining, but keeping pace. He was stronger, and his paddles dug deeper, but he was also heavier.

They continued onward, sapping the last of their strength as they once again reached Schoodic Point.

With one last mighty stroke, Trevor dug deep into the starboard waters and lifted his oar to dig into the port side. Just then his right plastic paddle came unlatched from the metal rod and floated helplessly away from him.

Julia laughed as she scooped up the paddle and made her way toward him, a mischievous look on her face.

"I'm in trouble!" he called. "Help! I need reinforcements!"

"Oh yeah, you're in deep, mister! Shout all you want; there's no one to save you now!"

Trevor tried to use his remaining oar like a canoe paddle, but it was no use. He spun crazily to the left, and Julia was alongside him in seconds. Their friends hooted and hollered in the distance at Trevor's impending demise. Holding her own oar like a baseball bat, she took aim as he resigned himself and stretched out his arms as a willing target. The oar hit the water perfectly, casting a huge spray in a graceful arc and soaking her companion.

Julia laughed as water dripped down his forehead and onto his wet shirt. He smiled with her, shaking the water from his head.

She paddled alongside him until the boats bumped one another. She handed him the missing piece that had led to his downfall.

"Don't mess with the master," she said smugly.

His eyes locked with hers, and she quickly turned away and began paddling again, trying to shake off the sense of longing she saw in his gaze, the vague ache that matched what she felt in her heart. Her eyes drifted to the ring on her left hand as she paddled away. Julia found herself cursing her wandering heart. *What is wrong with me anyway?* She either had to take off Miles's ring and tell him no or quit flirting with Trevor. She couldn't have it both ways. It wasn't fair to either of them.

"Any chance we'll have some semblance of order before my brother and his wife arrive?" Julia asked Trevor.

Jake and Emily would be arriving within weeks, and it seemed that every wall, ceiling, and floorboard in the old house was torn up. Trevor and three local electricians were rewiring the house, gearing it for modern conveniences.

"We're doing our best, Julia. This is a big project," Trevor said.

"I'm not getting on you. I know you're working hard. But Jake was just a little boy when we were here last. He can't even remember what Torchlight looked like. Emily, of course, hasn't ever laid eyes on it. I hate to have their first impression of the place be that it's a disaster."

"From what you've told me, your brother is too laid back to slap a judgment on it like that. You've told them we're in a major rehaul zone, haven't you?"

"Yes. But this is their belated honeymoon. They haven't been anywhere but that Montana ranch since their wedding day. I don't think they'd be coming now if Emily hadn't insisted Jake get away and see his only sister. It was like she had to pull teeth to make him take time off. I knew I liked her for some reason."

Trevor smiled down at her from his ladder perch, then turned back to his work, peeling layers of old wallpaper and slamming through the plaster as he followed the trail of the ancient wiring.

He looked back, his face chalk white from the dust of his work. "We'll work on it, Julia. Maybe we can at least be done tearing out the old stuff and making such a huge mess. But we won't have the new wires in before next week. They'll have to live with what we're living with."

"Okay. Just do your best."

"As always."

They were interrupted by the doorbell, which rang and stuck. As the loud ringing echoed through the house, Julia ran to the front door, opened it, and banged on the doorjamb three times, unsticking the bell. "Sorry," she said to Tara with a smile. "As you can see, there's another project every time I turn around."

"You should've let me bring lunch."

"Nonsense. You must feel like you spend your whole life cooking for everybody else. I thought it was high time someone cooked for you."

"I knew we'd be friends as soon as you sat down on my barstool," Tara said as she entered and looked around. "I didn't know you were going to destroy the ol' girl. I thought you were going to fix her."

"It takes a lot of destruction to reconstruct. Come on into the kitchen. It's the one room that already has semimodern wiring, so it's escaping this phase. I'm using it as my haven." As they walked out of the foyer and into the large blue-and-white room, a loud crash sounded upstairs, rattling the copper kettles hanging from the ceiling. A muffled voice could be heard above them. Julia went to the bottom of the stairs and called up to the electricians at work. "Everyone okay?"

A dusty man in white coveralls appeared at the upstairs railing and looked down at her with a broad smile. "We're okay. Mack was just looking down at Tara in the entry, and he fell off his ladder."

Julia smiled back at him. "Tell him it serves him right for gawking at my friend while I'm paying him."

"I will."

Julia grinned at Tara, who had listened to the exchange from the kitchen doorway. "You'd better stay in the kitchen. I can't afford to have the men lookin' after you and not their work."

"What can I say? I have to beat them off with a stick."

"Life's rough."

"What's for lunch?"

"Shrimp salad. Sound okay?"

"Sounds great."

Julia pulled from the refrigerator two plates piled high with salad and took a freshly baked loaf of French bread from the pantry. She and Tara each tore off a chunk of bread and ate it, unbuttered, as they sat at the kitchen counter in the relative peace of the room.

"I'm glad you could come today, Tara," Julia said. "I wanted you to see what we're doing here. If I weren't so obsessed, I'd make it into town more often to see you."

"Well, as soon as things get under control, I'll expect to see more of you." Tara took a bite, chewed, and swallowed. "You make a mean shrimp salad. If this inn doesn't make it, you can always come in and help me at the restaurant."

"I might have to take on a summer job if the place keeps sucking up money at this rate."

"I can't begin to imagine. Luckily you hired a handsome and talented overseer early on."

"He has been a blessing. I don't know what I would've done if you hadn't sent him my way."

"I bet."

"Tara…"

"Oh, don't tell me you haven't kissed him! I've seen how you two look at each other."

Julia lowered her voice and made a face at Tara. "No, I haven't. We don't have that kind of a relationship."

"Why not?"

"Hello? Is anybody in there? Do you remember that someone proposed last month? Why would I be kissing another man this week?"

Tara pointedly looked at Julia. "I hadn't heard that you called Miles to say yes."

"No. I haven't yet. But I'm wearing the ring."

"There's still hope."

"Tara! You're just getting to know me. Why are you so sure Miles is the wrong man?"

"I'm not so sure Miles is wrong for you. It's just that Trevor"— Tara's eyes went to the door—"Trevor seems so *right*. It's as though you two were made for each other, and everybody can see it but you."

"Well, I don't think he's as interested as you think."

"Oh no?"

"Tara Waverly, if you know something I should, you'd better lay it on the table."

"Sorry, I'm just here for a friendly lunch date, not to get into the middle of some warped love triangle."

Julia put her head in her hands. "Don't call it that. Trevor and I are just friends."

"Okay. But you're the friendliest friends I've set eyes on in a long while."

Julia and Tara finished their lunch and decided to climb the lighthouse stairs with their coffee. Tara beamed. "I haven't been up there in months!"

"I told you, you're welcome anytime."

"I know. I just don't want to barge in on your privacy."

"Don't be silly. Come whenever you want. If it makes you feel better, call first."

They entered the building and climbed all the way to the top. "Next time, bring along some oxygen for me," Tara said, taking in deep breaths of air.

"You're the one who always came up here," Julia said, panting herself. "I thought you'd remember to bring your own supply."

"Guess I forgot."

Julia smiled at her friend. She was so vivacious that everyone took an immediate liking to her.

"So, have you found out any more about your great-great-grandfather's return?" Tara seemed to be as interested in Anna's journals as Trevor was. Julia kept them both abreast of the news as she read, sometimes sharing portions aloud. It felt as though they were eyewitnesses to history. Julia was pleased that both friends shared her passion for the journals.

She took a sip from her coffee cup and looked out at yet another spectacular and clear spring day. It was sunny, yet seemed even colder without the clouds and heavy fog that were more characteristic of this time of year.

"I've been reading a lot from Anna's journals lately."

"With Trevor?"

"With and without him."

"What's been happening?"

"Shane came back. But he didn't make as much money as he thought he would. Instead of gold in his pocket, he returned with wild ideas about building faster ships—ideas we know made the family fortune—but, living in a tiny hole of an apartment, with a bun in the oven, Anna had a mighty hard time supporting his wild schemes."

Julia stared down at the waves crashing beneath the lighthouse, transfixed by the rhythm: *Crash, cascade, swirl, drain, build. Crash, cascade, swirl, drain, build. Crash…* "Still, I've got to hand it to her. Instead of beating him into submission and making him take a *real* job, she let him take his time and figure it out. She decided that ideas don't cost money; it's the building that costs money."

"I'd have said, 'Honey, go get a real job,'" Tara put in.

"Me, too. But Anna let Shane chalk stripes to simulate planking all over the apartment while she made him dinner night after night, until he headed off on another voyage around the Cape to pay the bills. They lived for months, months that turned into years, in a striped one-room apartment while great-great-granddaddy tried to find an investor.

"Still, Anna held on. She saw the glint in his eye and his passion for the sea. She knew he was smart—really smart. She trusted that. And she was so much in love she couldn't resist letting him follow his dreams. I admire her so much. I admire their love."

"Is that as far as you've gotten?"

"Anna gave birth to their first child while Shane was at sea. The baby picked up one of the zillion plagues that circulated through those poor neighborhoods. Can you imagine? Anna desperately tried to keep her child alive in sub-zero temperatures while, at the same time, wondering if her husband would ever come home. She was in a strange place and very far away from her family. How lonely. How *desperate*. I think God made people stronger back then."

Tara stared out at sea, as transfixed by the Donnovans' story as Julia. "But he came home. He came home and got an investor and made his fortune and built this house."

"Yes. But not before their first child died of smallpox. Shane came home to find that the daughter he'd never met had been buried for two months. And Anna was near death herself. He vowed that he'd never leave her alone again while she was pregnant. By some miracle she got well, and they grieved together. Fortunately, Anna got pregnant again two months later. That's as far as I've gotten."

"I want that kind of love, that utter devotion," Tara said simply.

"Yeah," Julia agreed, lost in a story a hundred and fifty years old.

After a moment she returned to the present. "What about Ben?" she asked carefully.

"Ah, the man needs a knock over the head to see the woman right in front of his eyes. But what a man he is. If he could get over grieving the loss of Sharon, I might have a chance. It doesn't look good now. I keep getting my hopes up. When we went sailing two weeks ago, we had a fantastic day. But as soon as we docked, Ben put up his walls and went back to keeping me at arm's length. Kayaking to Acadia was fun too, but he didn't let me in like he did the day we went sailing."

"How'd Sharon die?" Julia asked quietly. "I know she was your friend."

"Boat accident. Ben was out fishing while Sharon went sailing. She got caught in a late summer squall and never made it back. It was horrible. We were very close. Mike was only five years old. But that was ten years ago. Sharon would want us all to go on. I'm crazy about both of them, but I can't seem to get through to Ben."

"Why is love never easy?" Julia asked, looking into the fog swirling in front of the lighthouse.

"I don't know. I'd say if men weren't so darn cute I'd bag the whole relationship thing." She spotted Trevor down below, making his way to the cottage. "You can't tell me you're not even attracted to Trevor."

"I have to admit, he has this sort of raw magnetism that hypnotizes me at times. I'm drawn… I'm just not convinced it's anything more than a crush or a convenient reason to put off making a decision about Miles.

"Trevor's as much as said he's just passing through. I can't fall in love with a nomad! Miles is safe, known. Life with Trevor could be one surprising ride after another. But how do I know he'd want to stay with me any longer than a year?" She sighed heavily. "My whole future rests on this one decision."

"Isn't it strange how a person's choices help determine life's path for hundreds of others? Let's say you marry Miles; you and he live here for a while, then he gets tired of it, and you move back to San Francisco where's he's happier. Maybe you have kids; maybe you don't. Or…maybe you marry Trevor and live happily ever after here in Oak Harbor. Meanwhile, your daughter falls madly in love with an older man—my stepson, Mike DeBois, who has always lived just down the road. She calls me Auntie Tara, and it's a natural progression. You and I are ecstatic, of course, because now we'll be family…"

Julia burst out laughing. "You have one powerful imagination."

"I'm serious, Julia. You have to think how these things affect others, too. Just think. If you hadn't come to Oak Harbor, I wouldn't have begun work on my cookbook. I never would have considered trying."

"Do you have something to send yet?" Julia asked.

"I brought ten recipes, an outline listing a hundred others, some sample artwork to surround the ingredients, and last, but not least, a container of beans sealed for overnight air shipment. All I need are your connections."

"Tara! That's so exciting! You should have said something earlier. Let's go write the letter and get it out today. I'll be your agent."

"Okay, Ms. Agent, lead the way."

CHAPTER ELEVEN

*A*fter their lunch at Torchlight, Julia made a point of spending time with Tara a couple of times each week. She found the woman's wholesome, easy demeanor a welcome change from the gruff camaraderie of the workers and the tentative truce she seemed to have with Trevor.

Within a week, a friend of Julia's father sent a letter and contract via Federal Express to Oak Harbor. Tara wasted no time in getting over to Torchlight to share the good news.

She knocked loudly on the door and, when no one answered, reluctantly rang the insistent doorbell. Julia came tearing down the stairwell and threw open the door to pound three times on the jamb. The reverberation of the doorbell ceased.

"Tara, you know better than that…"

"I tried knocking! I have fantastic news! They want my cookbook!" Tara rushed into Julia's arms, ignoring the dirt and plaster dust on her clothes. "I owe it all to you! Thank you!"

"Tara, I'm so happy for you! I can't believe they turned out a contract so fast! Usually it takes *months*. Must have been those beans."

"I can't believe it either."

"Well, I knew you could do it. Now come in and tell me all about it. It's time for a break anyway." The two headed into the kitchen where Julia put the teakettle on the stove and struck a match to light the burner. "So tell me."

"Well, your father's friend went wild over the beans. They want me to write and illustrate the cookbook! As soon as it's done, I'm to go to New York and personally hand it over. At that point, I'll meet with their publicist and advertising manager. They think the whole idea is bound to get a lot of attention since I run a small restaurant in— Here, let me read it…" She pulled the letter out of her pocket. "'Since you run a successful restaurant in such a picturesque little town, we will want to do a photo shoot on location. Afterward, please arrange adequate help for your restaurant, since there will be some traveling involved in publicizing the book. Anticipate at least a month away and a fifteen-city tour.'"

Tara looked at Julia over her tea. "A fifteen-city tour! I haven't been farther than Boston in my entire life!"

Julia smiled back at her, genuinely pleased at this turn of events. "Like you said, isn't it strange how one move affects so many others? Think of Ben! This might be just the thing to shake him up a little and help him see who's right in front of his eyes. A beautiful, vivacious, talented woman, about to be the queen of the cooks!"

Torchlight's massive library contained mostly old classics, so two days later Julia went to the tiny local library to return a book about restoring homes. She entered the tiny building and saw Trevor immediately.

He sat at an old oak table, thoughtfully staring up at the portrait of Anna rather than at the book that lay open in front of him.

"I thought you were going for supplies," she said quietly.

He started and flushed a little in embarrassment. He gave her a small shrug. "It is remarkable. The family resemblance."

Julia looked up at the portrait of her great-great-grandmother standing on the rocky beach in front of Torchlight, her eyes looking to the sea. Anna bore a haunted, forlorn look, but her stance was steadfast.

Julia tore her eyes away. "What are you doing here?"

"Catching up on my reading—electrical systems and all. Did you hear the final bill for the heating and plumbing?"

"I'm afraid to ask."

"Over twenty thousand."

"I figured. You were pretty close to that on your original estimate. Well, I better get back. If I'd known you needed something, I would've picked it up for you."

"That's okay. I'll see you back at home."

Outside she couldn't resist a peek back into the library through the window. Trevor wasn't reading. He was staring at the painting again.

Ten days before Miles was scheduled to return, Julia's brother Jake and his wife, Emily, arrived at Torchlight. Julia spotted them as they pulled through the gates, and she rushed past Trevor in her excitement to get downstairs.

Jake parked in front of the house in a brand-new blue Ford truck, which he and Emily had driven cross-country. He hopped out, smiled at his sister, and pulled her into his arms for a huge bear hug. He then twirled her around, laughing. "You get more gorgeous every time I see you, sis."

She smiled up at her towering sibling. "It's good to see you, little brother." Julia turned to Emily, opening her arms to her new sister-in-law. "And Em, you look great. This marriage stuff is agreeing with you!" They embraced for a long moment and turned with luggage in tow back toward the house.

Trevor opened the door and met them on the porch. Jake set down his bag and shook hands firmly with the man as Julia introduced them. "Trevor, this cowboy is my brother, Jake, and this is his wife, Emily. Jake, Emily, this is my general contractor and Torchlight's savior, Trevor Kenbridge." Jake smiled broadly, and Trevor returned the friendly look. Shyly, Emily shook Trevor's hand, then followed her husband into the house.

They paused in the grand entry. "Wow," Jake said. "It's as wonderful as you said. Looks like a disaster zone now, but it will be great once you get her fixed up."

"I knew you'd say that! You should've seen this place a week ago. We've been concentrating on basics like hot water and lights. You'll have to come back next summer if you want to see her restored to her best."

"You're right, Jules. I can see she's going to be fabulous."

"Come on, I'll show you to your room."

Within two hours Jake had changed and was working beside Trevor on the wiring in the basement. In the last three days, Trevor had taken the time to reinstall wallboard in the places where he had ripped out and replaced wiring. Although the walls still needed to be replastered and painted, at least they were intact. Julia appreciated his efforts.

Emily and Julia were making dinner in the kitchen when Emily ventured, "So Miles finally asked you, huh?"

Julia paused to look down at her finger. "I was going to tell you over dinner."

"Women always notice rings. Leave it to Jake, and it'd take him days to see it…even that one."

"My brother isn't the most observant."

Emily stopped tearing up lettuce leaves and looked at Julia. "Why don't you sound excited? I thought you'd been waiting for years to marry that man."

"I forgot how direct you are! That's why I liked you right away. I think Miles is a wonderful, handsome man. I'm just not one hundred percent sure about us anymore."

"But you're wearing his ring…"

"He's coming back soon for an answer."

"You should know by now if you want to be with him. You obviously have questions about it. I've never met Miles, but Jake seems uneasy about him. That sounds like gut instinct. When Jake asked me to marry him, I knew there was nothing I wanted more in the world."

"It's tough, you know? I've spent so much time with Miles. He's so right for me in so many ways. He's so…*consistent*. We know the same people…"

"The only people that really matter are you two. Jake and I had to resolve that matter ourselves."

"I remember."

"How is it now, here, where you don't know the same people?"

"We're struggling. I think that's the problem. Once we find our footing, we'll be fine. After four years in one place, I've shot off in a different direction altogether. Miles needs time to adjust. And then I think we'll be fine. We've waited so long… I think it's about time we got around to getting married."

"You sound like you're convincing yourself."

"Maybe."

"So you're going to say yes."

"I think so. I think it's right."

"I don't want to get in the way, Julia. But Jake loves you very much, and I care about you too. I don't want you to get hurt or make a bad decision. You should know it's right. You may have questions, worries, but deep down in your heart, you should know you want to spend the rest of your life with the man if you're going to marry him."

"Thanks for the advice, little sister. Now help me make the casserole, or we'll never eat."

At six o'clock Trevor and Jake emerged from the basement stairs and walked into the kitchen, laughing, at ease with each other. Julia smiled, pleased to see the two getting along so well.

"How'd it go?"

"We should have it finished tomorrow," Trevor said. "Your bro is an ace electrician."

"I didn't know that, Jake."

"One of the things you learn in architecture."

"And on the ranch?"

"I actually helped Matt rewire his stables last summer."

Trevor turned to go. "Think I'll go shower. See you all tomorrow."

"Come back and eat with us," Jake invited.

"Uh, no, I'll leave you three to catch up on family business."

Jake looked at Julia.

"Come on, Trevor," she offered. "You've had a long, hard day. What do you have ready in your pantry to eat? Spam?"

He laughed with her. "Nothing as good as that. I'll be back in fifteen minutes."

"Ten," Julia said, looking down at the oven timer.

"Ten," he agreed.

Emily set the table while Jake showered upstairs, singing so loudly the two women could hear him through the old air vents.

"He sounds happier than I've ever heard him, Emily."

"He is happy. It's doing what he loves, seeing his sister…"

"And being in love, huh?"

Emily blushed. "That could have a little to do with it."

"Or a lot."

Julia opened the china cabinet and pulled out plates and glasses. Then she grabbed the silver candelabra and six green candles. "We're celebrating, right?"

"Right."

When the men entered the dining room, Julia and Emily were seated on opposite sides of the table, talking. Only candles illumined the room. "Very nice," Jake said. "Two beautiful women and dinner by candlelight. Couldn't ask for anything more, could we, Trevor?"

"Not in a million years," he said, smiling down at Julia. "Well…maybe one thing more." He walked into the library, turned on Julia's stereo, and placed a CD in its holder. The counterpoint rhythms of Bach complemented the mood perfectly.

"Not bad for tuna casserole," Julia said, admiring the scene.

"I'll say," Jake said. "Should I say grace?"

"Sure," Julia said. She knew that Dirk and Rachel Tanner's faith had affected him as it had her when she had stayed with them.

After he finished, Julia questioned him about it. "So, Jake, are you making Mother happy and going to church?"

Jake smiled at Emily, and then his sister. "Actually, we go because we enjoy it, not to make Mother happy. It took me awhile, but the Tanners are a living example of faith in action."

"How are Rachel and Dirk?" Julia asked.

"Great," Emily said, beaming. "They're pregnant!"

"Uh-oh. Last I heard, Rachel was just getting her at-home business off the ground. Was this a planned baby?"

"She's thrilled," Emily said.

"She's just going to scale back the workload," Jake said, passing the salad.

The four ate, happily talking, laughing, and joking over their dinner. Finally, stiff after more than an hour in her seat, Julia suggested they move to the living room. Before they left the room, she dramatically opened the china cabinet to expose the secret passage. Then she showed them how the bookcase in the library moved in the same manner.

"Unbelievable," Jake said. "They must have had some architect for it to work after all these years. You guys get all the fun—I wish I had been here to explore that passage when you first discovered it."

"Well, I saved something else for you, little brother. I haven't been in the attic yet—and Trevor's only been up there to check the roof and insulation. Remember how we used to play up there as kids?"

"Barely."

"Well, if it has half the treasures we found in the passageway, it will be wonderful."

"Treasures?" Jake asked.

Excitedly Julia told Jake and Emily about Anna's journals, and she updated them on her findings.

"How about reading us some?" Jake asked.

"That would be great," Trevor agreed.

"You three get settled," Emily said, "and I'll bring in the dessert."

"Let's go," Julia said. They carried their plates into the kitchen, then they moved into the living room.

The evening was such a success, the four repeated it several times over the next few nights. Together, through hours of reading, they followed Anna and Shane as they tried to convince wealthy ship-builders to give Shane's best design a chance. Finally, five years after arriving in New York and three children later, Shane finally got his opportunity.

20 March 1845

Shane's time has come! And not a moment too soon. If I have to live out another year in this tiny apartment with these children, I am liable to tear my hair out. Our investor is one Charles Hammond, a wealthy gentleman with a love for the sea and a penchant for risk. A friend told me about him, and I must admit, I went to see him while Shane was still at sea. There comes a time when a woman must do what she must to assist her husband at getting ahead.

In my best dress, I went to call upon Mister Hammond a month prior to my Shane's return and, using the best of my feminine wiles and most of my wits as well, convinced him that it would behoove him to hear Shane out, at the very least.

I told him of Shane's ideas to create prows that will

slice through the water with little resistance. "It is the first cargo into port that draws the highest prices, is it not?" I asked him.

When Shane returned, I casually told him that I heard a Mister Hammond was interested in the ship-building process. He was out the door with his models and drawings the very next day. He returned with a cheque, his head in the clouds, and directions to a ship-yard in Boston. I shall have my house yet.

"So this is really the house that Anna built," Jake said.

"If she had eyes like her great-great-granddaughter," Trevor said, looking directly at Julia, "Anna's 'feminine wiles' left Hammond with no choice."

"Leave it to women to get things done," Julia said, ignoring his compliment as she resumed her reading.

8 June 1845

They are raising her! Huge trees are transformed before us into a version of the hundreds of models my Shane built, only a thousand times larger. The children play amongst the keel and scarfed ribs of the tall ship as if it were a common playground, not the culmination of their father's dreams. Young Shane traveled with his father to hunt for the perfect trees to form the stem and stern of this huge vessel. I am so proud of my husband! He stands and looks at her with love and compassion resembling that with which he gazes at me.

14 August 1845

It amazes me to watch the process. What once resembled a huge rib cage, now has received what they call the "skin"—the interior boards are called the "ceiling," and the exterior boards the "planking." Yesterday, caulkers began the tedious work of pounding in oakum using heavy mallets they call "beetles" and a wedge-shaped caulking iron. The oakum is a disgusting ropy material bathed in tar, which creates a sticky tangle of hair, perfect for keeping water from leaking through cracks. After applying hot pitch today, the caulkers told young Shane he could assist them in scraping off the excess tomorrow. He is so excited he can barely sleep.

10 September 1845

I have begged Shane, but he pays me no heed. There is no stopping his first voyage, though autumn is easing quickly into winter. Now that the sails have been sewn and the ship built so quickly, Shane cannot wait to launch her. Mister Hammond is no help. He believes the sooner we launch, the sooner he'll get a return on his investment. I love this little cottage we are renting, but it would be worth precious little if my Shane were to die at sea. Never have I had such a foreboding feeling about a trip. I cannot sleep! I can only pray that Jesus Christ will be with him through every foot of water. The thought is my only comfort.

Julia paused. "Should we call it a night?"

"I can't sleep leaving Anna like that!" Emily said.

"Read a few more entries," Trevor demanded.

20 September 1845

I overheard two gentlemen laying bets on the Courier. One insisted she will tip over as soon as she sits in the water. The other believes she'll make her runs to Rio de Janeiro faster than other ships and make huge profits in the coffee trade. The Courier does not hold as much as the traditional wide-bodied tall ships, but the second gentleman is correct: She will be fast. I believe in my Shane's designs.

It is my position to christen the Courier tomorrow before the launching. I would enjoy this honor much more if it were May and not September. I have such a heavy heart! How can I let him go? He's been on count-less voyages, but never have I felt so desperate. Even my new gown from Paris fails to cheer me.

21 September 1845

He is off. After a champagne bottle shattered against her bow and a quick kiss for me from my Shane, the Courier effortlessly slipped into the water. She did not tip over, and when all sixteen sails were hoisted and she moved off in all her splendor, I gave that betting gentle-man a very good look indeed. He seemed startled, as if I could read his mind, and moved off in a rush. As con-

cerned as I am for Shane, I could not help but get car-
ried away in the rush of excitement at seeing our
dreams sail. The Courier is a grand ship. I pray to God
that He will surround Shane with angels and bring my
love safely home.

"This feels like a good place to stop," Julia ventured.

Jake groaned from his position on the floor, where he had lain for an hour, totally relaxed. "I could listen all night! Can you imagine going back in time to meet Anna and Shane?"

"I feel like I have," Julia said.

"I can't believe Shane could leave Anna and his family for all that time," Trevor said quietly.

Julia picked up on his line of thought. "He had to do what he had to do. It was his dream—his livelihood."

"He could've found other dreams. If I was as in love as those two were, no dream could tear me away for months on end." He stared into Julia's eyes.

Julia broke from his gaze. "Well, I'd better turn in. You two 'guests' ready to pitch in tomorrow? If I remember right, company isn't allowed to lounge more than a few days at Timberline. Same goes for Torchlight."

"Sure," Emily said.

"I'd love it. Can we work above decks tomorrow?"

"You bet," Trevor said. "The air vents in the basement are taking longer than we thought they would. Let's take a break from it and work on something else."

"Good. I like you, buddy, but I'm sick of being in the dark cellar with you. That place gives me the willies."

"How are you at scraping old paint and wallpaper?"

"It was one of my postgraduate work specialties."

"Excellent. I think we can find enough work to fill our days for weeks."

"Maybe tomorrow we should explore the attic," Julia suggested.

"I think we've waited long enough," Jake agreed. "Let's do it."

The four bid each other good night and headed off to bed.

CHAPTER TWELVE

"C ome on, Tara. You're not going with us?"

"I'm sorry, Mike. I have to work on my cookbook. I'm afraid I won't be free for any trips for a good month or two." She looked above his head and met Ben's sad gaze. *Say something. Tell me you'll miss having me along. Maybe I'll change my mind.*

"The cookbook again, huh?" Ben said irritably. "When's it going to be finished?"

He's acting like a spoiled child denied dessert! "I'm about halfway there. But it's slowed down. I did the easy ones first. Do you want to see what I've done?"

"Nah. I can wait until you're finished."

Tara nodded, fighting to keep any hurt from her expression.

"I'd like to see what you've done, Tara," Mike said, looking from his father to her in exasperation.

"Maybe later," Ben interceded. "We have some fishing to do. It will be good to be just us. Two guys playing around." He put a strong hand on Mike's shoulder and directed him toward the door, then looked back at Tara. "Couple of months, huh? It will take that long to do?"

This time her frustration reached her tone. "It's a big project, Ben," she said. *You big oaf. If you cared a whit about me, you'd want to see it. Or is it that threatening to you?*

"Oh yeah. Well, maybe you'll finish faster than you think," Ben said simply. He put his arm around Mike again and led him away from the restaurant. Tara stood and watched them until they disappeared around the corner.

"Attic day!" Julia said, grinning when Jake and Emily finally came into the kitchen.

"Caffeine first," Jake muttered, still trying to adjust to the two-hour time difference.

Julia brought a fresh coffeecake from the oven and sliced them each a generous portion while Trevor poured the dark, steaming brew into big, blue mugs.

"I've been wanting to get up there for weeks to check out all the things I saw, but Julia wouldn't let me near it until you arrived," Trevor said.

"I wanted to share this with my baby brother," Julia said, pretending to be defensive.

"I'm glad you did! As soon as this caffeine hits my body, I'll be ready to explore," Jake said.

"Well, hurry up!" Julia said, filling her mouth with coffeecake.

"I'm hurrying, I'm hurrying."

By nine o'clock the four of them were up in the bedroom that had provided the original secret entrance to the passageway. In the opposite corner from the passage, the entrance to the attic was cut from a portion of the wood ceiling.

Trevor set his ladder and began to climb. Jake's voice stopped him. "Trevor, would you mind if I went up first?"

Trevor quickly descended. "Not at all. Sorry. I should've thought of it myself."

Jake climbed the ladder and shoved upward on the door. It gave way easily, and he climbed a few more steps to peer inward.

"What do you see?" Julia called.

"Not much. Hand me that lamp."

She handed him the battery-powered camp lantern.

He disappeared into the attic. "You guys gotta see this," they heard him call. "Come up!"

Julia followed, then Emily, then Trevor. They all stood on the old flooring, stunned as they looked around.

"Isn't it amazing?" Jake asked quietly.

"I knew it would be," Julia said.

Trevor moved toward an ancient, grimy window on their right. "Be careful where you walk," he warned, looking at the wide-board pine beneath him. "A lot of this looks rotten."

He took a rag out of his back pocket and wiped the dirt of a hundred years from the glass, allowing more daylight to shine through.

Over the decades, spiders had filled the room with intricate webs. The light shining through caught each strand, and the group looked at them for several long moments before Jake made the move to start cutting them down.

Once he had cleared a pathway well into the enormous attic, everyone began to explore.

Broken furniture was strewn everywhere, packed away by former occupants who had lacked the right handyman to fix them. Gnawing mice had done quite a bit of damage to the exposed pieces, but many of the buried ones were completely intact.

Emily found the first real treasure. "Julia, come here!"

Julia went over to her sister-in-law. Emily pulled several perfectly preserved straw bonnets from a wooden trunk and set one on her head. "Look, they're all clean and dry!" She looked like a turn-of-the-twentieth-century china doll.

Julia selected a hat decorated with a fabric rose and intricate ribbons and placed it on her head. "Wouldn't these be wonderful hanging on a wall downstairs? What a collection!"

"Check this out! Only six planets!" Jake called. He held in his hand a nineteenth-century orrery, a pre-Neptune model of the solar system. The planets hung suspended on separate wires that were attached to the central sun, enabling each one to swing around in its approximate orbit with a squeaky push from Jake.

Trevor discovered an old United States flag, badly eaten away, with only thirteen stars on its blue field.

In a corner, Julia found suitcase after suitcase full of old letters and postcards from friends and family who had traveled around the world. Trevor joined her in her examination, fascinated by what people had seen more than a hundred years before he had visited the same locations. "There's a year's worth of evening reading here after we finish Anna's journals," Trevor said, smiling over at Julia. "Think of the pieces of the puzzle in here!"

"It's wonderful!"

They spent all morning opening boxes, exclaiming excitedly over old navigation maps, antique sextants, crates full of Shane's hand-carved ship models, family pictures yellowed with age, and countless other finds.

Julia was the first to speak up about her hunger. "Hey, you guys, I'm starving. What do you say we break for lunch?"

The others reluctantly agreed, deciding to bring a few boxes down to look at more closely in the light of day.

As they munched on sandwiches in the kitchen, Julia was struck with an idea. "Say, Trevor...what if we renovated the attic, making it a private floor for my use? It would give me a place to escape to when the inn is full. We could make it into a sitting room, bathroom, and bedroom." As she envisioned it in her mind, her face was alight.

"Uh-oh. Suddenly I see my job description expanding—"

"No! Think of it! That high-pitched roof would make a really dramatic room. We could install long, side-by-side skylights to let in the sun. The basement is more than adequate for storage space. That way, we could make the existing master bedroom a honeymoon suite."

"It could be pretty nice," he nodded.

"Let's give it some thought."

"You might want to look at your finances," he said. "Maybe wait until next year to refurbish the attic—it's a disaster. Did you see those walls? Hog-hair-reinforced plaster. It's crumbling all over the place despite their inventiveness. And the flooring...like I said, it needs to be totally redone. Not to mention the insulation—"

"Oh, come on, Trevor. Are you saying you're overwhelmed?"

"No. But if you get married, we'll need to get the main house in some sort of shape in time. After that, it'll be up to you and your new hired man."

He let the words drop carefully. Wasn't she putting him through his own torment with her indecision over Miles? Two could play at that game.

Julia frowned and glanced over at Jake and Emily, then back to him. "New hired man?"

"Well, yeah. I'm not going to stick around forever."

His casual tone obviously angered her. "I thought as much. Can't pin down the wanderer, huh? Where are your dreams 'calling' you now?"

Jake and Emily moved to leave, uncomfortable with the conversation and where it was heading. "Let's go for a walk," Julia said, following after them. "The current hired man has work to do. You guys are on vacation."

Ben had tried to accept the fact that Tara needed time for her project. But when she wasn't at work on Tuesday night, he felt inexplicably cross.

"Come on, Dad. My show's on in fifteen minutes." They had finished their dinner ten minutes earlier, but Ben still sat across from his son in the restaurant booth, silently nursing his Coke.

"We'll go when I'm good 'n' ready," Ben growled.

"What's wrong?"

"I don't understand how Tara can just leave the restaurant like this. Doesn't she understand that it's not the same without her?"

"I thought dinner was as good as usual."

"Not me. It's missing something."

"You miss Tara."

Ben scowled at his son. "Let's go, smart aleck."

Ben paced in front of Tara's house that night, wanting to go up and knock at her door but unable to bring himself to do it. He wanted to see her—not just through the window, but up close—but the thought of needing to see her frightened him. *If I could just say hello, see how she's doing...* He continued pacing.

He saw Tara rise from her easel, stretch, and move to the window to open it. He knew how stuffy that kitchen could get. In doing so, she looked out at him.

"Who's there?" Tara called out, obviously frightened but trying to sound tough.

Ben couldn't let her stay scared. Sheepishly he emerged into the light of the street lamp.

"Ben?"

"Hi."

"What are you *doing?*"

He walked toward the window. "Just dropped by to see if you were okay."

"Oh. Well, why didn't you just come on up instead of scaring me half to death?"

"I don't know."

She went to the front door and walked out onto the porch. Ben paused at the foot of the steps.

"You want to come in for some coffee?" Tara nodded toward the house.

"I don't think so..."

An uncomfortable silence fell as the two struggled with their thoughts and feelings. Tara spoke first. "Look, Ben, maybe you haven't figured this out. So let me just say it. You're here because you care for me. You can't admit it, even to yourself, so you stay hidden in the shadows. The sad thing is that even in the light of day, you're still hiding in the shadows. And I'm tired of it." She paused. "We're not just friends anymore, are we, Ben?"

Still he said nothing. He felt choked, speechless, as her words of truth sank into his heart. Things were not going to stay the same; indeed, they had already been altered. But he wasn't ready for a change!

Tara began pacing. "Maybe I'm dreaming this whole thing up. Maybe I'm way off-base…" She paused and looked at him. "No. I know that's not true. Ben, I miss Sharon too. But we can't deny what's developed so naturally between us. God is giving us the chance of a lifetime, but we're both too scared and too tongue-tied to take it.

"Look, if you're ever ready to hold my hand or take me in your arms for more than a sailboat ride, then let me know. Until then, I don't want you in my shadows."

With that, she marched up the steps and shut the door firmly behind her.

Scowling again, Ben walked home, heavy in thought.

Julia awoke instantly, sensing that someone was in the room with her. Sleepily, she opened her eyes and saw him leaning against the doorjamb, gazing at her as if transfixed.

"Good morning, sleepyhead," he said. "Sorry if I invaded your privacy. The door was open."

"That's okay. What are you doing?"

"Watching you," he admitted, looking into her eyes warmly.

"You know, you're so peaceful and still when you sleep, it's a great chance to really look at you." Julia silently sat up, not knowing what to say. She no longer felt any of the anger that had burned so hot the night before. What right, after all, had she to hope that Trevor would stay? She still wore Miles's ring.

"Come on," he said. "It's nine o'clock. Jake and Emily and I can't drink any more coffee or we'll start bouncing off the walls. We thought we'd go down to your grandfather's old shipyard and look around, then work this afternoon."

"So you're still going to be working around here, huh?"

"Look, Julia, things got a little out of hand yesterday. I said some things I didn't mean."

"Didn't mean?"

He shifted uncomfortably under her gaze. "I have some things to sort out for myself. We can talk about it later, okay?"

"Okay. Well, then…I think going down to the shipyard to take a look around is a great idea. After all, Jake and Em are on vacation, right? Can't make 'em slave all the time."

"I'll go tell them." Trevor flashed her a grin and turned to go. He turned back to look at Julia. Her long, tousled hair fell in tangles around her nightshirt-clad shoulders. Her eyes, refreshed after a night's sleep, loomed large, and her lips were rosy from her chewing on them unconsciously under his stare. "I have the most beautiful boss in town," Trevor said.

"You say that to all your bosses," she returned, then bit her lip, wanting to snatch back the flirting. She was messing with him. It wasn't fair.

"Yeah. Juan in Rio was particularly cute," Trevor said. His smile lit up his face.

I have the most gorgeous employee in town. "Fifteen minutes?" she asked him.

"Ten." He left her doorway, whistling.

Julia arrived a full fifteen minutes later, smiled innocently at Trevor, and grabbed a bagel from Jake's hand as he was about to take a bite.

"You haven't changed a bit," Jake said.

"She isn't very punctual either," Trevor said, looking at his watch.

"You guys ready yet?" Julia asked, as if she had been waiting for them all morning.

They walked out the front door, and Julia exclaimed in surprise as she sighted four bicycles standing in front of the porch. "It's a perfect day for a ride! Where did you get them?"

"I borrowed them from Tara and Ben. Jake and I went to get them while you were still lying in bed and Emily was making breakfast."

"You guys are wonderful."

The morning promised to be uncommonly warm. The temperature had already reached sixty degrees. As Julia raced out of the compound, she felt free and alive. "I haven't ridden since I was a little girl!" she called over her shoulder.

"They say you never forget how," Jake said. He pumped hard to pass his sister on the highway and called over his shoulder, "I think horses are easier though."

"Ha! That's all I need."

"You should try it."

"I'll come to Montana for that."

Jake led the way, with Julia right behind him. Trevor seemed at peace keeping pace with Emily, and the two rode side by side chatting. Jake slowed just enough to allow his sister to ride beside him. "Gorgeous day, huh?"

"It is." The highway curved toward town as it edged the water. Occasionally waves crashed against the tall granite cliffs, sending a fine mist their way. Beside the road, fat green buds had burst into sunny yellow Forsythia blooms. Maples, once the fire-red of autumn, were budding again. Here and there were the last blossoms of purple crocuses and daffodils.

"I can't wait to restore Torchlight's garden," Julia said.

"That will be beautiful. Em and I'll have to come back this summer to see it." Jake cleared his throat. "Jules, can I talk to you about something?"

She nodded. "Sure."

"What's the deal with you and Trevor? He's the best guy I've ever met for you. So why are you wearing that chump Beckley's ring?"

"I've been meaning to talk to you about that. First of all, Trevor is just a friend. And Miles is not a chump. I'm in love with him."

"You could have fooled me."

"Does this ring look like a joke?"

"No, it doesn't. Listen, Julia, I know you're thinking of saying yes to Miles. But don't do it! That guy is a loser. I know you think you love him, but maybe you're too close to see it. There's something about him I just don't trust." He looked over his shoulder to his wife and waved with a smile. Emily and Trevor waved back.

He dropped his tone. "Now this Trevor fellow, he's a prince. I liked him as soon as I saw him. Maybe no one else will tell you this, so I will. You two are made for each other."

"Jake, I think you're overstepping your bounds. I told you, Trevor and I are just friends. Besides, he could up and leave at a moment's notice. He's not husband material."

"Oh, he just feeds you that idea to protect himself. If you're thinking of marrying someone else, why should he lay his heart on the line? I was upstairs when he was supposed to be waking you up. I watched *him* watch *you* for five minutes. The man's in deep. I think you are too. You're just too confused to see it."

"Okay, Jake. You've said your piece. Now leave it. I have to make my own way."

"All right. Just make wise choices, big sister. You have a lot of money in your pocket right now, since you hit the big 3-0 and got your share of the family loot. Ever consider that Miles just wants a wealthy heiress for a wife?"

"Jake!" She wanted to stop and yell at him, but didn't, fearing that Trevor might overhear. She lowered her voice. "Did you ever think that it would make more sense that Trevor was after me for my money than Miles? Miles has his own nest egg."

"Trevor's not that kind of guy! You know it as well as I do. Miles, on the other hand—"

"Is working hard on his business to make a good life for us. He told me!"

"Where will that life be, Julia?"

She had no answer. "Let's drop this, okay?" she asked, feeling suddenly weary.

"Okay, for now. Look! Road to the shipyard dead ahead!"

Chapter Thirteen

*J*ulia had spotted the old shipyard two months earlier, and the foursome found it with little trouble. The road was overgrown with trees and brush, but a few weathered signs pointed them in the right direction. As they maneuvered around potholes and foliage, the road suddenly opened up into a large expanse of shoreline.

According to Tara, the two schooners that were languishing in the water had been abandoned in the thirties. At one time they had each had spars for four masts, but the masts were completely gone from one ship, which was also nearly overtaken by barnacles, and were reduced to but two and a half on the other. The second ship appeared to be mostly afloat, even though the planking was popped around the curves of her bow and she listed slightly to starboard.

Jake let out a long, low whistle while the others stared at the vision from the past.

Trevor was the first to speak. "These ships are younger than Shane's would've been, but they're still intriguing, huh?"

"I'll say!" Jake said. "Let's go aboard!"

"Let's!" Julia agreed excitedly. "If we're careful, we just might be able to reach her along the old pier."

Trevor shook his head. "I don't know, Julia. She looks mighty rickety to me. I don't think it's a good idea."

"Come on, Trevor! Don't be a wimp! Let's check her out. It's the next best thing to a real clipper."

"I hear there's a restored version in Portland. We could go down there tomorrow…"

His words fell on deaf ears. The Rierdons were already making their way toward the dilapidated pier. Emily looked back at him and shrugged. "There's no stopping them now." She turned to follow Jake and Julia.

With a sigh, Trevor parked his bike alongside the others and ran to catch up with them. "I don't like this," he muttered.

The pier stopped just ten feet shy of the old ship. Between the dock and the starboard edge of the ship stood six pilings that, though slightly wobbly when pushed, appeared to be basically stable. Julia turned around with an adventurous glint in her eye.

"It looks like we're out of pier," Trevor tried. "So much for that idea."

"Not so fast, Trevor. Come on, you've hiked dozens of dangerous mountains around the world. You're not telling me this intimidates you!"

"I've hiked with experienced trekkers. I haven't done a tightrope act on moving pilings to a rickety old ship…with two women."

"So that's what you really think! I bet Em and I'll make it over easier than you guys."

Trevor sighed and looked at Jake. "You think this is wise?"

"What's the worst that could happen? Maybe I'll get to see my big sis take a dive into the drink. Sounds fun to me."

"This water is forty degrees. Not very fun."

"Trevor! Why are you being such a spoilsport?" Julia looked at him with irritation in her eyes.

"I just have a bad feeling about this. I can't explain it."

"I'll go first." Julia gave Trevor one last puzzled look. "You were the maniac on the highway—and the one who dared me to go into the hidden passageway at Torchlight. Suddenly lose your nerve?" She turned away.

He grabbed her arm and immediately wished he hadn't.

"Come on. Let go." Her eyes flashed with anger.

"Julia…"

"I'm perfectly capable of making decisions for myself."

As they stared at each other, Trevor knew she wasn't just speaking of this moment. It was as if she was trying to convince herself.

He released her reluctantly. "I'll go first." He brushed past Julia and climbed up the first piling, which was still attached to the pier. Leaning over to the next weatherworn post, he found his balance and stood. After taking a deep breath, he moved forward, working his way from one piling to the next. On the last piling, he turned to gloat and almost fell when the old cutoff log moved a few inches under his weight. The trio laughed, then held their breath until he was safely aboard the ship.

Julia was next, then Jake. Trevor had expected Emily to refuse at the last moment, but the woman showed surprising nerve and easily shimmied up and over the piling.

He was distracted from Emily's last step aboard by Julia's excited exclamations. "Check it out!" she said, looking up the tall mainmast. "Can you imagine climbing this bad boy to the crow's-nest?"

Trevor stood by her side and took a careful look at the wood. "I bet this is one of the last old-growth pines that were forested."

Jake and Emily worked their way over to Trevor and Julia, maneuvering around black holes in the floorboards that looked particularly foreboding. "I read that Maine was once famous for giant white pines," Jake said. "The Brits used to come and select the best for their own masts. Until we drove them out, that is."

"How'd they get the trees from the forest to the shipyard?" Emily asked.

"Well, at first the pines along the coast kept them in good supply. But after a while, there were too many ships being built, a lot of them by Shane Donnovan."

"Gramps didn't do much for the environment, did he?" Julia said sardonically.

"Better sail-powered ships than oil tanker spills."

"Then where'd they get their wood?"

"They had to go deeper into the north woods to cut them, drag them to the nearest river, and wait for ice-out."

" 'Ice-out'?" Emily asked.

"They'd log all winter," Jake explained, "bring the felled trees to the river's edge, and when the water rose in the spring as the snow melted, the river brought down all that lumber to the seaside towns below. Gramps suddenly had his building material."

"You got all that from the history books?" Julia asked.

"Some. Plus I found Shane's logs in the library late last night."

"You're kidding."

"Nope. He was more prolific than Granny. Twelve books, bound in oilskin. Mostly ship stuff. Latitude, longitude. You know, the works."

"Oh, Jake! That's so exciting! Between Anna's and Shane's writing, we can piece together a large part of their lives," Julia said.

"Well, Anna's writing is much more interesting than Shane's. He just sticks to the logistics. Anna is the one who gives us the real scoop."

"Leave it to a woman," Trevor said, looking down at Julia.

She smiled back at him, then raised her eyebrows impishly. "Let's go explore."

"Julia, this deck is barely holding together."

His warning was ignored. She was off.

He was moving toward Julia, carefully watching her as she looked over the edge of one gaping hole to the deck below, when the rotting boards beneath her groaned and gave way.

Letting out one short, frightened scream, she vanished before his eyes.

"Julia!" Trevor shouted again, his heart frozen in fear.

There was no answer.

"Hold my feet!" he directed. Jake could only nod in agreement and comply.

Edging out to where she had disappeared, Trevor stretched to his entire six feet four inches in length, but still could not see. He looked back at Jake, who held his ankles firmly, then forward to the rotten boards in front of him. "I'll have to stretch farther to see! Hold tight!"

"You won't go anywhere," Jake promised.

Gritting his teeth, Trevor gingerly pulled himself forward, half anticipating the same crack and plunge that had sucked Julia into the ship's depths.

The wood held. Carefully, he peered over the edge of the huge hole. "Julia!"

"I'm…I'm here!" she cried.

As his eyes adjusted to the light, he could see her directly beneath him.

"Are you okay?

"I think I've broken a leg. What scares me the most is that I think I might fall through to the next deck if I move a muscle."

"Okay. Stay still. I'll be right back. I promise." He called over his shoulder, "Jake, pull me back!"

Jake moved with such force that dozens of large splinters edged into Trevor's shirt and chest. Consumed with fear for Julia, Trevor was oblivious to the pain. He stood and removed a Swiss army knife from his pocket. Moving to the ancient ropes still attached to the mainmast, he cut in at a place where the lines had begun to fray. As he worked, he explained the situation to Emily and Jake.

"Emily, I think Julia's going to need medical attention. If you can make it back into town on your own, go see Tara at the little restaurant. Tell her what happened. She'll know who to call."

"I'm on my way."

"Jake, once I've got the rope cut, we'll make our way to the next deck. I think it's our best bet. She's halfway through that level and is liable to break through at any moment."

"I'll go look for a way down."

Loaded with adrenaline, Trevor pulled a large section of the old sail down and struggled to cut away the rope he needed. "Julia!" he called through gritted teeth. "Talk to me!"

"I'm here!" Her voice sounded faint, in spite of its intended bravado. He had never heard her sound so vulnerable. It made him frantic to get to her.

"Are you cold?"

"Yes! How'd those sailors keep warm?"

"They didn't go belowdecks unless they had to!" At last the rope gave way. Trevor caught his breath and fought the urge to simply jump through a nearby hole to the deck below. He wanted his hands on her now. He wanted her safe beside him. *Dear Lord, I'm in deep here. Help me out. I don't want her to die. I'll tell her how I feel, I promise. Please show me the way.*

"Over here!" Jake called.

Trevor coiled the rope and threw it over his shoulder. "Coming! Julia, we're on our way!"

Jake had found the stairs that led belowdecks. Trevor descended into the darkness and then paused to let his eyes adjust.

"Well, it's about time." Julia tried to keep her voice light.

Jake moved to Trevor's side. "Julia? Are you okay?"

"I'm alive. Just feeling stupid for getting us into this mess. Listen, boys, we have a problem. These boards feel like they're about to give way."

"Here," Trevor edged toward her as far as the solid flooring would allow, and threw her the rope.

It fell a foot shy of her.

She leaned toward it in an effort to grab hold.

"Julia, no!" Trevor yelled.

As she moved, the last boards splintered, and Julia once again disappeared belowdecks.

"No!" Trevor and Jake yelled together. The sound of a sickening crash and the splash of water greeted them. Without worrying further about the stability of the deck, Trevor ran to the second hole and peered beneath him. The shaft of light from above shone through to the oily water below. Julia was not in sight. There was only a flurry of bubbles rising to the surface and bursting.

"She's not coming up!" Trevor yelled, frantic. "Stay here with the rope! We'll need you!"

With that, he slipped through the hole, hanging on to a buttress that held firm. Hoping he would not land on top of her, Trevor released his grip, falling nearly twelve feet before slicing through the icy water. He plunged, deeper and deeper. His muscles contracted in protest at the change in temperature as he swam for the top.

Breaking the surface, he gasped for breath and called out to her. "Julia! Julia! Do you see her, Jake?" He whirled around, unable to determine where she had gone.

"She has to be under still! Maybe she's caught on something!"

Trevor inhaled deeply and dove again into the black waters. He could not see a thing. He reached out in all directions, desperate. *God! Please help us!*

He felt nothing. He had to come up for air. As Trevor broke the surface, his teeth chattered uncontrollably.

"Nothing?" Jake called, with terror in his voice.

Trevor ignored him, inhaled again, and dove deeper. He was about to come up again for air when his hand brushed through a wave of what he thought might be hair. Fighting the need to emerge for oxygen, he moved closer to where he had felt the silky strands and caught Julia's arm. She was limp, not responding. He pulled, but she did not budge.

She was caught.

Trevor had no choice but to go up for air and then return. He felt like crying out. *She's dead! Good Lord, how can she be dead?* His head broke the surface, and his lungs sucked in the air they demanded. He no longer heard Jake's anxious yelling. Trevor inhaled deeply, held his breath, then dove again, fighting to concentrate on the techniques he had learned as a scuba diver. *Let the air out slowly to alleviate the pressure.* Tiny bubbles escaped his mouth in a steady stream.

A strange calm surrounded him as he once again dove down to Julia. Instinctively he swam to her feet and felt along them until he found what held her. One leg was bent awkwardly, while the other had broken straight through the bottom of the ship. Fingering the edge of the wooden board with both hands, Trevor placed his feet against the mossy boards of the ancient ship and yanked with all his might.

The board gave way. Trevor grabbed Julia's arm and swam for the surface. When both their heads came up, Jake let out a shout of relief. Trevor fought to keep Julia's face out of the water, carrying her in a lifeguard hold toward a portion of deck that remained intact.

He reached the deck and quickly pulled Julia out of the water. Panting, he immediately began CPR, pausing only to check for breathing or a heartbeat. Nothing. "Come on, Julia. You can't leave me now! We have work to do. Think of Torchlight. Think of me! I haven't even gotten the chance to tell you how I feel. Come on, Julia. Come back to me! I need to tell you…that I love you."

"I'm coming down!" Jake yelled.

"No! We'll need you to pull us out!

"Please, Father, help me." Trevor pinched Julia's nose, tilted her head, touched her cold lips with his own and blew air into her lungs until they rose. He repeated the procedure several times. There was no responding breath, no heartbeat.

He returned to her chest, and finding her sternum, carefully pumped as he had been taught years earlier in high-school CPR class. "How many times do I do this?" he called to Jake, who was practically hanging upside-down in an effort to see what was happening.

"Eight. No, five. I don't remember! Please, don't let her die!"

Trevor stopped at eight and moved his lips back to hers. He blew two quick breaths into her lungs and then resumed his efforts to resuscitate her heart. "Come on, violet eyes," he said, pumping rhythmically. "Come back to me." Two more breaths.

Panting from his efforts, Trevor paused to check for vital signs. Was that a hint of a breath? A heartbeat? No. He resumed his work. He was placing his hands above her sternum once more when she sputtered and coughed, choking on the water inside her lungs.

"Julia!" He leaned her on her side as she fought to get air and rid herself of the water that gagged her. Weakly, she waved her hand, wanting to lie back again.

He leaned over her. "Are you okay?"

She nodded painfully, unable to speak, and continued to cough.

Trevor let out a whoop. "She's okay! Jake, she's okay!" He looked into her eyes. "You look like a drowned rat, but you're still the most beautiful sight I've ever seen."

Julia could only manage a weak smile before fading out of consciousness again. Trevor listened carefully to her heart and watched her breathing, relieved as they gained strength. "I think she's okay, but she's out again. We'd better get her to the clinic."

"I think I hear help arriving up top," Jake said.

"Good. We'll need it to get us out of here."

The volunteer emergency response team came equipped with a long ramp, which they extended from the pier to the ship's edge. Calmly their leader cut away rotting boards on the far side of the hole with an ax and peered through at Jake. "What's the situation?"

"Trevor and my sister are another deck down. She went into the water and is unconscious. She woke up a minute ago, but now she's out cold again. Trevor says she's breathing, but thinks she's going into shock. He can't be far behind her. He was in the water almost as long as she was."

The chief paramedic directed several men in setting up a pulley system, to which they attached a long length of nylon rope and a yellow plastic gurney. The mainmast served as support. The paramedic tied another rope around the mast, then easily wove a makeshift seat for himself out of the other end. Wrapping the end of the rope snugly around his arm, he dropped through the hole without a word.

Hanging as easily as if he were on a tire swing on a hot summer's day, the paramedic paused briefly beside Jake to make sure he was all right. Then he let out more rope and descended further down and out of sight.

One man's walkie-talkie came to life as the paramedic gave the men directions. Another man chopped a bigger cavity through which the gurney could easily slide. Placing the ax in the gurney, the men lowered it to the next level, where Jake worked to enlarge the hole in his deck as well.

The men had Julia on the main deck within five minutes, Emily cried out as they carried her sister-in-law past. She decided to accompany her, entrusting the fate of Jake and Trevor to what appeared to be an accomplished team of rescuers.

Julia regained consciousness shortly after reaching the clinic. Two nurses in white had stripped her of her soaked clothes, dressed her in a dry gown, and tucked her under a heap of blankets.

The patient looked over at Emily, who held her hand. "Guess I should lose some weight," she said.

"Guess we better be more careful when we explore," Emily said. "I'm glad you're alive, Julia. That was a close one."

"I'll say. I'm not even sure what happened."

Jake overheard her response as he entered her room and the second team rushed past with Trevor in tow. As they passed by Julia's door, Trevor called out to her, but the attendants pushed his gurney on by, ignoring his demands to stop. Except for the splinters in his chest he was all right, but hospital protocol demanded they give him a complete exam.

"I'll tell you what happened," Jake said, turning back to his sister. "That man"—he pointed out the door where Trevor had passed— "risked life and limb to save you. You can't tell me he's not in love. And if you pass up a man who is so crazy about you he'd be willing to die for you, then you are not as smart as I thought you were. If you could've seen that man move like I did, you'd take off Miles's ring right now."

"Jake, give me a break. Let me catch up a minute before I make decisions that will affect the rest of my life."

"Your life! You wouldn't be alive if it weren't for Trevor!"

"Jake," Emily said quietly. "Ease up, huh?" She turned toward Julia. "I've called Miles, told him what happened."

"Thanks, Emily. Look, Jake. I get it. I owe the man my life. But if every woman married the man who saved her life, you'd have lifeguards who were also polygamists. If Trevor's right for me—and I'm right for him—we'll figure it out. Now, I just need to be alone!"

"At times, Julia, God has to speak louder to some people than to others. You might want to consider this a lightning bolt."

Julia awoke the next morning to a vase full of long-stemmed red roses. She reached for the card with a smile. "My heart stopped when they called with the news. I cannot live without you. Please say yes next week. I want you safe at my side for the rest of our lives. Your loving future husband, Miles."

Ah, the constant question. What to do with Miles? She admired the red blossoms and thought how romantic and sweet it was of Miles to do something like that. But it had been Trevor who had been at her side…this time. Jake, Emily, and Trevor interrupted her thoughts when they entered her room.

"She's awake!" Jake leaned down to give her a kiss on the fore-head.

"How are you?" Trevor asked, genuine concern in his voice. He sat on the edge of her bed as Jake moved away. Trevor held a gigan-tic bouquet of forsythia blossoms in his arms, but seemed to forget about them as he gazed at Julia. She had seen enough in the mirror to know she looked bruised, scratched, and generally beat-up.

"I'm a little stiff. This cast is gonna kill me. How will I get around?"

"Well, fortunately, you hired on the buffest of the buff, the strongest of the strong…yes, Hercules the Handyman."

Emily giggled as she sat down on the other side of Julia's bed. "You must've had a whole team of guardian angels around you yes-terday. Do you realize that?"

"I know it. I'm a lucky one. God must have plans for me yet." She turned back to Trevor. "Are you going to hunt down a vase for those beautiful flowers, or are you taking them back home with you?"

"I'll find a vase. Ever the boss, huh?"

"Sorry. Thanks for bringing them."

"That's better. You're welcome. I'll go ask the nurse for a vase." He moved off, and Julia watched the doorway a second after he was gone.

Jake cleared his throat. Julia looked at him. "There's the difference between Miles and Trevor. Trevor braved the thorny brush to gather the best flowers he could find to bring you. We had to practically drag him out of here to get some sleep last night. And he woke us up at six o'clock, bright-eyed and bushy-tailed, ready to come back over.

"Meanwhile Emily had made the obligatory call to Beckley. He received the news—even sounded worried—and placed his order with the nearest florist. Has he called? Did he think about making a quick flight out here to check on you himself? Perhaps."

"Come on, Jake. I'm not in any shape for an argument. He did call. He was really concerned. And you should read his sweet note," she said, gesturing toward the flowers. "Maybe you're just too closed-minded to give him a chance to express himself."

Trevor interrupted them when he came back, carrying the long forsythia branches in a vase full of water. He placed them on the table behind the roses, where they peeked out in golden splendor, brightening up the room considerably.

"The doctor says you can head home tomorrow. If you're up to it, we thought we'd take the convertible and cruise down the highway. Give these mountain hermits a better idea of what they're missing," he said.

"Sounds great. What time can I go?"

"The doctor's going to come in and talk with you."

On cue, a beautiful woman in a white lab coat entered and smiled at the roomful of people. "Hi, Julia, I'm Dr. Chambers."

Julia shook her hand. "So how bad is it?"

"Not too bad. You've fractured the lateral malleolus of the ankle. The cast should fix you up as good as new."

"How long will I be in this cast?"

"Six weeks or so."

"Six weeks!"

"Sometimes it takes longer."

"Longer!"

"I'd say we should take it off in six and see what we find," the doctor calmly continued. "I want to keep you in another day for observation. You can probably go home tomorrow. When you do, try to rest your leg as much as possible. And if you have to walk, use these crutches." Julia's dismay did not deter the doctor for a second.

"You're a lucky woman, Julia. In the last five years, we've had three kids in here who've had accidents on that ship. One has no mobility below the waist. Another died. You're fortunate you escaped with just a broken leg." With that, she left the room.

Feeling chastised for their foolishness, they sat for a moment, thinking about the poor choices they had made the day before. After a few moments, Jake began telling jokes, trying to break the somber mood. When Julia finally dozed off, the others decided to head home and allow her to rest. Trevor was the last to leave. Checking to make sure the Rierdons were out of hearing distance, he walked back to Julia's side. Tenderly, he sat beside her bed, picked up her hand in his own, and kissed her fingers, staring at her while she slept.

He rose. "Heal quickly, my love," he said in a faint whisper.

Julia opened her eyes as he left the room. *Heal quickly, my love.* His words raced through her mind over and over again.

Chapter Fourteen

*W*hen the trio arrived at the clinic the following morning, Emily brought a change of clothes for Julia to wear home. A nurse had washed her hair, and Julia looked much better.

"Now take it easy this week," Dr. Chambers directed. "Stay off that leg as much as you can for seven days, and keep it elevated."

"I hear you," Julia said. "Guess I won't be a whole lot of help to you for a while," she said to Trevor. There was a note of tenderness in her voice that made him look at her twice; her gaze confirmed what he had heard, and he felt his heart pound.

The doctor left, and Emily was the first to take action. "Okay, Jake. Will you go get the car and bring it around to the front? Trevor, you can grab the flowers and wait at the entrance while I help Julia get dressed."

They all jumped up and got to work as directed. Trevor privately wondered what would've happened if Julia or he, or both, had died in the murky waters. He shook the heavy feeling off as he stood outside, his arms full of flowers. In one arm, he had the roses. In the other, the forsythia.

He looked from one bouquet to the other and remembered his fervent promise to God to tell Julia how he felt. *I love her. I love her! I have to tell her.* He wondered if it was the right thing to do. Wouldn't a confession of love confuse her? First she had to decide whether or not she loved Miles. Trevor could not muddy the issue. Could he?

Julia came out in a wheelchair. She looked down at her cast, which stuck out from underneath a pair of Bermuda shorts. "Pretty, isn't it? And no wisecracks about my winter-white legs."

"No wisecracks from me," Trevor said as he peeked through the huge bouquets in his arms, admiring the shape of her bare leg, despite its scratches and bruises. "Julia, maybe we could talk—"

At her waistband, a cell phone rang out. "Oh. Sorry. Miles FedExed it. Wanted to make sure I would always be able to reach him." She pressed a button, silencing the ringing phone. "Hello? Oh, hi, Miles. Yes, I'm fine. Jake and Emily are taking me home now. Well, they are after we take a drive. I wish you were here too. Listen, may I call you back later? Thanks, love." She hung up the phone and looked back to Trevor.

"Come on, Kenbridge. No need to walk twenty paces behind me."

"Yes, my liege," he managed to joke. "I'm coming."

Julia turned and smiled, and they both laughed.

Mike sat on a barstool, miserably spooning chowder into his mouth.

Tara came over. "All right, Mike, what's up?"

"Nothin'."

"Come on. What's going on?"

"It's my dad. Ever since you guys got in that fight the other night, he's been in a bad mood. He says I shouldn't come in here so much and bug you."

Tara tousled Mike's hair. "Look, your dad has to come to terms with a bunch of stuff, like letting go of your mom enough to let me in. It's not easy, Mike. He's been missing her for a long time now—we all have.

"But now he has to stop mourning her so much that he doesn't push the living out of his life. I couldn't stand the games anymore, you understand? If we're just going to be friends, that's fine. But if we're going to be more, let's get on with it. You and I are ready for it. But your dad is still making his way. Let's pray for him that he makes the right decision, regardless of what we want, okay?"

Mike nodded gravely. "I hope—"

"No, Mike. Let's not hope anymore. Let's just wait and see. Let's wait and see what God and Ben come to."

Mike nodded again and then slipped off his barstool. He paused and looked around the empty restaurant. "Do you think you could say a quick prayer with me, Tara? I'm not much good at stuff like that."

"Come here," she said gently. She leaned over the counter and took his hands in her own. "There's no such thing as a bad prayer, Mike. God hears us, no matter what we say or how we say it. To his ears, it's all music."

"Still, I'd feel better if you said it."

She nodded and smiled at him softly. They bowed their heads. And there, in that tiny restaurant, the two prayed that the Almighty would move a man that they could not.

Julia, Trevor, Emily, and Jake spent the afternoon canvassing the southern coast of Maine, despite the cold turn in the weather. Few others were out on the highway, due to the fog and threat of rain. They talked little, simply thinking how blessed they were to be smelling the sea air; to be seeing the waves and trees and the rough granite cliffs beside them.

Julia looked over at Trevor, absently watching the scenery speed by, and was especially glad he had survived his rescue of her. Gently she took his hand.

He looked at her in wonder.

"Thank you," she whispered.

Tears unexpectedly welled in his eyes. "You're welcome," he whispered back.

"Hey, at the hospital, you said you wanted to talk."

"Yeah. Forget it. It was nothing."

The question hung between them. He knew it. She knew it. But neither seemed to have the strength to broach it.

She looked back out to sea.

When Jake and Emily left a few days later, Trevor still hadn't told Julia how he felt. That night, she invited him to join her for dinner and a reading of Anna's journals. He accepted, slightly dizzy at the thought of being alone with her once more. Work on the house had slowed as Trevor continued rewiring the mansion while helping Julia recuperate. She had spent most of the last week reading Shane's logs, catching up to where they had left Anna.

Excitedly she told Trevor that Shane's first voyage had been a huge success. "He didn't die at sea! As much as Anna hated to see him go, I was half expecting him to disappear then and there."

"Woman's intuition?"

"I think there's something to be said for it."

"Me, too. Did Shane eventually die at sea?"

"I think so. I can't remember if he died or just never came home from a voyage. I guess we'll find out. But I'm dreading that part. I can almost feel their love, and I can't stand for it to end."

Trevor looked down at her intently. Julia was inspecting the new wiring in the living room, admiring the clean work. "I'll see you in an hour," he said. "I'll take care of dinner. You stay put."

"Yes sir."

Too tired to cook himself, Trevor drove to town and picked up lasagna, salad, and French bread at Tara's restaurant before going back to the main house. He thought of how he'd nearly lost Julia a few days earlier and would probably lose her completely when she agreed to marry Miles. The image of her wet, limp body in his arms, not breathing, haunted him. Could Miles take care of her as well as he? Would he have jumped in after her? Or would he have just called for help, waiting until it was too late?

Trevor tried to put Miles out of his mind, not wanting to become angry and ruin his evening with Julia. He parked his motorcycle and, grabbing the picnic basket from the back, ran up the stairs. He was startled to see Julia opening the door.

Her hair hung down in a golden waterfall, and her violet eyes, accentuated by her long lashes, smiled back into his. The bruising and swelling of her face and arms were, for the most part, gone. She wore tights, bunched up at the top of her cast, and a fisherman's sweater that was long enough to meet the top of the white plaster. Even with the cast, she still managed to look lovely.

"Come in. You could've taken the car, you know," she said.

Trevor found his voice. He brushed past her nonchalantly, heading for the kitchen. "I know. I had to get my motorcycle fix. Every once in a while I just feel like taking off. Haven't been homebound like this for years. It felt good to be out on the road."

"I can understand that," she said quietly. After a pause, she followed him into the kitchen on her crutches. "After all, you've just come off a twelve-year odyssey into the world. I'm surprised you don't feel more claustrophobic than you do."

He pulled out the bread, salad, and main course. "I've had some serious distractions, so I didn't really notice. You know, with the house and everything."

"I know. The days are flying by. There's so much to do it seems I just get up, shower, and eat breakfast, and then the next thing I know, it's time for bed!"

Trevor reached for some dishes from the cupboard and arranged their meal on two separate plates. "As you can see, I hired Tara for the evening's dining experience."

"A fine choice. Let's eat in the living room. Then I won't have to move after dinner. Call me lazy."

"Okay, Lazy, grab those crutches and follow me. The living room it is." Trevor picked up the plates and led the way, choosing to settle into the wing chairs where Julia could put her leg up on the ottoman, beside a roaring fire. They ate and talked, mostly about Jake and Emily and all they had been through before getting married.

"I miss having them around," Trevor said.

"Me, too. They're good company."

"How about updating me on Anna and Shane?"

"Well, they've just moved to Maine. I think the last time you listened, it was three years ago in Anna's journals. The *Courier* not only made her first voyage a success, but she also had many more afterward. With the California gold rush in full swing, the need for fast ships around the Cape was at an all-time high. Gramps headed off to Maine to build his own ships after he and Mr. Hammond had a dispute.

"Anna was worried that Mr. Hammond would just keep building Shane's designs. But, fortunately, Shane had some improvements in mind. Those ships we saw at the ol' shipyard turned the shipping industry upside-down. He just kept making faster and faster ships."

"What journal are you on?"

"Number six."

"Well, let's hear some! I feel like I've been missing out."

"Okay. Can you grab me that brown journal from the table in the library?"

"On my way."

Julia admired Trevor as he went to get the book. He wore jeans and a dark-blue, long-sleeved T-shirt that complemented his muscular build. His motorcycle ride had left him with flushed cheeks, making him look even healthier and more vibrant than usual. She looked away as he returned.

As soon as Julia had the journal in her hands, she carefully opened it and began to read.

> *14 May 1848*
>
> *We launch the Donnovan tomorrow! My joy would be complete in this latest creation if old nightmares didn't still plague my mind. Since the Wave Runner went down last year directly after launching, Shane insists*

upon captaining the first voyage of each ship. He is convinced that he could have saved the Wave Runner had he been aboard. Any mention of the ship brings horrible memories of watching her go up in flames inexplicably. Those poor sailors jumped, so frantic were they to disembark, as the beautiful ship became a huge fireball. Nearly all hands died.

With memories like that still fresh in my mind, I cannot find the strength to argue with Shane. I simply want to banish all talk of her and try to forget. It is my recurring nightmare that Shane will be aboard when one of his ships succumbs to a fierce storm, is taken over by pirates, or once again goes up in flames. In my heart of hearts, I believe he would prefer to go down with the ship rather than abandon her.

15 May 1848

I must confess this. I wish to be with child for one reason only: to keep Shane at my side. I have not awakened with such fears in my heart since we launched the Courier. I tell myself he survived that; he will come home from this voyage as well, fit as a fiddle. But my heart does not believe. It cries out. I feel my Lord is telling me something, but Shane will not hear me.

He gave me a present last night, a wool burnoose from Morocco that he picked up on his last trip and has kept hidden. It is beautiful. The cloth is a rich black, the edges trimmed in satin. He placed the cape over my *shoulders and set the hood over my head. Lifting my chin, he looked into my eyes. "Wear this and look for me from the cliffs each eve I am gone," he said. "I will be speeding home to you, unable to think of anything but my beautiful wife awaiting me."*

I told him of my fears. He said only, "That is why I must have you watching for me, willing me home. God will hear our prayers and reunite us. Do not be afraid." He left this afternoon, aboard the Donnovan. She is his crowning glory, the most impressive ship he has ever built.

Trevor cleared his throat nervously. Julia looked up in alarm, never having seen him so ill at ease.

"Want to hear something very strange?" he asked.

"Okay…"

"When I was in Morocco four years ago, I picked up a burnoose that sounds identical to the one Shane gave to Anna."

"You're kidding!"

"I'm not. I'll be right back." He hurried out the door and returned, panting, several minutes later.

Trevor held the cape out to Julia. She gasped. "It is beautiful. I can see why Anna was so excited."

"It's for you."

Julia looked up at him, shaking her head. "Oh, Trevor, I can't accept such a gift from you."

"No. You must. I picked it up four years ago with the distinct thought that I would meet the right person to wear it. Who better than you?"

She could see that there was no changing his mind. "Thank you," she said softly.

"You're welcome. When I leave here, it will warm my heart to think of you wearing it above the cliffs, just like Anna."

Julia was speechless. The word *leaving* felt like a sudden punch to her gut, taking her breath away. Struggling for composure, she sought the right words. "So…so you're thinking about leaving soon?"

Trevor rose, looking out into the black night and obviously listening to the waves. *Crash, swoosh. Crash, swoosh. Crash, swoosh.* He stiffened before turning to say, "Well, sure. Can't stay on forever. Believe it or not, this house will someday be in ship-shape. And with you and Miles marrying this summer, you won't need me hanging around."

"Don't be silly," she said. "Of course we'll need you."

Trevor heard the "we" distinctly. His heart sank like a rock. *She's made her decision. There's no hope.* He feigned weariness, stretching broadly. "We'll see how things turn out. In the meantime, I'd better get some shuteye. Thanks for the dinner company. See you tomorrow morning."

"Thanks for the lasagna. And the burnoose."

He disappeared into the night without another word. Grief consumed him. He wanted to get out of the house before she detected his feelings from his expression.

Julia sat in the chair, staring at the cape and listening to the waves, for a long time after he had gone.

Miles's arrival came as a relief to Julia. His presence would force a decision and end her agony of having to choose between him and Trevor. Trevor. She had admitted her feelings to herself at last. *But I can't really choose between a man who is committed to me and one who could disappear at the drop of a hat. Trevor hasn't said anything to make me believe he'd ever stay.* She pushed the memories of his touch and words at the clinic out of her mind.

Miles walked up behind Julia as she washed dishes at the sink, and he pulled her into his arms. His touch was warm, comforting. "I've come to a decision about moving. Have you also come to a decision, my love?"

His choice of words made Julia wince, and she grabbed another pot to scrub. She forced a smile and looked at Miles calmly. "Getting very close. How 'bout I tell you over dinner?"

"Fine. Can I help you?"

"No thanks. I've got it."

"Should you even be on that leg?"

"I'm fine, Miles."

"Well then, do you mind if I look around at the progress you've made?"

"Go ahead. I'll join you in a few minutes."

While Miles observed the work that had been done downstairs, Ben worked with Trevor in the attic. Fishing had remained fairly stable, but Ben wanted to start picking up extra work before the season ended. Working at Torchlight meant making some extra money to put toward Mike's college fund.

Trevor carefully cut a length of thick pink insulation and placed it in between the empty framework of the roof. When it caught on a nail and ripped, he groaned and kicked a beam in irritation.

"What's eating you?" Ben asked.

Trevor paused, then knelt beside his friend. "I'm sorry. I hate working with this stuff, and I'm on edge already."

"Beckley's back, huh?"

Trevor's eyes met Ben's in surprise. The man understood, even though they had never talked about his relationship with Julia.

Trevor looked at the floor. "It's eatin' me alive."

"I sort of know what you're going through. I'm so torn up over Tara I can barely sleep. One part of me wants to go propose to her right now. The other part holds me in place. I don't ever want to mourn another wife. I couldn't take it."

Trevor placed an encouraging hand on Ben's shoulder. "So we're in the same spot, eh? I thought I was the only one too chicken to confess."

"Confess?" Miles questioned, his head just rising through the attic door. He climbed all the way up and brushed off his fine suit in distaste. "Now what would you working boys be talking about?"

He looked directly at Trevor. His eyes held none of the congeniality that his voice bespoke.

Trevor stood and nodded once. "Beckley," he said without warmth. He never took his eyes from the newcomer's.

Ben stood beside him. Miles looked to him. "Name's Miles Beckley. And you are?"

"Ben DeBois." He held out his hand, and Miles shook it firmly.

"Well, Ben, I think your friend and I have something to discuss. Would you mind?"

"I think I'll go grab a soda. Want one, Trev?"

"No thanks."

Miles and Trevor stared at each other until Ben descended the attic stairs and was out of earshot.

"Now, Kenbridge. I'm thinking there's a change in Julia I don't like. She's more distant than usual. I believe you might be trying to get between us. And I think I arrived just in time to hear something about you 'confessing.' What exactly did you mean?"

"None of your business."

Miles pulled his lips together tightly. "I think it is. Your confession wouldn't involve my Julia, would it?"

"Maybe." Trevor inched toward Miles, silently daring him to make a move.

"I told you to stay away from her."

"And I decided to ignore your advice."

"I won't tolerate any meddling by some lowlife, bloodsucking wanderer. You're not good enough for her."

Trevor laughed without smiling. "And you are? You are the most shallow, superficial loser I've ever met. You've been away too long, Miles." He let Miles draw his own conclusions as to his meaning. Given his rival's jealous nature, he hoped the hook would sink deep.

It did. Miles's fist came from nowhere and landed squarely on Trevor's jaw, sending him flying backward into a bale of insulation.

Trevor bounced up and went after Miles in a fury. Ducking a wild punch, he landed his own fist to Miles's gut and then hit him in the face with his knee. He'd learned to defend himself in more than a decade of traveling.

Miles paused to catch his breath, then came after Trevor again, tackling and throwing him onto the rotten boards. With their combined weight and momentum, the wood gave way, and the two fell through the old plaster ceiling of the northwest bedroom with a great crash.

They both rolled, coughing after impact and gasping for air in the dust-filled room. Trevor rubbed his shoulder painfully as Miles stood.

"What is going on?" Julia asked, furious as she looked from the men to the hole in the ceiling.

CHAPTER FIFTEEN

*M*iles pointed down at Trevor. "That man implied you two had something going on! Of course I went after him!"

"You did *what?*" she asked Trevor.

He was troubled. How could he explain without implicating her, yet remain truthful? There was something between them. Surely she knew it as well as he did. But he hadn't meant to force the issue. Miles had just driven him crazy with his superior attitude and ways. Trevor took a deep breath. "I can see why he thought what he did, but I certainly didn't intend to give him the *wrong* idea."

"What idea did you intend to give him?"

Trevor swallowed, dreading her reaction. "That you and I had been developing more than a friendship."

"There you have it!" Miles said proudly as Ben peeked around the corner.

"Now wait a minute—," Trevor began.

"You actually led my boyfriend to believe that we were having an affair?"

He stood his ground. "Aren't we? Of sorts?"

"What does that make me look like?" she seethed.

"Well, how do you explain it? How many times have we been close to kissing? It has to have passed through your thoughts too—"

"I thought you were more honorable than this!"

"There, you see, darling—"

"And *you!* Miles, I thought you were beyond actually getting into a fistfight with someone. You can't be totally innocent in this. You come here to tell me you're moving to Boston, and while I'm still digesting the news, you take on my general contractor and break through a bedroom ceiling within fifteen minutes after arriving. I can't have you around if this is how you act. I need this house *repaired,* not torn apart."

"Julia, I'm—," Trevor tried again.

"Don't! Don't either of you talk to me!" She stormed out of the bedroom on her crutches. "Ben, make sure they don't tear each other apart," she directed from the hall.

Their friend nodded and tried not to laugh as he looked at his plaster-covered, dumbfounded charges.

Early the next morning the buzz of the doorbell pulled Julia away from her private thoughts. She moved to answer it, knowing it would be Miles. She had sent him away the night before, too weary to deal with him or Trevor. *I don't feel up to it this morning either.* It was drizzling outside, matching her mood. *I just want to be alone. What had Trevor been thinking? An affair? Maybe an emotional affair, but he was just as responsible. And it was idle flirting. Nothing had come of it. Why bring my almost-fiancé into it?*

Miles stood on the porch, dripping wet. He gave her a winning smile.

"Come in," she offered grudgingly.

He wiped off his coat and hair, scuffed his boots on the mat, and entered. He looked down at her sorrowfully. "I came with a peace offering." Reaching under his trench coat, he pulled a golden kitten from a large pocket. "She's for you." The animal mewed pitifully at the loss of Miles's body heat.

"Miles! She's darling." Julia took the kitten from his hand and cradled her against her chest.

"Julia, I was way out of line last night. I'm sorry. Something about Trevor makes me crazy. I don't know why I let him get to me."

They stood in the entryway awkwardly. She looked down at the kitten, who was digging her claws into her sweater, pulling herself up to rest under Julia's chin. Julia sighed. "Here, take the cat. I can't manage her and my crutches. Let's get a cup of tea and talk."

His face lit up with hope. "Right behind you."

Miles's thoughtfulness softened Julia's heart a bit. The spontaneity of the gesture surprised and delighted her. They sat in the kitchen, where Miles insisted on fixing tea for both of them. The kitten purred in her lap as Julia watched him work methodically.

Miles carefully placed their cups on the table, then sat beside Julia and took her hand. "Julia, I hope you don't make your decision based on my behavior yesterday. I swear to you, I don't know what came over me. It won't happen again."

She removed her hand and touched his face gently. "Let's forget it ever happened, Miles. Just give me a little more time."

"How much more, Julia? Shouldn't we get on with this? I want you as my wife. I want to know I can count on that."

I know. I want someone I can count on too. Hadn't Trevor betrayed her? Hadn't Miles moved to protect her honor?

Julia looked down at the tiny kitten sleeping in her lap. *But hadn't Trevor merely stated the obvious? The truth of the matter?* "One more week. I promise I'll answer you then."

Two days later, Trevor and Julia still had not spoken. After Miles left, Trevor swallowed his pride and went to her.

"Look, Julia, it was wrong of me to bait Miles," he said. *How can you choose him over me? You should hear how he talks about you! You're more than a trophy to be won!*

"That's it?"

Trevor stilled his desire to voice his excuses. "That's it."

"Why?"

"Why?"

"Why did you bait him?"

"I don't like him. He doesn't like me. There was bound to be a pretty big confrontation sooner or later." *Because I love you.*

"How old are you? Fourteen? I thought you were smarter than that. You goaded him just for the sport of it."

He looked away.

"Please get to work on the new bedroom walls today. I want them completed by next week so we'll be on schedule." Her tone was icy.

"They'll be done," he said.

Miles appeared that following weekend, in very different style. He was extremely happy, having just secured his position in Boston and an agreement to work halftime from home—which he assumed would be Torchlight. For once, he was not wearing a business suit. Most surprising of all was his mode of transportation: a red pickup.

"Testing it out," he explained as she came out to the porch to greet him. "Maybe I can afford one for you and one for me now that

I have the new job." Miles picked Julia up, hugging her and gently swinging her around in a circle. "How's the leg?"

"Hopefully healing. The cast is coming off soon. I can't wait."

"It must be tough getting around this old place while partially incapacitated. Still, it seems as if you're managing all right."

"Thanks to Trevor," she said quietly. Seeing his frown, she changed the subject quickly. "Miles, you look great," she said, admiring his jeans, boots, and long-sleeved cotton shirt.

"Yeah, well, I thought I'd try and look the part since I was coming for your big answer after you put me off last weekend. Thought I'd really try and fit into your dream this time."

"I don't know what to say…"

"Don't say anything unless it's a yes… Let's go inside and decide what we can do around here for fun, with you in that cast."

She had never seen Miles so happy, so excited. *Maybe he's finally coming around. Maybe I've been right all along. Maybe he is the best man for me. Look how he's trying.* She remembered how she'd felt when she first fell in love with Miles.

He stood behind her and embraced her warmly, kissing her from her neck to her cheek. She giggled and nudged him away, finding his high mood contagious. "I've missed you," he growled.

Julia sat down on the second step of the entry stairs and watched him as he went to get his bags. She could not bear to tell him that she'd had second thoughts. *This is right,* she told herself. *This is right.*

"How 'bout I fire up your grill and fix us a couple of steaks for dinner?"

"Sounds fun," she said. "I haven't had anything off the barbecue for eons. I'll do some potatoes and salad."

"No, you won't," his voice playfully ominous. "You are the

injured party here. I can make a salad and potatoes as well as you."

"Miles! What has come over you?"

"Well, let's see. I doubled my salary in one year. I'm thinking about buying a truck. I have an entire weekend to devote to my bride-to-be, and it just feels good to be here again. How can life be better?"

"I like this change in attitude. Is it only temporary? Will you be back to your obsessive self tomorrow?"

"No ma'am. I've turned over a new leaf."

Upstairs, Trevor watched stoically. *He's playing the part to lull her into saying yes. Why can't she see it?* He was so angry, he turned and punched his fist through the wallboard he had just finished plaster-ing. *Maybe I better punch a couple more holes up here rather than be tempted by Miles's perfect face.*

After his fury was spent, he sat leaning against the damaged wall. *Why, God? Why me? Why did I have to fall in love with the one woman I can't have?*

Two hours later Trevor finished repairing the holes and put his equipment away for the night. He was surprised that Julia and Miles had not left the house for dinner. He discovered them on the living room couch, nuzzling and talking quietly.

"Sorry to interrupt," he said stiffly. "I'll be out of here in a minute."

Miles stood, looking smug. "Things progressing well, Kenbridge?"

"Counting your assets before Julia's even said yes, Beckley?"

"Trevor!" Julia said, angry at his insinuation. "Miles is simply try-ing to be polite."

"Sorry, Julia." He looked down as she struggled to rise, then met Miles's steely gaze. "Guess I'm not as taken in by Miles's facade as you seem to be. What is it? The flashy truck? His one attempt to drop the business suit? He's a fake, and you can't see it."

"Trevor!" she said again, really angry this time.

"Don't worry, darling," Miles said soothingly. "No harm done. We know the truth. I think Trevor here just wants to drive any wedge he can between us."

Julia looked at Trevor, obviously stunned by his behavior.

Trevor walked out without a word.

The next morning Trevor watched as Miles drove out of the front courtyard, probably on his way into town for the daily paper. The *New York Times* and *Wall Street Journal* made their way to Oak Harbor around ten o'clock each morning, and he bet Miles could not live without them.

Trevor ran upstairs to Julia's bedroom, knocking loudly and, in his zeal to speak with her, entering without waiting for her permission. She stood in front of her full-length mirror, wearing the burnoose, the hood covering her head.

He stopped, forgetting what he had to say. Her image hearkened back to a hundred years of romance, love, and hope. "You...you look exactly like Anna."

Julia ducked her head, pulling off the hood and struggling with the button at her throat. "Trevor!" She shifted self-consciously under his gaze.

"Look, Julia, I'm sorry. I blew it last night. I had no right to say those things. Your decisions are your own. I've kept my views to myself all this time. I haven't told you... What I mean to say... Last night… Well, last night, I just lost it. I realized he was here for your answer, and I haven't even had the guts to tell you how I feel about you. I took all my frustration out on Miles."

She gave up on the burnoose button and looked out the window. "I said yes," she said quietly.

"You said *what?*" *No! Not before…*

She turned to face him. "I said yes." She raised her chin, daring him to challenge her, hoping he would challenge her?

"I see," he said, his voice low. "When's the big day?"

"August."

August. He struggled for breath and looked her in the eye. "I hope you've chosen well, Julia. You deserve happiness."

He turned to go, then paused in the doorway. "I'd like to stay on through the summer, if we can make it work out. I'll be out of your hair before the wedding."

She raised her hand unconsciously, as if to cry out for him to come back, but the engagement ring on her finger silenced her. Julia turned back to the window and pulled the hood back over her head as the tears began to flow.

Dear God, am I doing the right thing? Last night it felt so right. Today it feels dead wrong. Please, please help me.

Once Julia's cast was off, she was able to work in the garden. She and Trevor had been fairly successful in avoiding each other over the past weeks, and the workers were definitely making progress. Trevor had decided to attack the job of stripping and repairing the hardwood floors, as well as the grand staircase, so Julia decided it was better if she worked on the garden.

Four men worked with Trevor on the floors inside while another assisted Julia in ripping out long-dead foliage and pruning overgrown bushes. She figured that by August the garden would be in full bloom, a glorious place for the small reception she and Miles had planned.

The house still needed to be painted and wallpapered, but all in all, it was coming together. Lonely since she and Trevor had parted ways over Miles, Julia spent more and more time with Tara.

Lately Trevor had not even asked how Anna was faring. It obviously pained him too much to think of those happy evenings, watching Julia delve into her ancestors' past.

They passed each other with mumbled hellos, completely ill at ease in each other's presence. Tara watched how both Julia and Trevor acted but kept her observations to herself. Everything in her wanted to shake Julia until she showed some sense, but Ben had talked her into remaining silent. *Humph,* she thought. *What does he know about love?*

Early one evening Tara drove to Torchlight with the five forsythia bushes and fifteen rosebushes Julia had ordered a week earlier. Julia had made some headway in the old cutting garden, and Tara could already see it would become an appropriate centerpiece to the spectacular grounds of the future inn.

Julia opened the door and greeted Tara with a hug. "We have to take refuge in the kitchen again. The boys brought in professional sanders to take off all the paint and grime. They'd kill me if we got any dirt in the other rooms after they worked all day to get every speck off the boards. Tomorrow, they seal her back up."

"They'll be beautiful. I can't wait to see it all finished!"

"Me either. Then we'll work all fall, painting, wallpapering, and furnishing the other rooms."

"So Trevor still has quite a bit of work ahead of him."

"Trevor's going to leave before the wedding," Julia said, keeping her voice light. "We both think it'd be best if he left a week beforehand. He and Miles just don't get along, and I don't want anything to ruin my big day."

"Even if the groom at the end of the aisle is the wrong man?" Tara wanted to take the words back as soon as they were out of her mouth, but now she was committed.

Julia turned, looking confused. "What do you mean by that?"

"I guess I'm the only one around here watching you two die a slow death because you're not together. You've both lost weight—"

"My cast—"

"Julia, it isn't your cast. It's the weeks you and Trevor have been at odds. If you could see the man! He sits in my restaurant and plays with his soup until I tell him to get out. He scares the other customers. Even Ben can't reach him, and they were beginning to be good friends. As far as I can tell, he just stays holed up in the cottage, coming out only for work and church.

"And you! Your hair is dull, your face is white, even though it's summer. If I didn't know better, I'd think you were sick. But I know what's wrong. Your hearts are screaming at you, and you are both too stubborn to listen. No, I take that back. Trevor has tried to listen. But he doesn't want to make the decision for you. He's reached out as far as he can, but you reach back with a swing of Miles's diamond ring to his stomach. He can't hold on much longer."

Julia tried to find the words to express what she was feeling. "I just think I'm doing the right thing. I can't think about pulling out of the wedding. Miles has tried so hard—he's ready to move to the East, for me. Besides, Trevor's never told me how he feels. I don't *really* know he loves me."

She sounded desperate, trying to convince herself.

"Don't you, Julia? Don't you know?"

Tara couldn't help it. She'd miss Ben, Mike, Julia, and the others, but she was thrilled to be going. After her visit to Julia, she had decided that everyone needed to make their own decisions, their own way in life. She was. She couldn't control anyone's life but her own. She couldn't make Ben say the words she longed to hear. She couldn't force Julia and Trevor to see the love between them. All she could do was walk her own walk.

This was her first step. She'd turned in the final manuscript weeks earlier, and she was on her way to Los Angeles, Seattle, Minneapolis, Chicago, and New York to do some advance promotion. She was scheduled to appear on thirteen local cable television shows as a guest chef.

She kissed Mike quickly on the cheek and hugged Julia goodbye, then nodded at Benjamin. "Good-bye, Ben."

"Be careful," he said gruffly.

"Yes," she said tightly. "I will."

She turned and hopped into her aging Volkswagen Bug and turned the key.

"Good one, Dad," Mike said. "You couldn't come up with anything better than 'be careful'?"

"Leave it alone, Mike."

"You all take care," Tara said, taking a moment to look each one in the eye.

"Go with God," Julia said.

"I intend to," Tara returned, feeling the first spark of life in her heart in some time. She stepped on the gas and left her driveway, as well as her nearest and dearest. Time away, that's what she needed. Time away.

That afternoon Julia left the lighthouse and walked along the granite-strewn shore, deep in thought. Tara had left Ben because he couldn't say the words; she was leaving Trevor because he couldn't say them either. But what about her? Wasn't she a part of it too? Couldn't she say the words herself? See if she was the only one who wondered if they could have made it, had not Miles been a part of the picture?

A fisherman's sweater kept her warm as the sun sank, and she stared out at the blue-green summer sea. The wind blew, and she closed her eyes, raising her face to it. *Talk to me, Father. Help me to hear.*

Julia heard nothing but the familiar sounds of the ocean. Taking comfort in the soothing music of the Atlantic, she stared and stared out to sea.

"Julia." The word sounded like a plea, a deep desire expressed, a cry of agony on his tongue.

Julia turned. She had not expected that he would follow her, yet she was not surprised to see him there. "Trevor."

She fought off her desire to fall into his arms. *Miles.* She'd come so far with him, it wouldn't be fair.

But Trevor moved before she could speak, pulling her to him.

She paused, surprised, then she clung to him, unable to resist, never wanting to let him go. They held each other for several long moments before he spoke. "I've missed you," he said huskily.

He moved away slightly, bending down to kiss her, but she stepped away. "No. Don't. I'm sorry... I shouldn't have..."

"What are you talking about?" His voice was tender, pleading. He could obviously see the inner struggle written all over her face. "This is what we've both wanted. What we've both been waiting for." He pulled her to him again.

"No, Trevor. I can't. I can't!"

Trevor looked at her, hurt showing in his eyes. "I'm sorry," he mumbled, and walked away.

Julia turned back to the ocean, more confused than ever.

A week later, in Tara's Minneapolis hotel room, the phone rang.

"Ben! How'd you track me down?"

"I called that publishing house of yours in New York."

"How are you and Mike?"

"Gettin' on. How's the tour?"

"It's so much fun, Ben! I wish you could see it all with me. It's like exploring Egg Island, except, of course, they're cities. Not quite as picturesque, but full of history, and lots of things going on. Everything's so fast: cars, people, talk. It makes Oak Harbor look like it's in slow motion."

"Does that mean you're fallin' for city life?"

"Oh no. But it sure is fun to visit. I'm having a ball. I cook on the morning shows and then have the afternoons free to explore."

"Well, you're being careful, aren't you?"

"I've managed to stay alive so far, haven't I?"

"Yeah, well. I worry about ya."

"I know, Ben. You've always been good about protecting me. I wish you understood why."

He paused awkwardly. "Listen, I've got to go. Just wanted to make sure you were doing okay."

"Well, I'm just fine, Ben."

"Good night, then."

"Good night."

CHAPTER SIXTEEN

*H*omesick, Tara decided to return a day earlier than planned and went directly to Torchlight.

"Tara! What are you doing home?" Julia gave her a warm hug.

"I thought I'd sneak into town. I haven't seen Ben yet—didn't want to destroy the high of traveling as soon as I hit Oak Harbor. I wanted to get home and go sailing. I'm tired of cars and smog. I want the wind in my face! I cooked up a grand scheme on the plane home. Let's you and me go out to one of the islands and camp out. The weather's perfect. We could sail out this afternoon, spend the night, and come back tomorrow."

"I don't know. I've got a lot to do with the wedding coming up. The house is still a disaster."

"Oh, come on, Julia. Be spontaneous! In the cities, I saw people making the most of every minute. Sometimes, at our slower pace, we take each minute for granted, doing the same thing day after day. Remember how it felt to kayak in Acadia? Let's sail! Come on!"

"Well, okay."

"Meet me in half an hour at my house. I've got all the supplies. You just need a sleeping bag, pillow, and clothes. Bring enough for two nights in case we decide to stay out."

"Okay."

Tara was gone before Julia could change her mind.

The two headed straight for the boat docks, prepared the *Sea Maiden* quickly, and eased her out of her slip. The gentle summer wind billowed out her sail.

"Where are we going, you wild and crazy woman?" Julia asked the ship's captain.

"Bourgeois Island! My friends and I used to spend the night out there as kids. It's only an hour away."

Julia did her best to help, hoisting and letting down sails as Tara directed. The late afternoon sun was still warm, and Julia felt comfortable in her Windbreaker and shorts. The forecast called for continued warm summer weather with little precipitation; she had heard the report herself that morning.

"Did you tell Trevor where you were going?" Tara hollered over the wind.

"I told him you and I were going camping, but not where. We're not into long conversations these days."

"Men! Who needs 'em!" Tara smiled, but inside, she knew she and Julia were both thinking, *I do.* "Ben called me in Minneapolis. Said he wanted to make sure I was all right."

"That was sweet."

"It was fine. But why couldn't he say, 'Tara, I miss you. I need you. I hate it that you're away.'" She spoke low and earnestly, role-playing Ben. "Why can't he just shout it to the winds? 'I love Tara Waverly!' Do you know what that would do for our relationship?"

"I know."

"Yes, of course you do, because you're weeks away from marrying Miles and still wondering if you're really in love with Trevor."

Julia's brow furrowed in irritation, then softened as she realized the truth of Tara's statement. She stared into the sea.

"I'm sorry, Julia. I'm just all riled up."

"It's okay."

"We're gonna have a great time! I packed food for an army, and I know the perfect camping spot."

They anchored the sailboat on the southwest side of the island and rowed the dinghy, loaded with their supplies, to shore. Bourgeois Island was a tiny land mass, covered mostly by rock and a few stands of trees. "Over here!" Tara called, moving toward a cave near the pebbly beach.

"Isn't it perfect? Even if it rains, you're covered. The beach is right there, and a hundred yards to the other side is a natural spring." Tara set to work laying the fire while Julia went back to the dinghy for another load.

Julia felt as though she was on a Girl Scout camping trip and was glad she had agreed to the outing. The tension with Trevor had gotten worse, and she had suffered from four migraine headaches in the last month. She attributed them to the stress of planning a wedding, but when she honestly questioned herself, she knew the real problem: the unresolved question of the status of her relationships. With Miles. With Trevor.

Julia returned to the fire, arms laden with sleeping bags.

"Doesn't a swim sound good?" Tara asked as the sun sank low and the sky faded to a deep purple against the mainland.

"A swim? Are you crazy? It's dark!"

"You *have* to swim at night; the water glistens. Besides, it's warm this time of year. Come on. We'll swim and then eat."

Resigning herself to follow her friend's lead, Julia walked behind her, pulling off her Windbreaker and shorts and easing into the surprisingly warm water.

The pebbles slipped under her feet, tickling her, until she was in deep enough to swim. She and Tara dove, somersaulted, and swam for half an hour as the splintered moon rose and flecks of light glistened in the water.

"What makes it sparkle, Tara?" Julia was treading water alongside her friend, twenty feet from shore.

"Phosphorus. When we were kids, we pretended we were swimming with mermaids who spread stardust around us. It was magical."

"Still is. It feels great, but I'm freezing."

"Let's go in."

They swam to shore, roasted hot dogs and marshmallows over the fire, and settled into their sleeping bags by nine o'clock. It felt delicious to be away, to have time to think and reflect and consider her path.

"Tara?" Julia asked sleepily as she watched the glow of the dying embers on the shallow cave's ceiling.

"Yeah?"

"Thanks."

"You're welcome."

Julia and Tara awoke to a bright summer morning and bathed in the natural spring, then spent the day doing nothing but read, nap, and lie out in the warm sun. They agreed to spend another night.

"Won't Trevor worry?" Tara asked.

"Won't Ben?"

"I say let them worry. I left a message at the boat docks with the manager about where we were going. If they want to, they can track us down. Radio's not working, but they can sail on out if it's so important."

"Your radio's out?"

"Yeah. Meant to get it fixed after our trip to Egg Island, but I got busy with the cookbook and all. Don't worry. We have a good weather report. And I know how to read the sea. We have supplies—we can stay here all week, if need be."

"Tara, I can't stay here all week!"

"I said we *could*," she said with a scowl. "I didn't say we'd have to."

But the next morning the weather surprised even Tara. Instead of the sunny warmth that had been forecast when they left Oak Harbor, a fierce wind and a driving rain woke them.

"Uh-oh," Tara said. "I was stupid. I should've gone to the *Sea Maiden* and checked the barometer."

"It's probably just a summer squall, right? We can just wait it out."

"Yeah. Let's see if it lets up. If it doesn't, we should make a break for it this afternoon, or we will be stranded for a while."

They spent the morning laughing and playing cards by the fire, each looking periodically to the cave's opening to see if the storm was easing.

"Have you heard from them?" Trevor's voice sounded tight as Ben answered the phone.

"Tracked them to the boat docks. Manager said they were heading to Bourgeois Island yesterday to camp. You know, Tara didn't even call me to tell me she was back from her tour."

"Maybe she needed some time to herself. Do you think they'll head home for it today?"

"Nah. I think Tara's too smart for that. But it's s'posed to ease tomorrow morning for a bit, followed by a brand-new storm. She'll tune in for the forecast."

"I'd feel better if we radioed them with the news."

"I don't think they went out there to be bothered by us."

"Yeah, well, that's tough. I kept Julia from drowning once. I don't want her to die sailing in this storm."

Ben was silent. Only then did Trevor recognize his blunder. "Oh man, I'm sorry. I didn't mean—"

"No. That's okay. I'm worried too. I'll try to reach them again. They're probably in the cave."

Ben hung up and tried the CB radio again. Still no answer. Tara had promised him she would get that radio fixed. There was no way she had gone out again without doing so, was there?

"I think we better wait until tomorrow," Tara said as she entered the cave again. She wiped raindrops from her face and wrung out her short hair.

"Shoot. I really need to get back."

Tara looked back outside and then to her friend. "I'm sorry. I wanted to take you away for a break, not mess with your schedule. It might ease up. Let's wait for a bit."

The weather did calm eventually. The winds seemed to die down some and the rain stopped, although heavy fog remained on the water. "Let's go," Tara said decisively. "We're only an hour from shore—what could happen?"

Julia's thoughts went to Sharon DeBois, but she quickly erased it from her mind, trusting Tara's judgment.

"I don't like it, Trevor. They're still not home, and I can't get through to the *Sea Maiden*'s radio. It seems like this soaker's letting up, but a sou'easter's right on its heels. I think they'll make a break for it."

"Don't you think they'll check on the weather?"

"Tara will—but she's had trouble with her radio before. She'll check her barometer, but she might risk it. She's so gutsy she thinks she can conquer anything. They might get into trouble."

"You want to go after them?"

"My trawler's been through worse."

"They'll be furious at us for checking up on them."

"Probably no more miffed than they are already."

"True. When do we leave?"

"Now."

The *Sea Maiden* was making good time, but Tara was concerned about the storm she saw gaining on them. They wouldn't outrun it, no matter how fast they were moving. *Stupid! I was so stupid to leave the island!*

At the time they left, the intense fog had hidden the second storm. Its front-runner winds had soon blown away the low clouds, and it was all too clear what they were in for. She glanced at Julia, standing in front of the helm, huddled against the wind and surf's spray. *Stupid! I've not only risked my life, but Julia's, too!*

Julia watched the thick, black, angry clouds behind them as the storm began to break. She could tell from one look at Tara's face that they were in serious trouble. A mile away the skies opened up, and a blinding wall of rain sealed off their view of the island. Stronger gusts caught their sails and threatened to capsize them.

"Lean ho!" Tara yelled, and Julia leaned over the edge to counter-balance the wind in the mainsail.

"We have to get them down!" Tara yelled over the wind.

Julia went to the rigging and quickly pulled down the jib, but when she got to the mainsail, a knot caught in the lock that held the rope in place. She pulled and pushed and struggled with it but finally shook her head at Tara as the rain pounded down upon them.

Tara was moving toward her with a knife to cut it when another powerful gust of wind caught them. A huge swell lifted the boat at the same time.

The boat veered windward as if in slow motion. Neither woman could stop its momentum, and within seconds, both were in the water.

Tara came up sputtering underneath the turtled boat, caught in an air space.

Julia surfaced beyond the *Sea Maiden*, thankful for her life jacket. She swam as hard as she could toward the capsized boat, but the jacket's bulk impeded her progress. The wind was just too strong, and the distance between her and the boat became greater and greater.

Mike insisted he be allowed to come along, and Ben knew he couldn't leave him behind. *He loves Tara almost as much as I do.* The three men hopped aboard the old trawler. Ben was right; the old girl had seen worse storms than this. Her battered walls and peeling paint were testimony to her years of hard work and seaworthiness.

Trevor grabbed Ben's binoculars and scanned the horizon, but the gray wall of rain sealed off any view he might have had. They were off within minutes.

Tara struggled to free her arm that was caught in the lines of the capsized boat. When the *Sea Maiden* had gone over, the lines that had given Julia such trouble had created a tangled web that now held Tara immobile, cutting off all circulation to her fingers. She had dropped the knife in her fall, and the taut ropes kept her from simply untying a knot and freeing herself. *Please, God, keep my friend safe,* she prayed frantically. *I can't help her.*

Tara was only five feet from the emergency beacon, but, although she stretched out with all her might, the ropes and water kept her from reaching it.

Julia swam as hard as she could toward the boat, but she was tiring quickly. The swells were growing, causing the *Sea Maiden*'s sevenfoot keel to disappear for seconds at a time. Julia's arms begged her to stop. Her legs begged her to quit kicking. She wanted to lie on her back and simply catch her breath, but she knew that doing so might be her death sentence. It would take hours, days, to find her if she didn't stay near the boat. *Kick, Julia,* a voice inside her urged. *Kick.*

She began to kick again.

"*Sea Maiden.* Come in, *Sea Maiden. Sea Maiden,* this is *Atlantic Queen; Sea Maiden,* this is *Atlantic Queen.* Do you read me?" Mike repeated his message over and over again, trying different frequencies.

Please, God, he prayed. *Let her be all right. Don't let her drown like Mom. Please, God.*

"See anything?" Ben yelled to Trevor through the window.

Trevor turned around, his face grave, and shook his head.

Ben focused back on his radar scanner. "Come on, Tara. I know you're out here." His face was white. This scene was all too familiar. His prayer joined his son's.

Julia was close, but she was exhausted. *Father, please. Help me. I'm so close. I know you're with me. Give me the strength to get there. So close...* And where was Tara? She could see the keel of the boat, bobbing twenty yards ahead, but no sign of her friend. Was she lost? Adrift?

Under the boat, Tara grabbed a floating oar and punched at the control panel, hoping to hit the right button. *Come on, God, give us this chance. Help me.* She jabbed again at the console.

"We have a signal!" Ben yelled, his throat tight and his voice garbled. "We have a signal! It's gotta be them!" He turned the boat five degrees west. "We'll be there in minutes!" he yelled out to Trevor. "They're not moving! They must be in trouble!"

Trevor wiped away the water flowing freely down his face, then wiped Ben's field glasses as well. The rain was coming down in torrents. The trawler chugged through giant waves that rolled and pitched, and the wind plastered Trevor's slicker against his body. Leaning heavily against the helm cabin's wall, he scanned the horizon in the new direction they had taken.

His glasses caught the *Sea Maiden*'s keel and, at the same time, his heart leapt. *No. Please, God, no.*

Mike saw the boat from inside the cabin. "No!" he screamed. *"No!"*

Ben caught his arm. "Wait and see, Mike," he said sternly. "Wait and see!" Inside, his heart cried out its own fear.

Julia's hand brushed against a nylon rope and then lost it. She searched frantically. At last, she caught it again and held on. The rope, attached to the boat, caught and held after giving out several feet. *Thank you, God!* she prayed silently, desperately trying to catch her breath.

The trawler was nearly beside her before she heard Trevor's voice cry out over the roar of the wind. He was over the edge of the boat and into the water before her mind could process what was happening. Mike appeared on deck.

"Dad! Julia seems okay, but I don't see Tara!"

Ben appeared then too, his face grim.

"Hold us alongside her, Mike. I'll find Tara." He left the cabin without waiting for a reply. After throwing Trevor a rope to secure the sailboat to the trawler's side, Ben dove over the edge himself, into the side of a huge swell. He came alongside Trevor and Julia.

"Tara!" Julia cried weakly.

Ben grabbed her arm. "Where is she, Julia?"

"I don't know!" she shouted miserably.

"Have you seen her since you capsized?"

"No!"

"I think she might be underneath!" Ben said to Trevor, who was treading water beside them. "Here, take my jacket. I'm gonna check."

Ben fought for a breath against his tension-filled chest and dove. *Please God, not again. Let her be alive!* His hand caught the mast and he followed it upward, emerging in the air space beneath.

"Ben!" Tara cried.

"Oh, thank you! Thank you, God! Tara, baby, are you okay?" He swam to her and before she could answer, gave her a long, deep kiss.

She smiled broadly at him, her eyes full of wonder.

"Tara, I was so scared! I couldn't stand the thought of losing you. I love you so much!" He kissed her again quickly.

"Well, it's certainly taken a lot to get you to admit that," she said, smiling, despite another swell that bathed her face in seawater.

"I know, baby. I'm sorry. I should've told you months ago. I guess God had to knock me upside the head before I could see it. The thought of losing you… Well, here, let's get you out first. They'll think we both drowned. We'll talk later."

He swam to the far side of the ship and dove down to release an emergency kit still strapped in its place. He surfaced, pulled a knife out, and quickly cut Tara loose.

She swam to him and kissed him with all the passion she had buried inside her for years.

It was his turn to smile at her. "Come on. Let's get out of here."

"Where is Ben?" Julia asked through chattering teeth. Trevor had pulled her aboard the trawler and wrapped her in a blanket. She leaned over the side, searching for her friends.

Trevor was about to dive in again when they emerged.

"There they are!" Julia yelled. She smiled at Mike. "They're coming 'round back now!" Julia knew it would be important to him to see Tara alive for himself. Mike grinned from ear to ear and raced to the back, reaching for Tara as soon as he saw her.

Sadly, they had to abandon the *Sea Maiden* where she lay. Given the storm, it was impossible to right the boat with her mast straight down, and only the small amount of air trapped underneath had kept her afloat at all. Their only hope was to recover her with a professional crew after the storm subsided—if they could find her again and if she survived.

But to Tara it was a small loss. She was alive! And Ben loved her! Mike stood at the helm while Ben sat by the heater, holding her in his lap. Trevor sat across from Julia, fuming.

Julia dried out her hair and looked up at him wearily. "Why don't you say it?"

"What?"

"You're obviously ticked. What?"

"You two should have known better!"

"Look, we made a mistake—"

"A mistake! This is the second 'mistake' to almost cost you your life, Julia! What if we hadn't been out here looking for you? How long could you have held on to that rope? How long did Tara have?"

"We didn't set out to get into an accident."

Trevor stood and paced. "Of course not! But you were careless! You can't expect me to be around every time you risk your life!"

Julia looked up at him, angry now. The others watched in silence. "No, Trevor, I don't expect you to be around every time I get into trouble. How could I? You're such a vagabond that nobody will ever tie you down to one place! How could I expect you to be around? How could I count on you?"

"How did this subject turn to me? It's you who makes the bad decisions."

"So you've never made any bad decisions in life?"

"A few," he admitted without lowering his gaze. "But I never risked other people's lives too!"

"I didn't mean to!"

"Of course not! But you don't think through all your decisions, do you?"

Julia paused. "Are you trying to get at something?"

He paced the short floor several times.

"If you're trying to get at something, just say it, Trevor. I'm tired of the word games. You obviously are too. Out with it."

He stopped and stared at her. "Oh, why mess with it? I'll be out of your hair in a few weeks and then we'll both be better off, right?" He walked out the cabin door and into the storm without waiting for an answer.

"Right," she said softly.

CHAPTER SEVENTEEN

$\mathcal{T}$wo weeks before the wedding, Julia tried on her great-grandmother's wedding gown for the final time. The dress had been unearthed from an attic chest and remade to fit Julia's taller and shapelier form. Sara, Anna's daughter, had had fine taste. The dress was an exquisite mixture of silk organza, handmade lace, and tiny covered buttons. It had taken half an hour to get her into it. Remade, it fit Julia perfectly.

Trevor came in and found her standing at the top of the stairs in front of a huge antique mirror.

"What do you think?" she asked him. She continued to look in the glass, watching the reflection of his image, pretending his presence did not affect her. She reached for the veil and fit it over her head, arranging the netting over her face. *So this is what it feels like to be a bride.*

Trevor, deliberately and unhurried, walked over to Julia's side. He gently took her right hand with his left and pulled her around to face him. Julia simply stared up into his eyes. Ever so slowly, he traced a gentle course, from her fingers to her wrists, along her elbows and shoulders. His actions sent shivers down her spine.

"What are you doing, Trevor?"

"What I should have done months ago," he said, his voice low and earnest. Julia did not breathe as he continued to draw his fingers along the graceful curve of her neck. Silently, he pulled the delicate veil away from her face and settled it carefully over her head. Then he bent and met her lips with his own, kissing her first softly, then urgently, then softly again. His lips felt soft and sweet, not like Miles's hard, pressing kiss.

She stood, her eyes closed, smelling the scent of Trevor's skin, lost in the moment.

"Julia? Julia! What is going on?"

Julia spun around, not believing that it could be Miles's voice she was hearing. "Miles! Miles, what are you doing here? You're not due for another week."

"So, if I had waited, I wouldn't have seen you two kissing, is that it?"

"Miles—," Trevor began.

"You shut up and get away from her." Miles's face was red with fury; the veins on his temples bulged.

"Look, man, I'm the one who kissed her. She did not come looking for me."

"I should hope not! She's wearing the gown she'll be wearing in two weeks when we marry. I'd think it would be highly inappropriate for her to traipse around kissing any man who enters her path."

"Miles!" Julia was, in fact, feeling guilty, torn over the fact that she had enjoyed Trevor's kiss more than any other kiss she had ever experienced.

Miles ignored her. "Get away from her, Kenbridge! I knew you were after her from the start!"

Trevor stepped away from Julia and toward Miles. "Not a very smart man, are you, Miles? If you knew I had an eye for Julia, why'd you leave her alone for weeks on end? I wouldn't leave a woman like her alone. Nothing could keep me away. Not a job, not anything. She would be first."

"I didn't want to get in the way of her dreams!" Miles paused and composed himself. "I don't need to explain myself to you. The fact that I took unpaid leave to be here should say a lot."

"Yeah. One last week to really sell her down the river, huh? You're not interested in Torchlight for the same reasons Julia is. You just see investment potential. Maybe a condo here, maybe there—"

"Why you—" Miles lunged at Trevor in his best Ivy League football tackle position.

Not anticipating his attack, Trevor fell heavily under his opponent's weight, but caught Miles's fist as it sailed down toward his face.

"Stop it!" Julia yelled. "Knock it off!" She pulled at Miles's shoulders, allowing Trevor to land a punch on his jaw. Miles fell, moaning.

"What have you done, Trevor? Miles, are you all right?"

Miles rose to attack Trevor again, stepping on Julia's train in the process. She ignored the sickening rip of fabric and ran to stand between the men, pushing them away from each other. "Knock it off!"

"Julia, tell him to get out of here," Miles said.

"No, Julia, tell *him* to take a hike," Trevor said. "Tell him the truth. You're really in love with me."

She laughed at his arrogance. "Is that your declaration of love? I would've expected something much more poetic than a threat toward my fiancé. You'd better go. I think you've caused enough trouble."

"You can't tell me you're still going through with it! Come on! You've known I was in love with you since I first saw you. I love the way you love this old house, the hard work you put into it. I love your determination and grit. I love how you're loyal to the end and how you are the most gorgeous woman I've ever laid eyes on. Why else would I risk my life *twice* to save you?"

"As I remember, you begrudgingly saved my life. You told me not to think you'd always be around."

"That's not what I meant."

"That's what I heard. How much time have you ever spent in one place? Have you lasted longer than a year anywhere? Two? You say you would never leave a woman like me alone, but why? How could I trust a man who never stays? How do I know that that old wanderlust won't come knocking and you'll be off? I want a home, Trevor. And I want a man who stays."

"Julia, what are you talking about?" Miles sputtered angrily. "You're not actually entertaining thoughts of the two of you *together,* are you?"

"It's different, Julia!" Trevor ignored him. "I was led here. I think God *wants* us together. We've come too far from two totally different places. We've come through too much." His face begged her for a chance. "I don't have any intention of leaving."

"Not now, but maybe next year—"

"No. Not without you."

"You say that now…," she said, shaking her head sadly.

She looked at Miles, suddenly remembering he was present, and then to Trevor. "Trevor, can we talk about this tomorrow?"

"No," Trevor said angrily, furious that she could not admit to a love so obvious. "I can't live like this any longer. We all need a decision."

"I need…I need some time. I'm so confused!"

"A *decision*, Julia."

"Well, fine then, you force me to a decision! I'll keep my wedding date with Miles."

The following week would have been agony for Julia had she not had the wedding to distract her from Trevor. There were so many details, and she had, after all, made her decision. Seven days before the wedding, Julia awoke with a pounding headache and thought, *Today he'll leave.*

Trevor is leaving. Will I ever see him again? Oh, who needs him? I need a steady man who will always be there for me, not a rogue who is off and running at the drop of a hat.

Later, Julia stood in the library, cleaning the leather-bound volumes, when she heard the rumble of his motorcycle, the pause of its engine, the slam of the front door, his steady footsteps into the room where she worked, and his heavy silence at the door.

Julia allowed him to watch her for several moments, pretending she did not know he was there.

"I have to leave," he said, watching her miserably. In the soft golden light that filtered through the high windows, she looked angelic.

She paused, book in hand, but did not turn. "I know."

"I think it's best," he said awkwardly.

"I know," she repeated. "Will you leave a forwarding address?" Julia asked, fighting to keep hope from her tone. "I need to send you your final paycheck. Your things too, I assume."

"I'll write," he said.

She nodded and resumed her work.

He turned and did not look back.

"Come on, darling, we're late already," Miles said, as Julia paused to straighten her red cocktail dress. After months at Torchlight, she had grown unaccustomed to dresses and high heels, but Miles had wheedled her into wearing the outfit. "You look lovely," he said, brushing her cheek with his lips. "I'll be the envy of every man in the room."

They entered the private dining hall of a swanky San Francisco nightclub, where a roomful of Miles's associates hailed them with the clink of champagne flutes and cocktail glasses. Miles called the evening an "obligatory social gathering," a function that served to honor their impending nuptials and help him gain greater stature by throwing the party of parties.

Miles had outdone himself. Waitresses passed by continuously, carrying trays laden with Chinese pot stickers, salmon and cream cheese with capers and thinly sliced onion on tiny French baguette slices, shrimp on Belgian endive leaves sprinkled with fresh dill, melted brie on pastry, and three kinds of caviar. At the same time, waiters generously provided glasses of champagne and cocktails as fast as the guests could consume them.

By the time Julia and Miles arrived, the party was in full swing. Before long, he was off to talk with one of the senior partners at his former law firm, and Julia realized he would not return anytime soon. A friend of Miles made a subtle pass at her, and she looked over to where her fiancé stood. He was oblivious, concentrating only on the older man who was patting him on the shoulder and calling colleagues over to join them.

"Come on, honey," the man slurred. "Let's dance." He pulled her onto the dance floor. Julia knew Miles expected her to handle herself in these situations. This wasn't the first celebration in which she had been forced to take care of herself. It certainly would not be her last.

Three hours later Julia's feet were aching, and her back was screaming for her to go home and lie down. How quickly she had grown used to the slow and melodic pace of Oak Harbor! Julia longed to get undressed, pull on her old blue bathrobe, and snuggle into one of the high-backed chairs for a good read of Anna's journals.

Julia plastered a smile on her face for the cake cutting, a preliminary wedding festivity to compensate for the fact that few of Miles's coworkers would journey to the East Coast for his wedding. She was glad for any distraction from the drunken man who kept hanging around her as well as around her mother, Eleanor, who had just arrived and wanted to run through every detail of the wedding.

They sliced through the white frosting, but her eyes saw only the tiny bride and groom atop the layers. For the first time, she visualized joining Miles at the altar, and the image terrified her.

"Julia?" Miles paused with a bite of cake in front of her mouth, looking nervously to the crowd watching them. "Open wide, darling."

She managed to open her mouth and accept the morsel. Why do people getting married feed each other cake? What does it mean anyway? She felt cross and belligerent but smiled sweetly as she fed Miles his portion. His teeth loomed large, and she noticed how thin his lips were. Not like Trevor's. *How will I like a lifetime of kissing those lips?*

Julia fought a wave of dizziness as the people cheered and Miles smiled. Bits of frosting clung to the corners of his mouth as he dipped her low in a fancy dance move and kissed her again. She fought the revulsion. *What is happening here?*

"Mother," she said. "I need to go to the rest room. Come join me." They made their way through the huge group to the women's rest room. Julia gripped Eleanor's arm as soon as they were inside.

"Mother, I think I've made a huge mistake! I got dizzy thinking of kissing Miles, and the sight of him almost repulses me!" She sat down heavily in a plush couch. Cigarettes overflowed from a table ashtray beside her.

"Oh, nonsense, Julia! Haven't you ever heard of prewedding jitters? I had them myself. I didn't think I'd make it down the aisle. But look what I would've passed up! Your father is a prince, and so is Miles. You two were made for each other," she purred, sitting beside her daughter. "You just wait. Next week you'll be a different person. Be glad you're going through it now rather than during the ceremony."

"You wondered if Dad was the right man for you during the ceremony?"

"Well, yes. I had numerous suitors at the time, you see. I chose Jacob because he was my best choice. And I was right. You adore your father, as do I. To think I could've married that Jack Stanford… You should hear the tales I've heard! And I came so close to saying yes to his proposal! Just last week I heard—"

"Mother, did you love Daddy?"

"Of course I loved him!"

"I mean, were you totally gone, never coming back, hopelessly and forever in love with Daddy?"

"That's the love of schoolgirls! My love for your father was much more quiet, peaceful, reassuring."

Julia acknowledged the news without comment. Her folks had developed a pleasant union. But what had been sacrificed to get to that point? Had Eleanor denied a love that should have lived? Was Julia about to head down the same path?

"Listen, sweetheart. Everything's in place. You've known Miles for years. You'll have a happy marriage and all the things you deserve. Come now, we mustn't keep the guests waiting any longer. Your groom will think we've up and run off on him."

Trevor waited for his cousin Bryn to return. It was eleven, and he had been on the hot cement stairs of her brownstone apartment for hours. It was sweltering hot, and his clothes were sticking to every inch of him. Several of the other tenants had looked at him askance as they made their way into the brownstone. If he stayed much longer, the landlord would probably call the cops. He had meant to explain his presence, but lacked the energy.

Maybe Bryn was out of town. It was summer; she had talked about going to Alaska. Or maybe she had a shift at the hospital. He hoped that was it. He needed to talk to her. And a couch to sleep on.

At eleven-thirty, a taxi pulled up and Bryn hopped out, still dressed in scrubs. "Trevor!" she greeted him in surprise. He stood, wearily, to hug her. "What's wrong?"

He smiled ruefully. "Never could pass anything by you, cousin."

"Nope. Come in. You have your bag? I take it you're spending the night."

"That okay?"

"Fine, fine. Let's grab an iced tea and sit out on the fire escape. Try and grab some semblance of a breeze. It's hot, isn't it?"

"It's so hot I could fry eggs on the sidewalk."

"Come on," she gestured with a nod of her head. "You can tell me all about it." They trudged upstairs to her third-story apartment.

On the dining room table, her tapered candles had melted to sad droops. "It's gotta be a thousand degrees," Bryn moaned, pouring them both tall glasses of tea. "No sane people live in Boston during the summer without air conditioning."

"Only the insane and residents at the hospital, right?"

"Not next summer. If I'm still here, I'll be making the big bucks. I'm going to be sitting back in my high-design chair, listening to my stereo, with the air conditioner set at sixty. Cool as a cucumber," she said, raising her sweating glass of tea to her sweating brow. She looked him over, from head to toe. "So. Why are you here, unannounced?"

"I've blown it, Bryn."

"Well, that's nothin' new," she wisecracked. "Come on. Out to the fire escape with you."

He followed her out, and they settled onto the wrought iron-work. Bryn threw him a big, grungy pillow. "Not the first time you've retired out here?"

"Nope."

"Bryn, it's not safe."

"Trevor, you're here to talk about you, not me. Why aren't you at Torchlight?"

"I finished my work there."

"What about Julia?"

"She's marrying Miles Beckley."

"Ah. I see. You told her how you feel?"

"In a way."

"In a way?" Bryn asked, narrowing her eyes. "Didn't we talk about this? You were going to find a time, a place with her, away."

"It was never the right time, the right place," he responded irritably. "I tried! I told her, right in front of Miles—"

"In front of her fiancé? What was she supposed to say?"

He sighed, pulling another pillow to his chest as if it could lend him some comfort, shield off his cousin's attack. "If she really loved me, Bryn, she could have said so. I saw her later, when I said goodbye."

"When you said good-bye? What is she supposed to do then, beg you to stay?"

"Well, yes! If she loved me."

A man leaned out of his window below them. "Bryn? That you?"

"It's me, Phil."

"Can you keep it down? I gotta work tomorrow."

"Will do. Sorry, Phil. Good night."

The man left the window sill, muttering. Bryn and Trevor stared at each other in the shadows. "You gotta go back, Trevor," she urged in a hushed voice. "You have to tell her, once and for all, that you love her. Make it absolutely clear."

"I can't. You didn't hear… You didn't see me try. I gave her a chance."

"Did you? Really? Did you try every which way possible? What's she afraid of?"

"That I'll get tired of Torchlight and leave. She's freaked out over my traveling, as if that proves that I'll never settle down."

"So you left Oak Harbor." She let the words sit between them like an unwelcome visitor. "Trevor, she's thirty. She wants a home, probably a family. And you're the handyman who seems to be just passing through. What was she supposed to believe?"

"What else was I supposed to do?" he whispered angrily.

"You were supposed to stay."

"Well, I didn't do that, did I?"

Bryn took a long drink of tea. "Trevor Kenbridge, you have two choices. You can move on, and wonder about Julia all your life. Or you can go back, make it absolutely clear that you love her and will stay with her. She'll either send you packing or welcome you home. At least you'll know." She rose and fondly brushed the top of his head with her hand. "I'll leave a sheet on the couch. Won't bother with a blanket. I've got a shift in the morning. You'll be okay?"

"Yeah. I'll be fine." He reached for her hand and looked up. "Thanks, Bryn."

But when she left, he knew he was going to be anything but fine.

CHAPTER EIGHTEEN

*T*hree days before the wedding Julia sat atop the high granite cliffs and asked the question again. *Am I doing the right thing?* She looked at the bright summer blue sky and spoke to God, "I'm still waiting for a word from you. It's not too late. But it's getting really close."

She wore the woolen burnoose that Trevor had given her. She seemed to be spending more and more time out on the cliffs, searching for answers. Always she wore the burnoose. It gave her a sense of safety. It reminded her of Trevor and his arms around her shoulders.

Where are you? What are you doing? If only Trevor had chosen his timing more carefully when he declared his love! If only she had not sent him away! Julia sighed and closed her eyes as the wind filled the cape's hood. She still had no answers, just a heart full of questions.

She entered the house and, hearing Miles in the kitchen on the phone, went to the living room to pick up Anna's journal. Shane was overdue, and winter was fast approaching. Anna was overwrought by his absence.

24 October 1848

> *By all accounts, he should have returned at least a month ago. I tell myself that he is safe; in harbor somewhere south but unable to send me a message. Or perhaps that message is on the way now. I spend my days*

on the point, anxiously looking to sea, hoping the
Donnovan's majestic sails will appear on the horizon,
and glancing toward the frontage road to see if a mes-
senger speeds toward me with word of my love.

I spend my evenings in the lighthouse, making
sure the oil burns brightly. I could not have Shane
arrive home to a darkened torch. He needs to know I am
waiting, ready, hoping. The lighthouse man is angry
with me for hovering over his work, and the children are
underfoot when they join me. But I cannot care. I have
but one focus. Shane.

Where could he be? He would not have survived all
those voyages if he was meant to die at sea! Not when
finances are no longer a burden! Not when he has four
lovely children to watch grow! Not when he has a wife
who dearly needs him!

My heart is breaking. Oh, Shane, come home! I love
you! How I long for your arms around me again!

"Julia?"

Julia raised her head distractedly, tears sliding down her cheeks. Miles stood above her. "What's the matter, darling?"

She swallowed, trying to sort out the right answer. "It's Shane. Anna thinks he's lost at sea."

"I'm on the line, but I'm on hold. I might have to go at any minute. Do you think you should be reading such dark material practically on the eve of our wedding? I want a happy bride in three days—" Then to the receiver, "Yes, I'm still holding."

"Don't you see? Shane could be lost forever! Maybe this is when he dies! We know from family history that he died suddenly. But I know Anna now. It's like I can feel her pain. I don't want her to hope that he'll come back, because I know she'll probably be disappointed—"

"Richard! So nice to hear your voice! I've been meaning to speak with you about that case we picked up. I just learned…"

Julia tuned Miles out as quickly as he had turned from her tear-stained face. She shook off a feeling of rejection and went back to the yellowed pages in her lap.

12 November 1849

It is done. I have suffered the most desolate year of my life, hearing that my Shane is gone, but refusing to believe it. It is only now, after a second ship has sailed and returned. The reports concur.

He is gone.

He sailed out of Rio de Janeiro last year, anxious to get home to his family. He ignored his advisors when they warned him of a shift in the weather. Two days later the fiercest storm to hit the coast in twenty years was upon them. We can only guess that the Donnovan went down fighting, with Shane at the wheel, refusing to let go.

I want to be content with the fact that he died at a task he loved, no, lived for. Yet my heart collapses as the Donnovan's masts must have done on that stormy night, and my insides rip raw as the sails. My spirit sinks, much as her bow must have dipped beneath the angry waves, crushing any cries of hope. Devastation! Oh, total devastation!

*I remain the sole proprietor of the Donnovan
Shipyard. Indeed, we have built four clippers since
Shane took his leave. But the money means nothing. I
want my beloved back. I want his arms, his kiss, his
companionship. No money can replace him.*

*If it were not for my faith in Jesus, my torchlight in
darkness, and my children, my hope for the future, my
desire to live would cease.*

Julia's own tears dropped from her face and melded with the ancient tear stains on Anna's journal. How she must have wept! Julia grieved for her ancestor, feeling her pain. It felt much too close. She wiped her tears away hastily, fearful they would smudge her great-great-grandmother's pain-filled prose. "Oh, Anna." Julia looked out to the lighthouse.

She wanted to go back in time to comfort her. Such a love! Once again she donned her burnoose and went to the cliff.

Engrossed with his call, Miles did not notice her leave.

It was a lovely early August day. Julia's dress, now repaired, was perfect. The flowers in her garden were blooming, the chairs were in place, the string quartet was setting up. Tara rushed in and out, keeping a close eye on the process in the kitchen but not wanting to miss out on anything upstairs as her friend dressed for the wedding.

Emily was working on the tiny buttons on Julia's back. She glanced worriedly to her sister-in-law's downcast face in the mirror. After the fourth effort on the same button, Emily finally paused.

"Julia, what's wrong?" she asked.

"I don't know."

"My wedding day was the happiest of my life! Are you having doubts? What is it?"

"It just feels wrong! This can't be your average case of prewedding jitters. I've got the shakes." She raised her hand, showing Emily that she could not stop the trembling. Her diamonds glittered in the sun.

"How are you normally when you're center stage?" Emily asked quietly.

"Never anywhere near this bad. I'm in sorry shape."

Eleanor bustled in, interrupting their conversation. "Oh, you look lovely! I think you need a bit more blush though. You should be ready soon, Julia. We want the guests to be seated in half an hour, and the photographer wants to take some shots of you alone. He'll take precautions to keep you out of Miles's sight."

"Small miracles," Julia muttered.

"What?"

"I said, 'Special moments.' I want to savor each of them."

"Yes, well. Emily looks like she's doing her best to get you ready." She gave her new daughter-in-law an attempt at a smile. "I won't stay in your way. I'll go see how Tara and the kitchen staff are progressing."

"Thank you, Mother," Julia said wearily.

Emily went back to work on the buttons. When she got to the top, she turned and gathered Julia's veil, which was attached to a crown of pearls. The netting, dotted with its own ivory stones, ran the entire length of Julia's short train. For a garden wedding, the dress was a little long, but Julie hadn't wanted to pass up the chance to wear the romantic gown.

"Julia," Emily ventured. "If you don't want to do this…"

"No," Julia forced a smile. "I'm being silly. It's just the jitters. Let's go."

Emily carefully pinned the veil to Julia's hair, done up in a chignon. The hairstyle reminded Julia of the first night she and Trevor had dined together, then read from Anna's journal. How he had looked at her! It made her knees weak just to think of his warm gaze. Julia closed her eyes, willing away the image of him.

"This is the magical moment," Emily said. "Watch."

Julia did as she was told, watching her image in the full-length mirror as Emily climbed a chair beside her to unfurl the veil and place it in front of her face.

Looking through the netting, she did feel like a princess. A shiver ran down her spine. "Magical," she agreed.

"You look beautiful," Emily said. "The dress, your hair… It's like stepping back in time to watch Anna and Shane. You truly are stunning." Her eyes glimmered with tears, and Julia's eyes welled up in response.

"It's time, darling," Eleanor said, ducking into the room again. "The photographer is getting impatient." She left without waiting.

Julia took one last look out the window. The guests were arriving and being seated in the garden, facing the ocean. In front of them, she would join Miles for their vows. *It's all set. I'd be crazy to back out now. Trevor's long gone. Miles is waiting. The wheels are in motion. What's done is done.*

She turned to follow Emily down the stairs.

It was a warm summer afternoon, and a gentle breeze favored them. It was truly the perfect day for a wedding. The musicians began the familiar strains of Pachelbel's *Canon* just as the last guests took their seats. Julia wanted to catch Tara's arm as her friend brushed by with a quick "good luck." She wanted to stop Emily from starting down the aisle, leading the way for the bride. But her mouth did not utter a sound.

She fought to catch her breath.

Miles walked to the front, grinned back at Julia, and with his eyes, beckoned her to come forward. He looked handsome in his tuxedo, his brown hair glimmering in the sunlight. His eyes were full of hope. He was totally at ease.

Have we even talked in the last few days? It seems like he's always on the phone or away. Is that what our life will be like? More apart than together? She felt frozen in place, a smile plastered on her face, the guests looking at her with questioning eyes, the musicians repeating the last refrain so they would not run out of music before the bride arrived. Still, Julia leaned backward, not allowing her father to escort her down the aisle. He leaned down to whisper encouraging words to her. Miles's brow furrowed.

"It will be okay, honey," Jacob said. "You'll see, it will be fine. You've made a fine choice."

The soothing cadence of his voice thawed her frozen stature, and she allowed him to lead her down the aisle without further resistance. She trusted his voice, his tone. This was the man who had always cared for her and always would. He trusted Miles. Shouldn't she, too?

They met Miles in front of the small gathering. Jacob shook the hand of his future son-in-law. He raised Julia's veil to kiss her briefly on the cheek, then took her hand and joined it with Miles's.

This is it.

The minister began the words of the ceremony, but Julia lost track of what he was saying after the auspicious beginning, "Dearly beloved…"

Did Anna feel this way when she married Shane? It sounded as if he'd had to work hard to convince her. And look how in love they were! Maybe we can develop that kind of love! She looked up into Miles's face hopefully but saw nothing there to convince her.

The rumble of a motorcycle engine came to her ear, although Julia did not take her eyes from the minister.

"Miles Hanford Beckley, do you take Julia Sirene Rierdon to be your lawfully wedded wife? To have and to hold, in sickness and in health, for richer or poorer, so long as you both shall live?"

"I do."

As if in a tunnel, Julia watched from a distance as Miles placed the gold band upon her finger. Could they not all hear the engine? Could they not guess at the significance? Were they all deaf?

"Julia Sirene Rierdon, do you take Miles Hanford Beckley to be your lawfully wedded husband? To have and to hold, in sickness and in health, for richer or poorer, so long as you both shall live?"

"Do not say yes," a voice commanded from the aisle. The guests let out a collective gasp.

Julia turned to look at him. He had come back. Her heart sang; her eyes danced. He was home!

She looked to Miles. He was angry at the intrusion, worried that she might change her mind, wondering what was the proper action to take.

"Why are you here, Trevor?" she asked quietly.

CHAPTER NINETEEN

I think you know why I'm here," he said so everyone could hear. "I'm here because the farther away I got, the more you were on my mind. I'm here because the more I'm with you, the deeper I fall in love. I'm here because you are the smartest, most beautiful, and most incredible woman I've ever known. I'm here because I cannot imagine life without you, and I think you're marrying the wrong man. I'm here because I would like to ask you to be my wife, and I'm here to promise I will never leave you again."

With that, he bent down on one knee and brought out his own ring for her, a simple antique band of gold.

Miles, furious, made a move toward Trevor, but Jake held him back with a firm grip on his forearm and shoulder. "My sister needs to make a decision," he said. "And you need to let her do it without interfering."

Julia looked from Trevor to Miles to Trevor again, blind to her family and friends. Everyone held his or her breath as she contemplated her decision.

"I'm sorry, Miles," she said as she looked up at him, genuinely apologetic as she slipped off his ring and pressed it into his palm. "I never should've let it get this far."

"I'll say." He threw the ring to the ground as if it were plaster and stomped off. He paused for a moment, turned, and shook his finger at her. "You haven't heard the last from me," he said.

She ignored him. Her eyes were on Trevor, who remained on bended knee in front of her. The crowd was silent as they waited for the rest of the scene to unfold, but Julia concentrated only on the handsome man in his brown leather bomber jacket and white T-shirt. Here was a man who truly loved her. Here was a man who had the potential of being what Shane was to Anna. Here was the love of her life.

Julia reached out and took the worn band from his hand.

"It's about the same age as Anna's would have been," he said.

"An appropriate engagement ring," she said. She leaned down to stroke his strong, square jaw line gently. "I'm so glad you came back for me," she said.

He rose and, lifting her veil, kissed her soundly. "So am I. So am I."

Dear Reader,

Torchlight is the second book I wrote, and I wrote it after seeing a picture of a lighthouse in a magazine. The story spun itself from there. I loved the romance of "torches," as the sailors of old used to call lighthouses, and the obvious symbolism of Christ. Haven't you looked for his light when things were really, really dark? What a gift to have a Beacon that is ever present when we are in danger of crashing on the rocks.

My own family history fascinates me—thus the interest in developing Anna and Shane's own love story. Talk about high romance! They were so intriguing to me that I think I'll have to go back and write their entire story someday. My family were not sailors, they were immigrants from Norway and Switzerland; they must've broken their backs trying to tame the land as farmers in North Dakota and Montana. The quest by Julia (my great-grandmother's name) to refurbish the old family mansion was, in many ways, a quest to know, to understand, my roots a little better. I dug even deeper for those roots in my Northern Lights series. If you liked Shane and Anna in this novel, check out *The Captain's Bride*.

I hope that this letter at the end of each book will help you see a little more into my life and know that I deeply appreciate your support. May you always seek his torchlight in the darkness.

Every blessing,

Lisa Dawn Bergren

Write to me via my Web site!
www.LisaTawnBergren.com
or the old-fashioned way:
c/o WaterBrook Press
2375 Telstar Drive, Suite 160
Colorado Springs, CO 80920

If you enjoyed TORCHLIGHT, *be sure to look for other books
in the Full Circle series, available at your local bookstore.
Following are excerpts from two of those books:*
PATHWAYS *and* CHOSEN.

Pathways

CHAPTER ONE

C ome on, Bryn. Come out in the canoe with me. You haven't been out of this cabin for two days. And it's summer. You can study later."

"No thanks, Dad," she said, turning her back to him and trying to concentrate on her anatomy textbook. The longer she could bury herself in her studies, the faster this trip would be over.

She heard her father, Peter Bailey, walk to the front window. "Come on, honey," he said, a slight begging tone to his voice. "The rain's let up. We haven't even been over to the Pierces' to say hello."

Thoughts of Eli Pierce flashed through her mind. People thought that Californians were snobbish. Eli wouldn't give her the time if he had the last watch on earth. They'd played together when she was at Summit Lake with her dad the year she was ten, but when she'd arrived over her fifteenth summer, the guy had avoided her like a bad case of barnacles on a barge. Sure he was handsome, but Bryn had better things to do than get snubbed by a small-town jerk. "I'm just fine where I am," Bryn said.

"Suit yourself," he said. She could hear the shrug of defeat in his voice.

She wondered what her dad saw in this place. It took hours to fly to Anchorage from Southern California, and a couple more to drive to Talkeetna. Then they had to take still another hour to get the floatplane loaded with their gear and fly in to Summit Lake. Bryn heard the door shut behind her father.

All day to get here. She turned over and looked at the two-room log cabin, built by her father twenty years before. Her eyes floated over the hand-hewn logs and white, crumbling chinking. She lay in the bedroom in back, which held a bunk bed on either side. The front room was reserved for a tiny kitchenette and sitting area. It was dark, with no electricity, and it smelled musty, like an old basement blanket at her Grampa Bruce's in Boston. Bryn had to read by the light of a kerosene lamp when it rained during the day. No wonder her dad hadn't been able to get Bryn's mother, Nell, to come all these years.

She closed her eyes as the hollow, scraping sound of her father dragging the canoe off the rocks and into the water reached her ears. She wished she were home working a summer internship at the hospital, heading to the beach, catching a movie with friends—anywhere but here. In two years she would be twenty-two, a graduate from college with a degree in premed. And she would finally tell her father that their days at Summit Lake together were to be no more. She would, after all, be an adult, no longer compelled to please her dad, despite her own desires. He'd have to accept that.

A pang of loss pierced her heart and she frowned, then sighed. Probably guilt pangs. The guy just wanted some quality time with his daughter. She could at least make the most of this trip with him. Appease him, share with him, make the proverbial memory together. Dutiful daughters did such things all the time.

Bryn tossed aside her textbook and shoved her feet into shoes, hurrying to catch him before he was too far out. Bumping her head on the top bunk, she grimaced. "Dad, wait!" she called, hoping he would hear her from outside. She rubbed the top of her head and rushed out to the front room, then out to the lakeside where her father was already nearly fifty feet out. "Dad, wait! I changed my mind!"

Her father turned and flashed her a white-toothed grin. He was dark and handsome—Bryn's roommate, Ashley, referred to him as "the sexiest man alive," which always made Bryn's skin crawl. No matter how others saw him, he was still just Dad to Bryn.

"Oh good, Bryn Bear," he responded, using her childhood nickname. "I was already missing you." The warmth and welcome in his eyes made her glad for her decision. It seemed his eyes were too often full of sorrow and longing these days, although she couldn't think of a reason for such emotions.

Bryn turned and ducked her head in the cabin door, grabbing her parka from the hook inside. Summers in Alaska were notorious for turning suddenly cold, so she always kept the warm coat at hand. She walked back to the shoreline, pulling her long hair out and into a quick knot. Her hair was the same color as her father's—Indian black, Peter called it—and they shared the same dark olive skin. Her nose was his too, straight and too long. But her eyes were her mother's—wide and a bit tipped up in the corners. Smoky brown, a boyfriend once told her. "Just like the rest of you," he had whispered. "Smoky."

He was long gone. She had seen to that. Keeping a straight-A average at the University of California at Irvine was no small deal, and he had been in the way, always wanting to party and go out rather than study. But she wanted to graduate and go on to Harvard, at the top of her class all the way. It took discipline and concentration to accomplish that. And vision. No man was going to get in the way.

The canoe crunched to shore again. "Push us off, Bryn Bear."

"Okay," she said, wrinkling her nose a bit when her boots got wet and the cold lake water seeped through her socks and to her toes. While they glided backward, Bryn balanced on the bow, then carefully climbed in.

"There's a jacket and paddle beneath the seat," Peter said from behind her.

"Thought I was goin' on a ride," she tossed back.

"If you ride, you paddle," her dad responded. "Can't make an Alaskan out of you if you sit up there like a Newport Beach priss."

She pulled out the life jacket, pausing to flick off a rather large spider, then put it on and reached for the paddle. Just then a bald eagle swooped low, his long wings spread wide, almost touching the surface as his thick talons clutched a trout from the waters across the lake. "Wow!" Bryn said.

"Isn't it something here?" Peter replied. "I never get tired of seeing things like that. If only your mother would share it with me…" His voice trailed away, as if the admission were too painful to tell his daughter.

"You always wanted to live here, didn't you, Dad?"

"Summers anyway. Your mother wouldn't hear of it. Wouldn't even come and see it." There was a shiver of anger in his tone, frustration, as well as pain.

"It is a bit…isolated," Bryn said, wondering why she felt compelled to defend her mother. She considered her father's words as she dug her paddle into the water. She had to admit that it felt good to be out on the lake, out from the dank little cabin.

"The solitude is part of what I love," Peter said, finally breaking the silence. "The first day Jed brought me here, I knew it would be a part of my life forever."

Bryn looked about them at the small, shallow lake, edged here and there by thick, swampy areas full of reeds, with thick-treed snow-covered mountains that shot up on all three sides. A river fed into Summit from the mountain streams to the south. "This place is *wild*," she said, shivering. "Mom would not like it."

He was quiet for a moment, paddling. "I know. There's something about being here—it's so…primary, basic. Not your mother's style at all. Reminds a person of who he is and who he wants to be." He dug in his paddle again, and Bryn remained silent, waiting for him to go on. "Jedidiah said to me once, 'The bush teaches a man about what he wants and what he needs, and the difference between them.' Every time I come here, I remember. And I leave rededicated to discovering it in Newport, too."

Bryn's mind flew from this thin-aired, low-maintenance hideaway to their rather ostentatious home in Newport. Her mother had made a career out of volunteering with the Junior League and decorating their home with only the finest furnishings and accessories. "How did you and Mom ever get together?" She looked over her shoulder to see his rueful smile.

"We were more alike once. In college, I thought…" His words drained away like the water off of his paddle. "At some point, your mother changed. I changed." He halted, as if trying not to say too much.

"She's been pretty mean lately," Bryn said, digging her paddle into the water again. "Are you two okay? I mean, your marriage and everything?"

He was silent for a long moment. "Sure, Bryn. We're fine."

Bryn licked her lips and kept paddling, searching the approaching shore for the Pierces' cabin. The sounds of sharp axes cutting through soft wood carried across the lake, as they had since morning, and she caught sight of Eli and his father as they stood around an old, dying tree. Built the same year as the Baileys', the Pierces' cabin had been completed first, then Jedidiah and Peter had moved on to finish the Bailey abode. All in one summer. "We were young then," her father would say wistfully. But there was something in his eyes, in the way he held his shoulders slightly back, as if still proud of the accomplishment, that made her ask him to tell the story again and again.

Peter Bailey had met up with Jedidiah Pierce, born and raised in Alaska, in the summer of '62, backpacking through Europe. In Germany, the pair had stayed at a youth hostel overnight and went out the next day to try the locals' fabled Gewürztraminer. Frequently wineries set up tents along the road, and the duo stopped at the first one they saw. It was only much later that they learned they had crashed a wedding party, and the father of the bride had them tossed out.

From then on, the men were like blood brothers, and Jed, having spotted the pristine site on a hike years before, brought his new friend to Summit Lake the following summer. Both purchased several acres from Ben White, who owned much of the land surrounding the water. Ben was an older man who had been living alone on Summit since 1953, when he was discharged from the army. His home was at the northern tip of the lake. No one else owned land on the lake or lived in the small mountain valley.

"There she is," Peter said from behind Bryn. "I'm always amazed that I can't see their place from the water until I'm nearly on top of it."

Deep in the shadows, the cabin did blend wonderfully with the trees, hidden behind a copse of alder and white spruce.

Jedidiah stood up with his son, ax in hand, panting. They had been working on felling an old-growth, rotten spruce that threatened their roof in the next winter storm. He wiped the sweat from his upper lip and took a step closer, grinning. "I knew that must be Peter Bailey who flew in," he said. "And he's got Bryn with him. Man, what a beauty!"

Eli met his father's knowing eyes.

"She was always like catnip and you the tomcat," Jed said in gentle warning. "Watch yourself."

"I don't think she's interested, Dad. The girl couldn't even manage to say hello last time I saw her."

"She was a kid then. Now you're adults. And that makes your dance a little more dangerous."

"What're you talking about?" Eli asked crossly.

"Can't you see it? Trust a father's intuition then. Just watch your step, Son. Listen to the Spirit's lead," he said, looking upward into the sunlight filtering through the dense alder and spruce boughs. He slammed his ax into the tree trunk and left Eli's side to greet his old friend.

After a moment, Eli began to follow. As he walked down the path, he tried to get a covert look at Bryn. When he saw her grin up at his father on the bank, it made him pause and almost trip. The girl, who had been a fox at fifteen, had grown into a classic Greek goddess, with long, lithe limbs and dark, swinging hair—an uncommon grace in every movement. And when she smiled, sweet heaven, it made his heart hurt and sail back to the year he was sixteen. The year she wouldn't even speak to him. Too good for him, he had supposed. Their childhood friendship plainly dissolved.

Forcing himself to leave the cover of the trees, he approached his father, keeping his eyes on Peter Bailey, not risking a fall on his face in front of Bryn. Eli shook Peter's hand firmly, noticed the look of admiration in the man's eyes, his glance down to his daughter. And then Eli had to. Had to turn and look at her, greet her. Like an adult, just when he felt a keening teen shyness he hadn't encountered in years.

Eli reached up for his grandfather's airman's cap and pulled it off his head, slipping it under one armpit. He forced himself to smile and look into her eyes—the color of a beaver's tail in water. "Hi, Bryn," he managed.

"Eli," she said with another smile and a short nod. "Your dad roped you into a trip to Summit too, huh?"

"Every summer," he said, wondering at her words. *Roped?* This place was heaven on earth. The kind magazine crews scouted for catalog shoots. Thoreau would have died a happy man after he'd seen a place like this. He glanced out at the honey glaze on the water, the deep forest green of the mountains, the snow at the peaks that was almost lavender. "What's it been, four, five years?"

"Five years," she said, confirming what he already knew. "Dad can only make it two years between visits here. Every five years is right on track for me. I mean, it's pretty… *rustic.*"

"Ah, I get it," Jedidiah said, giving her a warm hug. "Californian would rather be at the beach? You're a sight, Bryn. Pretty as a state-fair queen. You must be proud, Peter."

"Couldn't be prouder. And she's smart as a whip too."

"Dad—," Bryn tried, obviously embarrassed.

"Straight A's, at the University of California."

"*Dad*—"

"So focused on her studies she won't even look at the guys," he said, punching Eli on the shoulder.

"Dad!"

"What?" Peter asked innocently.

Bryn sighed and passed her father, shaking her head. "Dad still thinks I'm a deaf teenager," she said under her breath to Eli, "so that he has license to say anything that passes through his head. Sorry."

"No problem," he said, watching her go by, catching the scent of vanilla and green apples. Her shampoo? A lotion? She sat down on a chair on the porch and looked out at the lake.

"My boy has his pilot's license," Jedidiah said to Peter, clearly not wanting to be one-upped. "Has his sights set on his own operation out of Talkeetna."

"Great," Peter said in wistful admiration, as if he wished he were the one starting a company in Alaska. He clapped Eli on the shoulder. "That your de Havilland?"

Eli looked past him to the old, restored Beaver on shore, knowing full well that it was the only plane in sight. "She's mine."

"A beaut!" Peter said. "I would've had you fly us in had I known you were looking for work. Your operation will be all floatplanes?"

"Float*plane,* in the singular form," Eli said, following his father and Peter up the path to the cabin. "Maybe someday I'll have one outfitted with skis, take the tourists to land on the glaciers, up around Denali, that sort of thing."

"Talkeetna's hopping. Must be twice as many people in town this summer as compared to ten years ago," Peter said, as if hoping he was wrong.

"Yeah," Jedidiah said. "Have a seat, everyone. I'll get some coffee on." Through the open doorway, over his shoulder he said, "Princess Cruises bring busloads of tourists into town now. You should see them, walking through, completely oblivious to the locals trying to keep on with everyday life. It's as if they think they own the place. And the trash they leave behind!"

"You know what they say," Eli interjected. All eyes turned to him. "An environmentalist is someone who already has their own cabin."

Peter laughed. "That's a good one. It's true." He looked back out to the lake. "I never want Summit to be discovered, changed. This is our place. Ours." He almost whispered the last word, and Bryn studied her father as if confused. She clearly was not as enamored with the pristine Alaskan valley as were their fathers or Eli. But the way she leaned back against the Adirondack chair, her hair falling out of its knot like a curling oil slick along the Kenai peninsula... She looked as if she belonged there. At Summit Lake. In Alaska. Whether she knew it or not.

"Where's Meryl?" Peter asked as Jedidiah came out, a tray of coffee mugs in hand.

"She's taking this summer off. Said us boys needed some man time." He smiled and offered the tray to each before setting it on the porch floor. "Truth be told, I kind of like our reunions after a little time apart." There was a twinkle in his eyes. "So how long you stayin'?" he asked, directing the question to Peter.

"A month, if I can keep her here that long," Peter said, nodding at his daughter.

She paused for a telling couple of seconds. "I think I can last." She paused, obviously thinking. "You know, Dad, a porch like this would help a lot." Bryn looked around at the overhang that extended from the roof. "Allow us to be outside more. Keep us from getting cabin fever."

Peter nodded, looking around at it too, walking over to touch a post as if already doing measurements in his head. "Been a while since we've made any improvements to the old place."

"I could bring you some supplies," Eli offered. "Headin' out tomorrow."

"We could harvest the poles and crossbeams ourselves," Peter said, throwing Bryn a cocked brow of challenge. "I think the boards for the roof would have to be flown in," he allowed, gratefully accepting a refill from Jedidiah. "Not as young as I once was."

"Not ready to hew your own lumber?" Jed teased. "Gettin' soft there, city boy."

"Yeah, yeah. I'm not soft, just smarter. I'd rather spend my month building and hunting and hiking and canoeing, rather than harvesting wood. We'll maintain the integrity of the cabin with a few native elements," he said, looking at Bryn again to see if she was in on the idea, "and buy us some relaxation time by getting Eli to fly in the rest."

"You can do that?" Bryn asked of Eli, forcing his eyes to hers. "Fly in a load of lumber?"

"Sure. I'll strap it to the Beaver's belly, compensate for the weight, and bring it right to your door."

"Can I go with him?" Bryn asked suddenly, casting the question toward Eli as much as to her father. "To mail my letters, pick up some supplies I forgot?"

"Bryn, we just got here—"

"Please, Dad. I'll just be gone a day. And you said yourself this would be a good project."

Peter cast anxious, narrowing eyes from Bryn to Eli to Jedidiah. "He's a good pilot, your son?" he asked of Jed.

"You know as well as I do that bush pilots are the best of the best. And he was trained by a couple of old-timers."

Peter sighed. "All right." He looked to Bryn and shook his finger at her. "But you ever tell your mother of this and there'll be you-know-what to pay."

"My lips are sealed," Bryn agreed.

"It's not you, my man," Peter said to Eli. "My wife was very explicit about her desire to keep Bryn out of small planes as much as possible."

"I understand," Eli said. "Tomorrow then, Bryn. At eight?"

"I'll be ready," she said, and Eli wondered at the glint in her eye. Had she changed so much in five years?

CHAPTER TWO

*A*t least you're talkin' to me this year," Eli said, unable to hold it in any longer.

From his side view, he could see her lips moving and he motioned to his headset, reminding her that over the noise of the de Havilland's engine, little could be heard without the headset. Her face turned red at having forgotten his instructions, and she pulled the microphone down and said, "I could say the same thing."

His eyebrows shot up in surprise, but he had to concentrate on the plane as he ran through a quick flow check and eased the throttle forward, heading toward the north end of the lake. There was a slight chop to the water, perfect for taking off and landing. He turned the plane into the wind. The Beaver shot along the length of Summit, picking up speed, swaying a little, and then they were aloft, clearing the riverbed below by a couple hundred feet.

Eli chanced a look at Bryn and she was smiling, clearly enjoying the ride. He picked up his radio mike and pressed the button. "Talkeetna radio, this is Beaver-four-two-six-Alpha-Bravo. We're leaving Summit Lake and headin' home. ETA is 0930 hours."

"Roger that, Beaver-four-two-six-Alpha-Bravo." With Denali just twenty miles away, he knew they would encounter their fair share of air traffic, it being the height of tourist season.

Once they settled into the flight, circumventing the towering Mount Foraker and heading toward Gevanni Pass to the southwest, he spoke into the headset microphone again, talking to Bryn. "What did you mean by saying you could say the same thing?"

She faced him briefly, her look incredulous. "You were the one who wouldn't say more than two words to me five years ago."

"Oh no. *You* were the one who blew *me* off." They looked at each other for a long moment, and their smiles grew. Eli shook his head. "Guess we both assumed too much, huh?" He cocked an eyebrow at her. "And I guess I was in love with Chelsea that summer."

"Yeah, well, that's a good excuse. And we were kids."

It was funny, hearing her say that. Eli still felt like little more than a kid, just on the brink of adulthood. He sometimes looked at himself from the outside, shaking hands and talking like an adult, and yet he felt as if he were playing a role, pretending to be grown up. Getting his pilot's license, establishing a line of credit, and purchasing this old plane were all new territory for him. But there was something about Bryn that told him she was born old. Something exotic and knowing.

Like catnip to a tomcat, his father had said. How had he known?

Eli Pierce was like a cougar cub in a cage, Bryn decided, covertly looking at him. One minute playfully showing off his floatplane, and the next minute holding back for some reason, as if he were pacing. The combination was charming, she decided. Intriguing. And his declaration that he thought *she* had blown him off five years ago had her at once confused and relieved. Confused that they had gotten so off track and relieved that he didn't believe her to be beneath him, unworthy of his attention as an Outsider, a cheechako, as the Alaskans referred to those from the Lower 48. Her fears had been for nothing.

Because as much as she didn't quite understand Alaska and its draw for her father, she knew she wanted to belong. She wanted at least to find acceptance here. She had always needed approval from others, she realized, regardless of their roles in her life, regardless of how much she didn't *want* to need it, chafed against the need.

Bryn stared out the window at the miles of rolling forest passing by below them, mostly lime green birch and black, pointy spruce, if she remembered the names right. She admitted to herself that it was curious, her simultaneous need for acceptance and her solitary life. Was there something deep inside her that kept her from reaching out, joining the circle? Something that would incapacitate her for the rest of her life? She hoped it was just a phase, just this time of reaching for her goal of becoming one of the best physicians in the country. Once that was attained, surely she would make room in her life for deep friendships, soul connections.

She didn't want to become her mother, distant and angry, constantly blaming her childhood for her miserable adulthood. Nor did she care to become her father, wandering and searching for something intangible, something that would lead him to happiness. Bryn chanced another look at Eli. He and Jedidiah had a way about them, a peaceful aura that calmed those around them. Maybe that was what drew Peter Bailey to Jedidiah. Her dad wanted a part of Jed's secret, that sureness about his life. Could it be the place? Alaska? Summit Lake? Surely such certainty about himself had to come from more than a sojourn to the great outdoors. But what?

"Penny...your thoughts," Eli's tinny voice came through her headset, broken up.

"It would take many pennies for me to share," she said. "How long until we reach Talkeetna?"

"Twenty, twenty-five minutes," he said, glancing out as if able to pinpoint exactly where they were. There were few landmarks other than winding, silver ribbons of rivers among the miles of trees. Did he know this wild, seamless country so well that he could identify each tree? Perhaps it was such familiarity that made him seem so at ease. She wondered. As they got closer to town, they saw more dwellings—summer cabins and year-round homes. "Up ahead," he said, suddenly. He dipped the nose of the plane and then pulled off some throttle to lose some altitude. "See? In…pond, two o'clock."

She smiled as a bull moose raised his head—the living mantel for a huge rack of antlers—with slimy bottom sludge hanging from either side of his huge snout. He shuffled out of the water, disgruntled by their passing, and the de Havilland sailed by. "How many of those do you see from up here in a summer?"

"Train bait?" he asked with a grin. "A hundred or so."

"Train bait?" she chanced, feeling every bit the cheechako.

"Trains kill about forty every year in this area alone. They're slow, they're big, and they like the open track. Easier going than the forest."

The rest of the trip was spent in relative silence, with only air traffic control coming through their headsets.

"Talkeetna," Eli said with a toss of his chin. In five minutes they were landing on a narrow stretch of the Susitna River and, in another five, were tied up. "Want to come with me to the lumberyard?" Eli asked her. "I'll have to get my dad's truck to haul the wood. He leaves it parked at the church. I'll be gone for about two hours."

"No thanks. I think I'll poke around town and mail my letters, pick up a few things. Meet you back here at, say"—she pulled up a sleeve to look at her watch—"three o'clock?"

"That'll be fine," he said, staring into her eyes a moment longer than necessary as if he could see through her, ascertain why she was reluctant to spend time with him. She wasn't even sure herself, except that he seemed dangerous, too risky a diversion from her carefully laid plans. She looked away, busied herself with gathering her belongings, and pulled her backpack up on one shoulder. "See you then, Eli," she said.

"See you then, Bryn," he returned, nodding at her once. She turned away first.

As soon as she was talking to her mother on the phone, Bryn wondered why she had called. Maybe it was the vague longing in her heart, the pervading sense of displacement, missing home, wanting that security Eli seemed to have—

"Bryn? Are you there?" Her mother's voice jolted her back to the present.

"I'm here, Mom. We're doing fine. I'm just in Talkeetna for some groceries and then heading back to Summit. Is there…is there anything you want me to pass along to Dad?"

A long silence followed. "No. No, honey. Tell him I said hello. I'm going sailing with the Bancrofts tonight. It's always awkward to do that sort of thing without your husband. I tell you, I just don't understand why he has to go off to the end of the world every other year."

"Maybe you should come up and see—"

"Oh no. I have no need to go someplace that has no running water or a decent toilet or a telephone."

"We heat water on the stove for a bath every day. It's kind of fun actually," Bryn said.

"I'd rather have hot water at my disposal without lugging it any-where. And listen to you! You sound as if you're actually enjoying it this year."

"I don't know if I'd call it enjoyment, but—"

"Are the Pierces still there? Have you seen Jedidiah's son?"

"Yes. He was sweet. We're getting along better than last time." She carefully held back the information that he had flown her to Talkeetna—her mother would never let Peter hear the end of it if she knew a twenty-one-year-old, just-licensed pilot had been in charge of her safety. There was no way to express in a way her mother would understand that Eli had a way about him that just made a girl trust…

"…that's good," her mother was saying. "Remember last time how crushed you were when that boy wouldn't say boo to you?"

"I was fifteen, Mom. I guess we had a misunderstanding. He was dating someone."

"Fifteen. My, it seems that was just yesterday. And now you're twenty. I miss you, honey. Want to come home? We could tell your father the truth—that you prefer being here in California to Alaska in the summers. He'd…understand."

He wouldn't. Her mother knew it as well as Bryn. "I don't think so, Mom," Bryn said gently. "I think…this will be good for me. Good for me and Dad."

"I…see," her mother said, a bit icily. Bryn had chosen. And it was the wrong choice, as if electing to stay was an admission of loy-alty to her father over her mother.

"I gotta go, Mom. We'll send you a report in the mail in a couple of weeks. We're fine. Don't worry about us, okay?"

"A mother always worries," Nell said with barely disguised irritation. "Take care of yourself."

"I will. You too." Bryn hung up the phone then, unable to rouse the words *I love you* from her lips with any semblance of honesty. She felt jumbled, confused, after her talk with her mom, as she always seemed to feel when they spoke. *Maybe this summer I can figure out exactly how I feel,* Bryn thought. *Maybe that's why I need to be here. To get my thoughts straight. To figure out where I belong. How I belong.* There was certainly time and quiet on the lake.

And Eli. He clearly knew who he was. "Comfortable in his own skin," as her Grampa Bruce would say. Maybe… No. She could never talk about such personal things with someone like Eli. He might laugh, or worse, feel sorry for her. *Poor, mixed-up Bryn Bailey.* Nobody at school thought of Bryn as mixed up. Everyone said she was so purposeful, focused. And she liked it that way.

She turned away from the phone, an open half stall against the side of Nagley's Mercantile, and left to mail her letters. She passed five college-age kids, probably river guides, who were laughing and playing around as they walked.

Suddenly she wished she were with Eli. Smiling and half flirting. Out flying or maybe hiking… Thinking about anything but her mother and her father and the widening abyss between them all.

What would it take to reach Bryn? Eli wondered, driving back to Talkeetna from Willow with Peter Bailey's wood and nails. When he entered town, he waved at the postmistress, walking with her toddler, then at Sheriff Ross. The tourists were out in force, and with Bryn not in sight, he turned down a dirt road to circumvent the crowd, heading back toward the river and his floatplane.

It took him twenty minutes to get the lumber properly secured under the belly of the plane. If Bryn didn't show up with too many purchases, they'd be perfectly balanced for the flight back to Summit. He rose, panting from the exertion of tightening the cinches, and wiped his hands on a cloth. He looked about for Bryn and spotted her approaching, only two sacks in hand—one a plain brown grocery bag and the other bearing the logo of a local T-shirt shop. It reminded him that she was only just passing through. Staying long enough to eat a few meals, but briefly enough that she needed a T-shirt as a memento. *Hang on to your heart, Pierce,* he told himself. *Pull back on the throttle.*

Two guys passed her and turned around to stare. She moved forward, oblivious to the strangers' admiration, focused only on him or the de Havilland. He couldn't tell which. There were some cute girls in town, but no one as amazing as Bryn Bailey. He knew it; those guys knew it. Bryn could be a model with her perfect features and long, shiny hair and curves right where a man appreciated them. A shiver ran down his neck to the middle of his back and out to his elbows and knees. What would it be like to take a woman like Bryn in his arms and kiss her? To feel her cling to him and press her lips hard against his? *Hang on to your heart, Pierce.*

She drew near and smiled shyly at him, her head slightly ducked. It made him want to hold her, to reassure her nameless, subtle fears. To kiss them away… *Hang on to your heart, Pierce.* The warning was clear, a holy urging from deep within, but he didn't want to hear it.

"Hi, there, pilot," she said, finally at his side. "I see you got the wood. All set?"

"All set. You can climb on in."

She paused on the float, one foot inside the doorway. "I was wondering, would you take me out hiking sometime this week? If you're not busy, I—"

"Sure. I'd love to." *So much for pulling back.* "I have a flying job over the next couple of days. How about after that?"

"Well, I gotta check my social schedule." She pretended to mentally mull over an intense calendar, finger to lip, eyes aloft. "Let's see, other than a promise to my dad for a daily canoe ride, I don't think I'm busy. So, Sunday?"

"Make it Monday. My dad and I hit church every Sunday morning, and that pretty much wipes out the day. Hey, you could come with—"

"That's all right," she said, climbing into the plane. "Monday will be fine."

"Okay." He climbed in behind her and buckled himself in, then grabbed the headset and put it on. He glanced at her, but she was staring outward, already quiet and thoughtful again. *Hang on to your heart, Pierce.* And this time the warning was as clear and alarming as a stall horn in the cockpit.

On Sunday evening Eli canoed over to the Bailey place to talk over the next day's plans with Bryn. She was out on the front stoop with her dad, holding a pole in place while Peter pounded in a long nail. With her hair up in a loose knot, soft tendrils falling to her neckline, and a body that in profile would make any man swallow hard, Bryn was as desirable as a mystery to a detective. And when she looked at him with those dark eyes that seemed to convey every whisper his heart longed to hear...

Eli wanted to know her—what motivated, moved, mortified, molded her. He forced his focus back to their project, suddenly conscious of Bryn's protective father and that he probably appeared to be gawking. *Am gawking.* The framework on the porch was almost complete, and appeared to be level and solid.

"Lookin' good," Eli called from the water, his eyes slipping back to Bryn. *The woodwork isn't bad either.*

"Thanks!" Peter greeted him. "Guess I haven't forgotten too much in the twenty-odd years since we built these places."

Bryn grinned at her father and then at Eli as he made his way ashore. "I think he was just waiting for my year to take this on," she said half accusingly.

"Hey, girl, it was your idea."

"So it was. But somehow I think it was yours all along."

Her father slipped his hammer into a belt loop and crossed his arms. "Now how do you figure that?" Eli picked up a rising note of tension and shifted, uneasy.

"I don't know… You've always been able to get me to do exactly what you wanted."

"Not me. Your mother maybe."

"Both of you," she said, picking a splinter from her hand. Eli noticed her nails were closely cropped, with small white half-moons on each nail bed. Perfect. Just like the rest of her.

"Hey, Bryn," he interrupted, not caring to be caught in the middle of a family disagreement. "I just popped over to talk about tomorrow. Want to head out early?"

"Sure," she said, still staring at her father. "We thought we'd go hiking, Dad. Okay with you if I abandon camp for a while?"

Peter looked from her to Eli, then back to her. "Just make sure you have the right gear and get back well before dark. Okay?" His focus was on Eli again, his intent clear. Alaska could be a dangerous place. *She's your responsibility, Eli. I'm trusting you.*

"No problem, Mr. Bailey," Eli said respectfully. He turned back toward the canoe, saying over his shoulder, "I'll see you tomorrow at seven, Bryn."

"I'll be ready." There was no hesitation, no qualm in her voice. She was brave and gutsy. He liked that.

"Good night," he said, already paddling away.

"'Night!" Peter called. Bryn was silent. And because she was silent, Eli knew he would be fantasizing about her whispering "good night" in his ear all evening. What was it about her? He stubbornly refused to look back toward shore.

For the first time since he'd started daydreaming about Bryn, Eli whispered a prayer heavenward. "Lord God, you have brought me to this place for a reason." He paddled deep and hard in a J-stroke, powerfully forcing the cedar canoe forward. "Help me to be your servant, to be who Bryn needs me to be, and not so focused on my most base desires." It was then that her declining his invitation to join them for church that morning came back to him.

Why hadn't he thought of it before? Peter Bailey had never been a believer, always telling Jedidiah that he lived a moral, if not a Christian, life. And that was enough. Memories of the two men sitting out by a campfire, debating theological questions, came back to Eli. Like father, like daughter.

He had assumed she was a believer. Hoped she was a believer. Hadn't wanted to think anything else, drawn into his attraction for her like...*a tomcat to catnip.*

The problem was that Eli was already rolling in the catnip.

"My dad calls you a bear magnet. Think we'll see one today?" Bryn asked, keeping up with Eli with some effort. It wasn't easy, at this altitude, but she was loath to admit it. There was an air of testing about Eli today, something she picked up the moment he collected her in the canoe. She wondered why.

"It does seem to be true—every time I go out I come across the closest bear. Must be something about my smell." He turned and grinned at her, handsome with a slight flush to his lower cheeks where the faintest stubble hugged his skin.

She raised her eyebrows, forcing her thoughts back to bears. "Great. So if we encounter a bear, Mr. Magnet, what are we supposed to do?"

"Grizzly, stay absolutely still. They perceive anything running away as dinner. If attacked, you play dead. If it's a black bear, you fight back. Don't try to climb a tree. They'll be right behind you, and trust me, they're better climbers. Grizzlies don't climb."

"Okay," she said slowly. "I'll just do what you do."

He smiled over his shoulder at her again. "Don't worry. I'm the bear magnet. You didn't put any citronella on, did you?"

She stopped, and he walked a few paces before stopping too, then turning around.

"You did?"

"Well, I had to do something to keep from giving these mosquitoes a unit of blood." She swatted around her head, suddenly hearing the high-pitched whine of the dreaded insect nearby. "Why? Don't tell me. Bears love citronella."

"Some bears." He frowned and Bryn frowned too, now truly

worried about a bear attack. Yet she was glad for the attention from Eli. There was a protective, loving way about him that made her feel more feminine, aware, alive.

"We're, what? Three miles out?" Bryn said, trying to return her focus to the task at hand. "Might as well get to the mining camp and then go home. Maybe the bears are in other territory today."

Eli scanned the horizon, suddenly all Eagle Scout. "Maybe. Just stick close to me."

No problem, she thought. It was about seventy degrees out, a perfect summer day, and Bryn concentrated on the beauty all about them rather than on her handsome guide or the bears that might want to eat them. Summit Lake lay on the western border of the Denali Wilderness, and from this vantage point, they could see much of Mount McKinley—which Eli preferred to call by the Athabaskan name *Denali,* "since that president from Ohio never even laid eyes on her"—and the rest of the Alaskan Range.

It was breathtaking—white peaks descending to dark silver-blue ravines and gullies, above green-brown tundra-covered "hills" that rivaled most of the Rocky Mountains in elevation. Bryn knew that many of the peaks were eleven to thirteen thousand feet high; Mount Foraker was over seventeen thousand; and McKinley, the queen, over twenty.

"What does *Denali* mean?" she asked, panting, following in Eli's footsteps.

"High One."

"That's appropriate."

"Highest point in North America," he said with a note of pride.

She stifled an *I know.* She wasn't stupid—she had scored 1490 on her SAT. But she sensed that he hadn't said it to be a know-it-all.

He simply loved this place. What was it about him that at once drew her—as though they had been lifelong friends rather than periodic acquaintances—but also repelled her—as if she were a complete cheechako?

"So you're premed," he said suddenly. "Want to be a generalist or a specialist?"

"Don't know. I have a few years to figure it out."

"I'd say," he agreed. "What makes you want to be a doctor?"

She mulled over his question, and the silence grew between them. Finally she said, "I think it's because I like to get to the root of a problem and fix it. Problems with the body almost always have a good reason for occurring, and a good solution."

He paused, letting her catch up to him, and opened up his canteen, then offered it to her. "You thirst, and you quench it. It's all very orderly."

She looked him in the eye, catching his obvious hint. "You don't care for the orderly?"

"I've found that my life isn't all that orderly. I want it to be, but it doesn't matter. It's messy and mixed-up and turned around every time I think I'm on the straight and narrow." He took a sip after her and then with the back of his hand wiped his lips. Bryn found herself staring at them a half-second too long.

"Isn't that aggravating?" she asked, taking a deep breath. She wouldn't let him distract her. "Don't you just want to make it right, make it straight, less messy again?"

"To some extent." He looked around, surveying the land like a one-man search party. "I've been spending quite a bit of time with Ben White. There's a reason my dad has been friends with him all these years. You should get to know him too."

She sat down on a nearby rock, her calves suddenly aching. "Why? My dad says he's just an old coot who's tucked himself away from the world. A religious fanatic."

"That's not how I'd describe him. Ben's wise. Smart. Caring. He's pretty remarkable."

"Because he raises bear cubs?"

"That's just part of the reason." Eli shook his head. "It's hard to explain. I'll take you to see him. He'll be back tomorrow. He's out on a Fish and Game assignment."

"What does he have to do with our conversation?"

Eli sat down on a neighboring boulder. "He writes a lot. He told me the trick to writing in a way that grabs readers is to note what is vivid and vital in life. And if you can take note of it and embrace it, whether you're writing about it or reading it, you'll enjoy it all the more." Eli looked at her steadily. His eyes were the color of the far hills, a hazel green. "When is life most vivid and vital for you, Bryn?"

Here, now was the first thing that came to her. She thought about sharing it with him but held back. He was right. Her days were not focused, not organized with a huge goal before her as she usually kept them, and yet she felt more…interested and…*whole* than she had in a long time. "It's a good question," she said instead, rising. "Come on. If we're going to get to that mining camp and back, we had better hurry."

Eli watched the thoughts pass through her dark chocolate eyes like a ticker tape through a stockbroker's hands. There was something moving her, changing her, making her think. She set off ahead of him, assuming their trail was dead ahead rather than veering to the right at the crags, moving on instinct. Was that how she always tackled a problem? Move forward and figure it out on the way?

"Uh, Bryn? We want to head over to the right. The camp should be about a quarter-mile farther."

"Oh. Okay." She modified her path immediately. "You asked me what makes me want to be a doctor. What makes you want to be a pilot?"

"You were up with me last week. You saw what fun it is, right?"

"Yeah. But what about the rest of the world, Eli? What about seeing Europe like our fathers did? Or China? Or New Zealand or Peru…"

"I'd like to see those places. Someday."

"Why not now? Have you ever even been Outside? To the Lower 48?"

"Twice. We went to see my grandparents in Chicago."

"That's it?" It was her turn to stop and study him. "Don't you ever wonder what you're missing? What's out there?"

He mulled over her question. "Guess not. Wasn't wild about Chicago. This is home, and I'm pretty sure it always will be."

She nodded but was clearly not assured.

"And flying… There's nothing else like it. When I was a kid, I wanted to be a hawk, circling, riding the wind. If I could spend all day in a glider, I'd be a happy man. The de Havilland and flying for a living is the next best thing."

He took the lead. "I might not have seen China yet, but I see something new every day. Isn't that what most people want from their work? Something new, to keep things fresh, interesting?"

"I suppose."

They crested the next hill and spotted the remains of a small mining operation—decomposing traces on the ground, a black, cavernous hole in the hillside, barely covered with metal fencing in a meager Forest Service effort to keep hikers and daring spelunkers out. There wasn't a whole lot to it. But beyond it, miles of treeless, green-gold tundra extended all the way to the base of the white mountains in the distance.

"This is it?" Bryn asked, staring down the gully to the sad remains.

"No," he said. He took her hand before thinking about it and waved to the horizon. "That's it." He stared outward, but his attention was on the connection between them. It felt so good, so right, that Eli suddenly didn't want the gesture to be casual; he wanted to hold her hand forever. He looked over to her.

She was gazing up with such a look of rapture that it seemed to Eli that she saw, really saw Alaska—the land he loved—for the first time. "Oh," she whispered, and her fingers tightened around his.

Bryn began to look forward to Eli's visits, his shy smiles and warm glances. So when he came over a week after their hike and invited her to go with him to meet Ben White, she agreed. Together they paddled up to Ben's cabin. His home was a bit more expansive than the other two Summit cabins, with a wraparound porch and wide windows on three sides. There were tidy wooden and stone steps that came down the hillside to the beach. Ben emerged as they neared and gave them a small wave, moving slowly, stiffly, to the stairs, to come and meet them.

"You all right, Ben?" Eli asked.

"Ah, fine. Just that darned arthritis acting up." He came closer and smiled tentatively at Bryn. "Must be Pete Bailey's girl. Spittin' image."

"I am." She reached out her hand. "Bryn. Bryn Bailey."

"Ben White," he said with a friendly nod. He was a short man, perhaps four inches shorter than Bryn, but compact and strong. About seventy years old. He was dressed in an old plaid shirt that had probably seen a decade of wear and jeans that had holes at the knees. But they were clean.

It was his eyes, kind and sagelike, that drew Bryn's gaze. "Come on up and share a cup of tea with me," he invited.

"That would be great, Ben," Eli said. He and Bryn moved forward, and Eli's hand moved to the small of her back, a polite gesture of pure masculinity. Women didn't go around touching each other there. She found herself wishing he wouldn't let it drop away. It was warm and comforting somehow. Oddly intimate.

"Have any bear cubs?" Eli asked Ben as they entered the house. The walls were plastered, making it lighter and brighter than the Baileys' cabin, and the floors were of wide, clear pine planks. She and her father had been debating the possibility of flooring their own cabin.

"Don't have any bears now. Those I went to see were dead before we could reach them. The guys down at Fish and Game tell me they're hoping to bring a couple by next week. Guess I'll be back to nursing a new set along."

"How many have you 'fathered'?" Bryn asked.

"Couple of twins. Several lone cubs." He set the pot on the stove, lit a match, and cranked the dial. A propane tank must be nearby, she surmised. He turned and reached for a few mugs from hooks and several boxes of tea, then set them on the table before her and Eli. "It's a crazy thing to do, but I enjoy it. Without me, those little critters would die. And there's a place on God's green earth for every one of them."

Bryn bristled at his mention of God. She remembered her dad's warning about Ben White, and she wondered if she would get the religious fanatic spiel now.

"Had a couple of problems with one young male," he continued. "He's wandered on over to Talkeetna and is liking the garbage smorgasbord rather than hunting. I have to figure out a way to get them used to hunting younger, so it's not such a shock. My females have done well, but this male—"

"How do you know he's yours?"

"Part of my deal with Fish and Game. I radio-collar them all. University tracks them for me. My job is to raise them up as a bear mother would. Wrestle with them. Take them out on walks. Show them how to dig for a spring covered with foliage or grub under a log, that sort of thing."

"How'd you get into it in the first place?" Bryn asked.

"Father was a vet and always fostering wounded or abandoned wildlife in New Hampshire. An owl with a wounded wing. A falcon. Ferrets. Anything you can name. We had a couple of bears when I was growing up. People brought him animals from all over the Lower 48. It became the family business." The teapot whistled, and he turned to take it from the stove and pour each a steaming mug. "Enough about me. How do you find Summit this year, Bryn? I wasn't around the last two times you visited. But I well remember the year you two were ten or eleven. Inseparable, you were."

She could feel the heat of Eli's embarrassment, but she concentrated on Ben. "It's pretty here. But a little…far away from everything for my taste."

Ben sat down and looked at her from over the rim of his mug. "Takes awhile. You'll see it eventually—what brings your father here."

"Besides a break from my mother?" It was out before she realized what she was saying, but there was something about Ben that invited confidences. His open kindness, lack of judgment.

He smiled and nodded, seeming to sense that now was not the right time for eye contact. "Alaska calls a body home. Your father's got it in his blood. I'd wager you'll soon have it in yours as well. Once it's in there, there isn't a way to get it out. No way to remedy the ache when you're away other than to visit. Or move here permanent."

Bryn smiled in confusion. "You make it sound like a disease."

"Some might call it that, yes."

He was puzzling, this wizened old man. She wondered what it was about Ben that her father had disliked, but for the life of her she couldn't figure it out. He was a genuine, sweet gentleman. Maybe Peter was afraid Ben would see into his soul as he was seeing into Bryn's. Afraid that he'd open up to the old guy when he wasn't ready to open up to anyone. Her thoughts floated until Ben brought another cup of tea.

They talked of Eli's blossoming business plans and his parents, about Bryn's studies, her mother in Newport, her grampa in Boston—it hit her then that Ben reminded her of her beloved grandfather. How she missed Grampa Bruce's smiling eyes and the way he would trace his old finger down her jaw tenderly when he was telling her something he wanted her to remember forever...

When their mugs were empty, Eli and Bryn said good-bye, promising to come back the following week to meet his "babies."

Eli followed Bryn down to the canoe, allowed her to get to the front, and then pushed off of a large rock without ever getting his boots wet. As they paddled away, he asked quietly, "What did you think?"

"About?"

"About Ben."

"I think he's a very nice old man. I don't know why my father doesn't like him."

"Why don't you ask him?"

"I might."

"Want to go fishing?" Eli changed subjects. "I can teach you an old Tlingit tribe method and catch you a passel of trout for dinner."

"Yes. I'd like that," she said. "But let's stop and get my dad's fly-fishing rod too. I want to try my hand at it."

"You got it."

Chosen

PROLOGUE

*S*amuel Roarke Jr. gazed out at the Mediterranean, thinking about the incredibly preserved sunken ship he had seen an hour ago. In his mind's eye, he could just begin to see what the ancient harbor must have looked like in its glory. He wished for the thousandth time that he could travel through time to stand beside Herod, observing his ways, his work, his wonders. *Thirty years before Christ was born.*

Sam glanced back at his partner, forcing his mind back to the subject of the ship. "It's gotta be Greek," he said.

Robert Hoekstra, head of the Center for Maritime Studies back in the States and current supervisor of Israel's Caesarea Maritima dig, nodded in agreement. "It's at least as old as the one they found off the coast of Athens. We need to fly in a consultant to advise us on how to pursue this part of the project. It's a thousand years older than anything I've had hands-on experience with."

"Christina Alvarez?" Sam suggested. He and Robert had recently discussed the innovative dive site protection system that Christina had developed while excavating the American Civil War wrecks, then perfected during work on nautical archaeological sites in the Caribbean.

Robert stood before him, rubbing his forehead, which was bronzed from weeks in the mild winter sun. "If she'll agree to it. That lady's got her fingers on more projects of economic importance than anyone else I know."

"It's that treasure hunter husband she hooked up with."

"I need to find myself a treasure hunter wife," Robert said, grinning down at his frayed, sun-bleached shorts.

"That you do," Sam said with a laugh. Then he grew more serious. "I think we can get her to come see this. If I know Christina, just the chance to check out a ship like this will bring her, at least on a consultant basis."

"Very good," Robert said, stroking his gray beard. "Give her a call right away. We haven't a day to lose."

JERUSALEM, LATE JANUARY

Alexana Roarke walked up the wide, grand stairs and handed her briefcase to the Waksf guard. No matter how often she went through the procedure of passing the guards at the gate of the Temple Mount—referred to by Muslims as the Haram el Sharif—she was irritated by the amount of time they took. The guard smiled in recognition and quickly searched the case, waving off his companion who moved to body-search her.

"Yes. She is too pretty to be carrying a bomb," the second guard said in Arabic, misunderstanding the first guard's wave. He smiled at Alexana in appreciation.

Her smile in return was perfunctory at best. Yes, she hated this process more each time she endured it. *Weaselly guards who think they wield so much power…*

"But sometimes they send their prettiest to do the dirty work," the second guard muttered as he scrutinized her, continuing his monologue as though he thought someone was listening. Warming to the power of his position, he pushed onward. "As I look at her more closely, I think she is not so pretty. Just blond. You always like the blondes."

"Be quiet, fool." The first guard switched to English. "This is Dr. Alexana Roarke. She has been summoned to meet with Abdallah al Azeh."

His cohort's eyebrows lifted in surprise.

She nodded at the first guard as he gave her permission to pass, then turned to the second. "I will be sure to inform Abdallah al Azeh that you do not like blondes," she said in perfect Arabic. She did not stay to watch his response.

Moving quickly, with purpose, she passed the El Aksa Mosque and the ornate, golden Dome of the Rock without looking twice; she had no time for sightseeing. Besides, the dramatic structures of Jerusalem had been part of her life for as long as she could remember.

A group of tourists passed her, straining to hear their guide who led them from one location to another. She felt sorry for the people who buzzed through Jerusalem this way, passing in a mad frenzy from one holy site to another. How could one truly come to experience this wonderful, crazy, complicated city in one week? The Temple Mount, or the Haram, had been breathtaking to her the first thirty times she saw it after grad school. Covering an area equivalent to five football fields in size, the monstrous structure could be explored for weeks on end.

But that was her archaeological head speaking. Still, there was so much to this place, the city Jesus had lived in and loved, the city she lived in and loved. Alexana drew in a deep breath of air, fresh from a light rain. It smelled like clean stones to her. She approached the offices on the northeastern corner of the Haram where al Azeh conducted business.

She racked her brain as she had done since yesterday for the reason Abdallah al Azeh—head of the Waksf and Islamic Affairs—had summoned her to meet with him, then shrugged her questions away, drew a breath, and knocked on the official's door.

A male guard opened it and nodded her forward.

Alexana stopped in shock at the inner office door. Standing to her left and right were two Mossad agents, easily identified by their trademark secret service aviator glasses. Sitting across the desk from Abdallah al Azeh was Abba Eban, head of the Israeli Antiquities Authority.

Eban was seldom seen in or around the Haram. Convinced that the Jews only wanted to destroy the Haram to rebuild their biblical temple, many Muslims would consider Eban's presence an act of treason by al Azeh. *The mystery deepens,* she thought.

"Come in, come in," Abdallah said, motioning to a plush, green chair beside Abba Eban. Both men politely stood. Abdallah watched Alexana sit and inquisitively study them.

"You wonder why we both wish to meet with you."

A tiny smile edged her lips upward. "To say the least."

"Alexana," Abba Eban said, smiling broadly. "Under the new peace accord, Abdallah has paved the way for an unprecedented dig." He paused dramatically, letting the information sink in. "We are to have unlimited access to Solomon's Stables."

Alexana drew in her breath sharply, struggling to maintain her composure. Not only was she sitting before the leaders of two long-standing enemy factions, men who heretofore would have been loath to be so near one another, but they both wanted to excavate. And the excavation was no ordinary dig. It was under the Temple Mount, the Haram, fiercely protected by Muslims for decades.

"Due to your longstanding reputation, the work done by you and your family in the region, and your ability to remain neutral between Palestinian and Jew alike," Abdallah said, "we have chosen you to be dig supervisor."

TREASURE (Book 4) • Ever since she roomed with Bryn Bailey *(Pathways)* at Harvard, nautical archaeologist Dr. Christina Alvarez has been obsessed with finding her ancestor's sunken treasure ship. Only one man—Caribbean treasure hunter Mitch Crawford—can help her, and he refuses to do so. But Christina's fight to win Mitch over may lead them both to a treasure more valuable than either of them ever dreamed.

CHOSEN (Book 5) • As supervisor of the Solomon's Stables dig in Jerusalem, archaeologist Alexana Roarke—grad-school friend of Christina Alvarez *(Treasure)*—knows she is in significant danger. Yet she will let nothing impede her excavation, not even the concern of handsome, world-renowned news correspondent Ridge McIntyre. Her stubbornness, however, could cost Alexana her life—and a future with the man she loves.

FIRESTORM (Book 6) • As a forest firefighting crew boss, Montanan Reyne Oldre—friend to Rachel Tanner and Beth Morgan *(Refuge)*—once led a team of courageous firefighters into a blaze that ended in tragedy. Now that the flames of love have begun to flicker between her and smokejumper Logan McCabe, Reyne must face the fears from her past and battle the raging firestorm that burns in her soul.